FORGET ME NOT

WILDFLOWER RIDGE 3

ELLE ASHWELL

GlitterInk PRESS

*For those who found their true family in friends,
and for those friends who've become family*

AUTHOR NOTE

While this is a sweet, sexy love story, some subjects may be upsetting for some readers. These include: brief mentions of a car accident causing death of both the main character's parents (in the past).

Depictions of farming practises, sexually explicit content and coarse language are also included. Please read with care and reach out if you require further information.

GLOSSARY

Wildflower Ridge is a New Zealand based sheep and beef farm and as such, this book uses New Zealand spelling and language. I've included some Kiwi-isms and farming terms in this glossary to help you out.

Bench - a kitchen counter

Bush - native forest

Hereford - a breed of beef cattle that is a reddish colour with white face and markings

Hokey Pokey Ice Cream - vanilla ice cream with small pieces of honeycomb. A Kiwi classic

Hot Dog - a New Zealand hot dog is a battered sausage on a stick

L&P - a lemon flavoured soft drink/fizzy drink/soda

Milo - A drink made from malt and enjoyed hot or cold, usually by Kiwi kids

Paddock - a fenced off field to keep stock in

Smoko - a work break

Tomato Sauce - similar to ketchup

Ute - a 'utility vehicle', commonly referred to as a pick up truck in other parts of the world

1

———

WILLOW

HUNTER WOODS WILL BE the death of me.

Specifically his ass in those jeans.

It isn't fair. He could have gotten ugly in the past decade. Anytime between the year we turned eighteen and now would have been great.

He could have gone bald, or have his grouchy frown etch great haggard wrinkles into his face.

But no, he's as fucking hot as ever.

I should climb out of my car and say hello. I should step in front of him and watch his eyes register that it's me, while never letting his frown slip.

Instead I slide lower in the driver's seat of my car and hold my coffee cup in front of my face, just in case he happens to glance in my direction.

He doesn't.

He hunches his shoulders against the autumn chill and continues striding down the footpath.

I sit in my car and stare at his ass and the way his jeans stretch over it and round his thighs.

I lift the coffee cup to my mouth and take a sip.

Fuck. Too hot. I hiss and place the cup in the holder.

I should start my car, pull into the street and drive home, but my gaze, as always, is drawn back to Hunter.

I should leave, but what I really want to do is fall into his arms, feel them wrap around me and have him whisper in my ear as he strokes a hand through my hair. Which is utterly and completely ridiculous.

He opens the door to Sugar and walks inside. I can see him in the bright little cafe. He strides straight up to Tilly Sheridan at the counter who smiles at him as she finishes organising the large order for the group before Hunter.

And shit. What if she mentions I've just been in there? What if Hunter turns to look around and sees me?

I took a needless risk coming here, but I didn't really expect to see him. I thought he'd be busy at work at this time of the day, not stopping for a coffee.

I'm not ready to come face-to-face with him yet. Not here. Not like this.

I've managed to avoid accidental run-ins with Hunter for the past ten years, only seeing him when I was prepared for it. I made sure I looked good and felt better every time.

But seeing him this morning, or worse, having him see me, I am definitely not prepared for it.

Not when I cried for the first three hours of my drive this morning. I cried until the tears ran out. One look at me and he'll know, even if the tears dried up long ago.

Because that's the thing about Hunter: he knows me, possibly better than I know myself.

Or at least he did once upon a time.

I PULL into the driveway at Wildflower Ridge and smile at the sign hanging above the gate.

Coming home always feels incredible, like a cosy, loving hug and a warm muffin straight from the oven.

Over the past year though, it's also filled with an aching sense of loss and longing.

I know Mum and my sister Olivia will be ready to welcome me home, like always, but Dad isn't here. It's been a little over a year since he died suddenly and I'm still not used to being home without him here. Every time I enter the kitchen, or head out on the farm, I expect to see him.

I expect to see him discussing some odd aspect of the farm management with Dallas, or making plans for the future with Olivia, or laughing at whatever antics Flynn has gotten up to.

Every time I realise he's not here and he's not coming back it's like taking a bucket of cold water to the face. Again.

I guess this extended trip home will get me more used to his absence. I hope so, because I can't keep living with the jump scares.

I cruise up the driveway, winding my window down to let in the fresh country air. I suck down a lungful of it and feel myself relax.

Even on a grey, gloomy day like today, there is no place I'd rather be than Wildflower Ridge.

I park my car next to Mum's and study the various vehicles as I climb out. Flynn's motorbike is here, so is Dallas's ute, Dad's old farm ute is parked down the end of the row with Olivia's car and a silver sedan. I have no idea who that belongs to.

Apparently I turned up right on lunchtime. Spectacular. I'd hoped I could time my arrival when the house wouldn't be overrun with people.

I should have known better. There's always someone here.

I take a deep breath, check my face in my car wing mirror and straighten. I can do this. I can walk in there and surprise them all with my visit. I don't need to tell them all about the rest of it. That can come later.

I stride up the porch steps, channelling the attitude I've fine-tuned after ten years in a city. It's harder to pull off wearing an old pair of trainers and leggings with a sweatshirt that's so frayed around the neckline I'm expecting it to completely give up and disintegrate one of these days.

I push open the door and follow the sounds of conversation to the kitchen where my family is gathered around the giant wooden table.

Mum sits in her usual spot, her hair loose around her shoulders and a cup of coffee in her hand. She's chatting to Dallas, our farm manager, who's sitting next to her, his arm around Katie who is leaning into him while talking to Olivia.

Across the table, Flynn and Abi are making moon eyes at each other. Abi runs the function venue here on the farm, while Flynn is a farmhand and also like family. He and Katie are

Olivia's best friends and he's Hunter's little brother. We're very tightly knit.

Flynn is the first to spot me, which is surprising considering it seems nearly impossible for him to tear his eyes away from his girlfriend.

"Willow!" he says as his gaze slips over Abi's shoulder and lands on me.

One word and the room goes silent, six sets of eyes turning to me at once.

Mum's out of her chair a moment later, wrapping me in a hug, exactly like I knew she would.

Tears prick at my eyes but I blink hard and push them back.

"What're you doing home?" Mum asks. "Not that we aren't happy you're here."

I shrug, hoping it looks more casual than it feels.

"The party," Olivia says to Mum.

"Party?" I ask, although I'm pretty sure I already know the answer. Dread fills my stomach.

"Katie and Dallas's engagement party. That's why you're here isn't it?"

And that's when I burst into tears.

2

—————

HUNTER

MY COFFEE HAS GONE COLD.

I pull a face then tip the rest out onto the ground, tossing the cup onto the ute tray behind where I'm sitting on the tailgate.

I'm parked at a roadside lookout on the outskirts of Kauri Creek, staring across the farmland spread out before me. In the distance I can just make out the closest town to us, Tōtara Grove.

This lookout is one of my favourite places and, simultaneously, one of my most hated.

Some days the potential of all that world outside Kauri Creek feels positive, inspiring and motivating.

On days like today, it's stifling, demoralising and overwhelming.

I should be at work in the middle of the afternoon on a Thursday, but I had a meeting at the bank and my boss let me have the rest of the afternoon off.

I'd appreciated it at the time. I regret agreeing now, because

I have a whole afternoon stretching ahead of me with nothing to take my mind off the complete disaster that was that bank meeting.

The meeting was supposed to give me some kind of purpose, but all it did was point out that, at twenty-eight, I have nothing to show for my life.

By the time my dad was twenty-eight he was married, owned a home and had me. My little brother Flynn wasn't far behind and neither were the two businesses my parents owned.

And sure, I own half a home. But my brother and I inherited half each when our parents died. It wasn't like I did anything to achieve that.

All I have is a job that I've just learned is going nowhere.

I don't even live in the house I part-own.

Because what do I need with a three-bedroom family home with a lawn big enough for kids to run around on?

Besides, Flynn has virtually moved in there with his girl-friend Abi, who's technically our tenant. They need a house with bedrooms and a big lawn. They already have Abi's daughter living with them half the time, and from what I've seen, Flynn's a great stepdad, so I wouldn't be surprised if more kids are coming soon.

It's weird seeing my little brother all settled down, espe-cially in that house. I don't know how he can handle being there again, living there, making Mum and Dad's room his own space.

Mind you, when Mum and Dad died he didn't lose his entire future alongside our parents. Not like I did.

I was just finishing high school when they died. I had the grandest plans of escaping this shit-hole town with my best friend. We were going to university, then to travel the world together. It was going to be the adventure of a lifetime. I never planned to come back. Not to live anyway.

Instead, I ended up with guardianship of a grieving four-teen-year-old with no way out of this town. And to top it all off, I managed to lose my best friend in the process.

I try to avoid thinking about Willow too often, because it *hurts*, and I don't like pain. Who does?

I sigh and bury the thoughts of her. I'm already wallowing enough right now. I don't want to be completely overwhelmed with despair over my life choices.

I did the right thing.

The right thing was staying behind for Flynn and letting Willow go. I don't regret either of those things. It was the best thing for the two people I love the most in the world.

I'd do it again and again if I had to.

They're happy now. Flynn is settled down with Abi, even if I don't fully understand their relationship.

And Willow ... she's happy too. Last I heard she had a great job in Auckland, putting her business degree to use, and was talking about getting married to her long-term boyfriend.

I slide off the tailgate, boots hitting the ground with a thud. Slamming the tailgate, I round my ute and climb into the driver's seat. Enough sitting here wallowing in my stupid feelings.

This is my life and I'm going to have to deal with it. Thinking about all the things that could have been isn't going to help.

I glance at the sheet of paper I'd scribbled numbers on during my meeting with the bank. What a waste of time.

I screw up the paper and hurl it across the cab. It bounces off the dash, ricochets and hits me in the forehead. Serves me right.

As I turn the key in the ignition, my phone lights up.

A text from Flynn, as though my thinking about him summoned him. We aren't really the type to randomly text, which is probably my fault, but I never know what to say to him. I've fallen into this weird space between brother and father and I never know how I'm supposed to act around him. Thank god for the Austin family, who managed to mostly keep us grounded and on the straight and narrow during Flynn's teenage years.

I shake the thoughts free and refocus on my phone.

FLYNN:

You're coming tomorrow night right? Have a surprise.

Tomorrow. I groan and tilt my head back, banging it against the seat.

Katie and Dallas's engagement party. Katie is one of Flynn's best friends and they both work with him at Wildflower Ridge, the Austin family farm on the outskirts of town.

But why do *I* need to be there?

I don't care that they're engaged. I was hoping Katie settling down would make her less of a pain in the ass, but I was wrong. I was very, very wrong. She still takes every opportunity to annoy me.

And a surprise. What the hell could Flynn have to surprise

me with? Unless him and Abi started on those babies even sooner than I expected? But would he announce that at someone else's engagement party?

That's not like my brother. Maybe he wants to tell me quietly.

I sigh and hit reply.

HUNTER:

I'll be there.

If not for Flynn's sake, then for Violet Austin, who'll be hosting the party. Willow's mum. The woman who kept me together after my parents died. I owe her everything.

3

WILLOW

I COULDN'T HAVE PICKED A WORSE time to crash-land back at home.

I completely forgot about Dallas and Katie's engagement party. I should have waited another week to completely upend my life.

But I'm here now, so I'm going to have to deal with it.

The kitchen clears out in zero point two seconds, with the entire team suddenly having to get back to work, which I appreciate. If I'd lost my shit and bawled my eyes out in the city I'd probably have a crowd of people around me to witness my meltdown. I appreciate that these people know that right now I feel stupid enough without having an audience.

Mum wraps me up in her arms, holding me tight until my tears have soaked her shirt. I'd really thought they were all dried up. Maybe the coffee I grabbed in town refilled the well.

"Come here, sweetie," Mum says, leading me to the table

and sitting me down in my usual spot. She flicks the switch on the jug and starts spooning something into a mug.

I sit at the table and stare at the empty seat to my left. The place my dad would always sit.

Mum places a mug in front of me—my favourite pink one with little purple flowers dotted all over it—then lowers herself into the chair across from me.

"What's going on, Willow?" she asks.

"Nothing," I say, wiping my cheeks with my sleeve. I don't meet her eyes though.

"Yeah, right." She lifts her own mug and takes a sip, her eyes never leaving me.

I wrap my hands around my cup and have a taste. Milo. My mum made me a Milo like I'm a little kid. It's exactly what I need though.

"I know you're not here for the party," Mum says, her voice soft.

"Who says I'm not?"

"Well you did, when you first got the invitation." She gives me a smirk, like she's won.

"Obviously I changed my mind." I don't want to sound like a brat, but I know I kind of do.

"So why did you walk in here and start crying?" She's teasing me, but it's gentle. Mum always knows how to read a situation, she always knows how to get the exact balance of softness without taking any shit from us.

I sigh and lie my head on the table. I should tell her and get it out of the way. That's what I'd planned to do, before I was reminded that Katie's engagement party is tomorrow. I'm not letting my drama ruin this for her or Dallas.

Neither Katie or Dallas are related to us, but Katie has felt like a part of the family since she moved to Kauri Creek when she was sixteen and almost immediately became best friends with Olivia.

Dallas has been the Wildflower Ridge farm manager for less than two years, but I know Mum feels like him and his five-year-old daughter Sadie are family, especially now that he's with Katie.

Mum's like that though. She's always been less about blood relatives and more about making your own family, especially after Hunter and Flynn's parents—her best friends—died.

She takes everyone in and treats them like family. It's one of the things I love most about her.

"I miss Dad," I whisper. It's not a lie, but it's not the full truth either.

Mum reaches across the table and strokes my head. "I know you do."

There isn't really anything else to say.

I lift my head and take another long drink of my Milo. "So, what needs doing for this party? Put me to work."

WHEN I OFFERED MY HELP, I had no clue what Mum had in store for me.

We own a function centre, yet for some reason the engagement party is being held at the house, instead of the venue that's set up for exactly this purpose.

But Katie and Dallas asked for the house, so I spent my entire day cleaning, making food and hanging decorations.

At least it gave me very little time to mope and dwell on my disaster of a life. Instead I scrubbed the bathroom until sweat ran down my spine and I could almost see myself in the sides of the bath. Why we needed the bath to be clean for a party I don't know, but it seemed like a good way to deal with my emotions.

I lay a final platter of snacks down on the table—sliced carrots, celery and capsicum with a bowl of onion soup dip— and step back to survey the spread.

Sadie, Dallas's five-year-old, bounds into the room. "Hi, Willow," she greets.

"Hey, Sadie," I reply with a smile. It's impossible not to around this kid. "I like your dress."

She beams. "Mama helped me choose it. Do you think Katie will like it?" She smooths the lavender tulle skirt, the iridescent sequins sparkling under the lights of our dining room. We pretty much never use this room, except for formal occasions, and it'll be where most of tonight's guests mingle.

"Katie's going to love it. You go see Violet in the kitchen, she's got special snacks for you."

Sadie glows at my confirmation that Katie will like the dress, then skips through to the kitchen, almost colliding with Flynn on her way.

"Woah, slow it down, sprout," he says, lifting a jug of punch above Sadie's head and managing to avoid spilling any of the brightly-coloured drink.

"Sorry, Flynny," Sadie calls back.

He shakes his head at me, his usual grin in place. "She's so excited. She's been bouncing off the walls all afternoon."

"That's really sweet," I say.

Flynn places the punch down on the side table. "And how are you?"

"I'm good," I say, forcing a shaky smile.

Flynn's hazel eyes study me for a moment, his face uncharacteristically serious, then his mouth kicks back up into a smile. "Have you seen Hunter today?"

I blink at his change of subject. "No. I've been here all day."

His smile explodes into a full blown grin. "Cool," he says. "I've got to go grab some drinks out of the fridge in the garage."

"I'll go," I say quickly, not understanding his response but nervous he's plotting something. I can hear voices near the front door though, and I need a moment to myself before I face these people.

I assume Hunter will be here tonight. The conversation with Flynn all but confirms it.

"What do we need?" I ask.

Flynn's gaze turns serious again but for barely a second. "One of everything, or whatever you can carry."

"Do you not think I can carry as much as you, Flynny?"

He laughs. "I'd never suggest such a thing, Will." He opens his arms and I automatically step into them. "It's good to have you home," he says as he squeezes me tight.

"It's good to be back," I mumble, not sure if I even believe myself.

4

____

HUNTER

I PARK my ute on the side of the driveway and walk the rest of the way to the house.

I'm early to the party, so I could park right near the house if I wanted, but I don't want to get blocked in. I'm showing my face because I owe it to Violet, but I'm not here for a long night.

I pull the collar of my jacket higher around my neck as I stride up the gravel drive. I wish I'd grabbed a beanie. It shouldn't be this cold already, but at least it's a clear night and not raining.

I pause when I reach the front steps of the house. I stare up at the place I spent half my childhood. We were always here. Violet and Henry were my parents' best friends. I learned to drive right here as soon as I was tall enough to reach the clutch in the old farm ute. I spent my weekends and school holidays working here, driving tractors or helping with the sheep at shearing time.

But, as familiar as the place is, I don't fit here anymore. Not since the night my parents died. I'd never, ever let Violet know I feel like this. But I lost more than just my parents that night.

And losing Willow felt like losing this whole place too.

I let out a long breath, but instead of heading inside, I turn and make my way around the side of the house.

The side door to the garage is slightly open, a dim light slicing through the gap. The light over the work bench in the back must be on.

My fingers wrap around the doorknob and I brace myself to open the door. I shove harder than necessary and the door flings back.

It bounces off something and something else hits the floor.

"Oof," a feminine voice says, then groans.

"Shit," I say, pulling the door out of the way and stepping around it.

Willow is standing right behind it, juggling bottles of fizzy drink in her arms. There's a bottle of L&P at her feet.

Willow is here. I didn't know she was coming. My feet stumble and my heart stutters, then races a million times its normal speed.

"Fuck. Fuck, fuck," she mutters.

"Here." I reach out with shaking hands, adrenaline surging through me, and pull a couple of bottles from her arms, setting them on the shelves running along the side of the garage. Willow places her bottles beside them.

I bend to pick up the L&P and when I straighten, Willow is rubbing her shoulder, twisting to try and see her upper arm.

"Fuck that hurt."

"I'm so sorry."

She finally looks at me and the moment her eyes connect with mine she freezes.

Her brown hair is shorter than when I saw her last. It's cut into a blunt bob that falls near her jaw. She's styled it into waves with little braids pulling back the strands around her face. It suits her and I love it immediately.

My gaze travels from her blue eyes, taking in the dress she's wearing. It's silky looking, a soft pink, and skims her body, highlighting the curves of her breasts and hips. The neckline dips low, showing off her cleavage.

She looks incredible, but also ... not like her.

The dress doesn't feel like her.

My Willow was all about cosy sweaters with jeans. Sometimes she'd wear mini skirts that showed off her legs and always made teenage me lose my mind. She wore sneakers or boots, not strappy high heels that look like they're killing her feet.

The only thing familiar about her is the gold bracelet wrapped around her wrist—a gift from her parents for her sixteenth birthday. I was there when she unwrapped it. I'm the one who fastened it on her for the first time.

The bracelet and her eyes. It feels like that's all that's left of the girl I once knew better than anyone else on the planet. The girl I once planned to spend the rest of my life with.

I drag my gaze back to Willow's, forcing my breaths to even out. She's still taking me in, the way I've been doing to her, and when her eyes finally snap back to mine she sucks in a breath.

"Hunter," she breathes.

"Are you okay?" I ask, my fingertips grazing the bare skin of her shoulder. It's slightly red, but doesn't look too bad. God, I shouldn't be touching her, but her skin feels incredible, even with the barest point of contact. Heat flares in my fingers.

"Yeah. Yep. I'm fine." She turns away, slipping out from under my touch, and my breath catches. The slip of a dress exposes her whole back, with ribbons crisscrossing over her skin to tie in the middle, right in the small of her back.

My fingers itch to reach out and tug the bow loose, to free the knot and let the dress fall away. To stroke down the length of her spine.

But I can't. Because Willow isn't mine.

"Why are you out here? The party's inside," Willow says, her back still to me as she collects the bottles again. She goes to take the L&P out of my hands.

"Maybe not this one yet," I say, avoiding her question. "I'll bring one in that isn't going to explode all over the person who opens it."

"Yeah, probably for the best. It'd be me for sure." She turns back to me. "I, uh, need to get back." She gestures with her arms full of bottles and I realise I'm blocking the door.

"Oh, yeah, of course. I'll be right behind you with a safe bottle of this." I step aside and after another long look at me, Willow bites her lip and scurries from the garage. Well, she scurries as best she can in those lethal-looking shoes.

I leave the L&P on the shelf and head for the fridge in the back corner, pulling out a fresh bottle. I grab a beer too and use the corner of the workbench to pop the top. I take a swig and skirt around Violet's car, still spinning from Willow's appearance. It's not particularly surprising that she used the party as an excuse to visit, but I'd normally hear about it before running into her.

At the far end of the garage I pull the elasticated cover off the vehicle that's stored here. I lean back against the bench, the L&P and beer sitting on the timber beside me.

I stare at the bright red 1974 Holden Torana. It was my Dad's pride and joy, aside from Mum, me and Flynn. He restored as much of it as he could himself, with Henry's help, and saved every spare cent to outsource any work he couldn't do. He did an incredible job and he loved this car.

It could be the solution to my problem, but I'm not sure I can bear to let another thing go.

I've already had to let go of my parents.

I've had to let go of Willow.

This is just a stupid vehicle, but for some reason it means something to me.

There are too many memories tied up in it—working side-by-side with my dad as I learned how engines work, the day we ran the engine for the first time, our first drive in it once it was finally finished, Henry driving Flynn and I home from our parents' funeral.

And the memory that's etched in my brain, no matter how hard I try to let it go: the night I kissed Willow across the front seat before driving her home and sneaking her into my room. The one night I was allowed to touch her the way I'd always wanted to.

The image of her tonight comes back to me, the desire to feel her bare skin under my hands again hitting me hard.

I'll never get to do that again.

I'll never have Willow the way I once did.

All I get are the memories of that one night and this stupid fucking car.

5

WILLOW

I HATE THESE SHOES.

I hate this dress too. I hate having to tape my boobs into place so I can wear it, I hate the colour and the fabric, I hate that no matter what underwear I wear, you can see the line and, trust me, I've tried them *all*.

I hate everything about it, but I still don't hate it as much as I hate these shoes.

Shifting my weight, I try to give one foot a break. All it does is make my other foot ache and burn. The straps are cutting into my feet and I need this party to be over.

I should simply take the shoes off, I really should. No one here will care. I'm in my own home for god's sake.

But the thought of it still makes me feel uncomfortable, like I'll be judged for it, even though I know that's not true. The person who would have judged me for it, the person who chose these shoes in the first place, and the dress, isn't even here.

I hobble back into the dining room and check everything is

in order. Guests are chatting, eating the nibbles and generally celebrating the happy couple.

Katie is looking stunning in a short white dress covered in iridescent sequins. Dallas is in dress pants and a dark shirt, looking handsome beside his fiancée. They're the perfect pair. Katie tosses her head back and laughs at something Flynn is saying while Olivia slaps his shoulder.

They're such good friends and I'm so glad they have each other. I watch wistfully for another moment as Abi reaches up to whisper into Flynn's ear. He leans down and draws her into a kiss so sensual I have to turn away.

I scoop up an empty serving bowl and carry it to the kitchen. I freeze in the doorway when I see who's sitting at the kitchen table.

Hunter.

And the most unlikeliest of companions, Sadie.

"They're kissing *all the time*," Sadie says as I step inside the room. "I know that's what happens when you're in love with someone, but there's so much kissing. Too much."

"I feel ya, kid," Hunter says, tossing a chip into his mouth. He takes a pull of his beer, his gaze landing on me as he does. His throat moves as he swallows, his eyes trailing down my body to my sore feet, then skimming back up, his expression never faltering. He turns his focus back to Sadie. "All this romance is gross."

Sadie agrees and Hunter taps his bottle against her plastic cup then takes another drink, this time finishing the bottle. It bangs against the table when he sets the empty down, the sound reverberating through me.

I realise I haven't moved from the doorway so I take a few wobbly steps into the room, placing the bowl on the bench near the dishwasher. When I turn back around, Hunter's eyes are on my shoes.

I haven't seen much of him tonight, aside from running into him in the garage. My shoulder doesn't even hurt from where the door collided with it while I was trying to figure out how to open it with my arms full, but I still feel the graze of his fingertips over the spot.

I expected Hunter to follow me back to the house right away, but he didn't. I know because I watched the door until Mum called me away to do something helpful.

I didn't see him come inside, but every time I've seen him tonight he's had the usual grumpy scowl on his face. He doesn't even bother to hide it anymore. I love that about him. Meanwhile, I'm over here wearing a dress I don't even like because someone else said they did.

"Sit down, Willow," he says, voice low and gruff.

"I'm good." I smile, but it doesn't reach the edges of my mouth.

Hunter frowns. "Those shoes are killing you," he says.

I sigh. I guess I'm not fooling anyone. I slide into the chair next to Hunter.

"They're pretty shoes though," Sadie says.

"Yeah, but pretty doesn't mean comfortable," Hunter grunts. "Here." He bends down and slides his palm down my calf, hooking my leg over his knee.

The touch feels scalding, and even when he moves onto undoing the tiny buckles around my ankles I can still feel the ghost of his touch. Hunter, however, appears wholly unaffected by the contact.

"Sadie, there you are," Flynn says, poking his head into the room, his eyes lingering on how close Hunter and I are sitting. At least he can't see my leg in his lap. "Come on, your dad's about to do his big speech."

Sadie gasps. "Then it's my turn?"

Flynn nods. "Sure is, sprout. You ready?"

Sadie nods and scrambles from her chair. Flynn shoots a grin in our direction, then disappears with Sadie.

I try to pull my leg back, meaning to follow the little girl back into the party, but Hunter's hand lands on my thigh.

"Wait," he says. The final buckle gives and Hunter slides the shoe off my foot, dropping it to the floor with a thunk. I let out a soft hiss as he skims his fingers over the red welts left behind. "You need to burn these fuckers," Hunter murmurs. "Other foot."

He reaches over and scoops my other leg into his lap. The angle forces me to turn my whole body and I sit and stare as Hunter sets to work on the other shoe.

He keeps his hair short now, probably cuts it himself over his bathroom sink. I miss the days when it was longer and used to fall in his face while he was working on his dad's old Holden. He would brush it back and inadvertently end up with grease smudges on his face. I mocked him about it relentlessly, but secretly I was melting inside at how incredibly hot he was.

He's still hot. Every time I see him I'm reminded of it, even with the buzzcut.

His frown deepens as the second shoe falls to the floor. "Fuckin' torture devices," he mutters.

"Yeah, but they're pretty," I say, trying not to visibly react when he rubs his thumb across the mark left by the ankle strap.

"They don't seem very like you," he says, glancing up, hazel eyes meeting mine. "Not really your style."

I pull my feet back. He lets them go without resistance this time. "What would you know about my style, Hunter? You barely know me anymore." The words come out snappish and I wish they hadn't. I'm not supposed to react to Hunter anymore. I'm not supposed to have him get under my skin and make my heart ache.

But I do, and it does.

I huff an aggravated breath, then leave my shoes on the kitchen floor and storm from the room. I slip out into the hallway, grateful I don't have to go through the dining room full of people to get to the stairs. I race up them, my silent feet a relaxing change to the heels that click on the hardwood floors with every step.

For a brief moment I hope Hunter follows me. I hope he comes after me. I hope he wants to know me again, the way we used to know each other.

But I'm not surprised when he doesn't.

History has proven that Hunter will never come after me.

6

———

HUNTER

SO I DIDN'T LEAVE the party early. I didn't leave at all.

Instead I drank too much, had a ridiculous conversation with a five-year-old who insists on calling me Uncle Hunter, and have ended up sleeping on the couch in Violet's lounge.

She offered me a bed upstairs, but the spare bedroom is all set up for Sadie and I didn't want Violet to have to find another spot for her.

Sleeping upstairs also felt too close to Willow. The couch feels too close to Willow right now, but by the time I pissed her off I'd already had too much to drink to be able to drive home.

I should have gone and stayed in the old shearer's quarters, but I didn't want to freeze my balls off walking down there in the middle of the night, plus I'm pretty sure my brother is staying down there and I don't want to hear what him and Abi get up to through the paper thin walls.

I'd asked him what his surprise was after a few hours at the party, when the unease in my stomach hard curled itself into a hard knot. He gestured to where Willow was chatting with Olivia in the corner, the two sisters leaning into each other.

"Willow's here," he said. "None of us knew she was coming. Or did you know?"

"No," I said. "I didn't know." Because Willow doesn't talk to me anymore. It was a nice surprise though, seeing her, being able to watch her with family and friends. It was painful too, especially when I touched her when I removed her shoes.

I groan and roll over, cursing at the random pain in my back from sleeping scrunched onto a couch. It's not the first time I've slept on this couch, but I didn't expect to still be doing it as an adult.

I've been lying here, pretending last night didn't happen, but it doesn't matter how many times I lie to myself about it, I can't shake the truth.

I said something stupid to Willow. I should probably apologise, but knowing my shitty track record I'll slip out of here before she's up and she'll be back to her real life by the end of the weekend, leaving me to mine.

There's soft music coming from the kitchen and I roll off the couch and make it to standing. There's bright sunshine coming through a crack in the curtains and it hurts my eyes.

I follow the music and the smell of something baking into the kitchen, expecting to see Violet standing over the stove.

Instead I see the full curve of Willow's ass in a pair of tight jeans as she bends down to pull something from the oven. I wish I could say my boner was just morning wood, but that would be a lie. That was already gone long before I made it into the kitchen. This one's all Willow.

I'm frozen in place, watching her as she pulls a baking tray out and slides it onto the stovetop to cool. I should go, before she sees me and we have to rehash last night and a lifetime of history.

But I don't have a chance to move before she turns and sees me.

She gasps, her hand coming to rest against her chest. "Holy shit. How long have you been standing there?"

I shrug. "Not long. I didn't want to distract you while you were holding something hot." I gesture to the tray, hoping my excuse sounds plausible and I don't look like I'm creeping on her.

"Why are you here?" She scoops up a coffee mug and slides into a seat at the table, eyeing me with suspicion.

"I slept here."

She blinks. "You did?"

"Yeah, Sadie got me drunk."

She laughs and the sound is pure magic. "You know where the coffee is," she says, leaning down to collect her shoes from where I dropped them under the table last night.

I pour my coffee and slide into the seat opposite her. She places the shoes on the chair beside her, then turns back to me.

I study her. The shimmery make up from last night is gone and she's wearing a dark red knitted sweater. She looks like the girl I remember.

My gaze catches on her necklace. A gold chain with a small pendant. I can't make it out from this distance, but could it be ... could it be the one I gave her?

Willow shifts and with a movement so subtle most wouldn't notice, she tucks her necklace inside her sweater.

It can't be the same necklace. She wouldn't still have the one I gave her. She definitely wouldn't be wearing it. No, the one she's wearing is probably some heinously expensive thing gifted to her by her boyfriend, the one she's talked about marrying someday.

I clear my throat. "I'm sorry about what I said last night."

Willow's mouth tips up at the side. "You were right." She sighs. "I hate these shoes." She gives them a distasteful look.

"Happy to burn them for you," I say, relieved she isn't still pissed at me.

"Fuck no. They were so expensive. Think of the resale value."

"Someone would buy your secondhand shoes?"

"Are you trying to imply there's something wrong with my secondhand shoes?" She arches an eyebrow at me and I have to lift my coffee to my mouth to hide my smile. This banter is ... unusual, and I love it. Willow seems lighter than she has in the past few years. More like the girl I remember, maybe. I can't quite put my finger on it, but despite tired eyes, she looks happy and relaxed, even in my presence.

"Never," I answer. "If you think someone will pay for old shoes then who am I to argue?"

"I'll let you know how much I get for them."

Silence falls between us as we drink our coffees. We've hardly spent time together over the past few years, not alone like this anyway. I don't know if it was a conscious choice on Willow's part, but I haven't gone out of my way to seek her out.

I know what I did. I never wanted to cause her pain in the first place, let alone make it worse by forcing her to spend time with me.

We technically parted as friends when she left for university at eighteen, but it's definitely not the friendship we had before then. Now it's more that we put on a good front for our families.

I finish my drink and set the cup back on the table.

"I should head off. Have things to do today," I say.

"Um, yeah. Sure." Willow fiddles with the handle of her coffee mug, then flicks her eyes up to meet mine. "It was good to see you, Hunter."

"It was good to see you too, Willow. It always is." I place my mug in the dishwasher and head for the door. "I'll see you next time you're back?" I ask, pausing at the threshold.

"Yeah ... next time," she replies, but she seems far away, like she's thinking about something else. Like she's moved on from me.

Which is fair enough. She *has* moved on from me. She has to have, considering she wants to marry someone else.

7

WILLOW

I'M PRETTY SURE the universe is making me pay a penance for walking out on my life. Why else would Hunter be repeatedly put in my path when I least expect it?

I've been so careful to avoid being alone with him and now it's twice in less than twenty-four hours.

And to make it all worse, I'm convinced he saw the necklace I'm wearing today: the one he gave me for my eighteenth birthday, back when we were both head over heels in love with each other but hadn't quite figured out how to tell the other person yet.

I never wear it when I know I'm going to see him, but I always keep it close.

My ex, Mark—the one who convinced me I should buy last night's dress and shoes—hated the necklace, and I suppose I understand why. He doesn't know how close Hunter and I really were—no one does—but it wouldn't sit right with me if he had a piece of jewellery from another woman.

I play with the necklace as I eat a cookie for breakfast. I woke up early after a terrible sleep and decided to make use of Mum's pantry full of baking supplies. I never bake at home, or … the place I lived. I guess it's not home anymore since I packed all my stuff up and stored it in my best friend's spare room.

Seeing Hunter this morning should have been more awkward than it was, but somehow falling into the pattern of snarking with him came easily, despite it being years since we've talked like that. I try to keep up a pretence around my family that nothing ever changed between me and Hunter, but I don't think they buy it. This morning though, it was believable. A shame really that no one was here to witness it.

Mum joins me as I'm starting on my second cookie.

She grabs a coffee and a cookie and sits down across from me.

"Thanks for your help yesterday. I always forget how much needs to be done. You'd think I'd have it figured out by now."

"It's all good," I mumble through a mouthful of cookie crumbs. "Glad I could help."

"Are you ready to tell me why you came home yet?" She arches an eyebrow.

"Katie and Dallas's engagement party," I say, then take another enormous bite.

Mum studies me then makes a little pfft sound. "Sure thing, Will." She reaches across the table to catch my fingers in hers. "You tell me when you're ready. Are you heading home tomorrow?"

"Um, actually I thought I might stay for a little bit." At least I already know she isn't buying the engagement party story, because if I'd only come back for that then I'd be on my way again tomorrow morning. "Or maybe a bit longer than a little bit?" I add.

"Oh." She blinks at me, momentarily stunned, then recovers. "Of course. You know you can stay as long as you like. Always." She watches me as she takes a drink. "What about your job?"

"I can work remotely for a some of it, but they're okay with me taking some time off. Apparently I'm overdue a lot of holidays."

"That doesn't surprise me. You spend a lot of time at work." She clocks the expression on my face and hastily adds, "Not that it's a bad thing."

"Yeah, it's not. And I know how much you and Liv and everyone else works around here. I figure I can help out a bit, maybe sort out some financial stuff to help make it easier for you guys."

Mum flops back in her chair. "That would help. We have things under control, but it's not exactly a streamlined system."

"You know you could have asked me to do this at any time," I say, not sure if I'm hurt that she hasn't. When Dad died I offered to come home for a bit, but Mum insisted I had my own life and we needed to carry on as best we could. Running the farm was never my career goal like it was Olivia's and at the time I was grateful I didn't have to step up like my little sister did.

But now … now I want to be near my family and figure out what it actually is that I want.

It doesn't take long for Olivia to join us for our extremely nutritious breakfast and once we've demolished most of the batch of cookies, I tag along as she heads down to the barn. She needs to check a few things on the farm this morning, since she's given Katie and Dallas the weekend off and I offered to help out. I won't actually be much help, but getting out on the farm seems like it'll be good for my soul.

We tack up our horses—Olivia on her big black gelding Bruno, and me on Scout, who is mostly ridden by Sadie these days. I used to have a horse of my own, but it doesn't make sense to have one when I'm hardly home. Maybe I should look at getting one if I'll be sticking around.

"So, how's Mark?" Olivia asks as she swings into Bruno's saddle. "How come he didn't come with you this time?"

I can hear the derision in her voice clear as day. She doesn't think much of Mark, especially when he didn't come home with me at Christmastime or Easter. I tried to explain he had other commitments, but the truth was, he didn't want to spend the holidays in some backwater town with my family.

"He didn't come because I broke up with him," I say, steering Scout past Olivia and heading for the main track out to the farm. I unlatch the gate and swing it open from the saddle, leaving it open behind me.

"Woah. Wait up," Olivia calls as she tries to hurriedly close the gate again. A moment later she trots up beside me. "You can't drop that bomb then run away."

"I didn't do either thing," I say. "It's no bomb, not for you anyway. You can't tell me you didn't see it coming."

"I actually *didn't* see it coming," Olivia says. "You've held onto him all through the past year, when all he seems to have done is let you down. I know I barely knew him, but that's all I saw. I just didn't think *you'd* see it."

I scowl. "He didn't always let me down."

"I'm sure he didn't." Olivia doesn't sound like she believes it though. "But what finally got you to dump his sorry ass?"

"He wanted to get married," I say, the unease churning in my gut again, even though I've already made the decision to end my relationship.

"Oh, the audacity," Olivia says with a mocking lilt. "How dare he want to marry my incredible sister? It's not like you haven't talked about marrying him before. Mum's already told half the town."

I groan. I should have expected as much. "He wanted to get married at this truly hideous venue in Auckland. It was right in the middle of the city, in a god-damned skyscraper." I turn to watch Olivia's reaction and it's as good as I expected.

"What. The. Fuck?" she growls. "He knows about this place, right?"

"Yep." I pop the 'p'. "And I'd already told him this is where I want to get married someday. Apparently he forgot when he got excited and booked a wedding venue without asking me first."

"Shiiiiit," Olivia breathes. "He didn't even take you to see it first?"

"No, but I actually meant he booked a venue without actually asking me if I wanted to marry him."

Olivia's jaw drops and I can't help the giggle that escapes me. "Why didn't you tell me?"

"I *am* telling you. Mum doesn't even know yet." I sigh. "Don't tell her. I'll get around to it."

"I won't say anything," she promises. "When did this happen?"

"Tuesday. I spent Wednesday packing up my stuff and moving it into Margot's place. Then she cut my hair off and I came home Thursday." I toy with the ends of my hair. "I knew it was over a long time ago." I drop my hand to stroke my fingers down Scout's neck and avoid looking at my sister.

"I couldn't handle the thought of more change. I wanted one thing that was going to stay the same. I thought my issues with the relationship were grief related. I hoped I'd eventually go back to enjoying Mark's company. But Dad ... it made me look at things differently. I am different now, and Mark and that life isn't what I want."

We ride side-by-side in silence for a few minutes before Olivia breaks it.

"Did he choose last night's dress?"

"Yeah, he did."

"Makes sense." She nods. "It didn't suit you at all."

"I hate it," I admit. "And funnily enough, you're not the only person to tell me it doesn't suit me."

Thoughts of Hunter crowd my mind: his steady gaze, his big, slightly rough hands gently removing the shoes from my feet, the way he trailed his fingers across the marks left behind, reverence in the touch.

Maybe he does still know me. It feels impossible that he could after all this time, but, on the other hand, I feel like I still know *him*. I feel like I always will.

We were the best of friends, virtually inseparable for eighteen years, and we've seen each other regularly during the ten years since, even if we never went deeper than surface-level small talk.

I miss what we had though; I have from the moment I lost it. I miss the friendship and knowing he always had my back, I miss the adventures we'd go on and the way we dreamed about our future.

I just miss *Hunter*.

8

———

HUNTER

AS USUAL, I spend my weekend doing chores.

I spend a few hours on Saturday at work, getting ahead on a restoration project we have going on. I don't need to clock in, but I have nothing better to do with my time.

Once I'm done there, I head out to the cemetery. It's been too long since I've visited Mum and Dad and Henry. I tidy around Mum and Dad's shared headstone, even though the council does a pretty good job at keeping the place nice, then I sit cross-legged on the grass and talk.

I don't know if Flynn visits them like I do. I have no idea if he comes here at all. There's never any sign of it—I'm pretty sure the handful of wildflowers are from Violet—but I don't leave behind evidence of my visits either.

It's not the sort of thing I can ask him about. We don't have that kind of relationship, and while I often wish it was different, I know it's my fault we've ended up barely being able to speak about our parents.

I talk about Flynn to *them* though. I tell them about Abigail and Sadie. I tell them about his puppy, Jett, that he got at the end of last year. He was supposed to get one a decade ago, but I couldn't handle the thought of being responsible for a puppy and my brother.

It might have helped though, and I regret not following through. Just another regret in a long, long list.

I talk about my job and the restoration project. I talk about my boss Walter's heart attack and how the business is now for sale. A business I thought I had the opportunity to buy, but it turns out a single, small-town guy like me can't afford to keep up with an offer from a big city investor. Why they want a crappy, rundown mechanic's workshop in a shit-hole town I don't know. All I know is my long-term plan is now worthless, unless I can find a substantial amount of money in a very short amount of time.

Saying goodbye to my parents, I head towards the more recent plots, finding Henry Austin's grave with no trouble. There's a bunch of wildflowers adorning the headstone, similar to the one on my parents'.

As I stare down at his name, I realise I've overlooked an option. Once upon a time I would have gone to Henry about my problems. I can't do that anymore, but there is one person I have left.

I slide my phone from my back pocket and pull up my text thread with Violet.

HUNTER:

Can I ask some advice? Maybe tomorrow afternoon? I'll bring coffee and cake.

I go to put my phone away, not expecting an immediate reply, but it buzzes before it makes it to my pocket.

> VIOLET:
>
> Sure thing. Don't worry about coffee/cake though we have enough here.

She says that about the coffee every time. And every time I turn up on her doorstep with her caramel latte and something delicious from Sugar. She hasn't turned me away yet.

ON SUNDAY MORNING I clean my tiny flat above Kauri Creek Motors—a perk of being the workshop manager.

The flat is tiny, and not exactly nice, but it's all I need. There's a small kitchen, a bathroom and bedroom, plus space for a couch and TV in the main area. I don't have room for a dining table, even a small one, but since I never have people over it's not a problem. The couch works as well as anywhere for me to eat my meals.

Once the place is as clean as it's ever going to get, I head down the street to Sugar and place my usual order, plus Violet's. They have a raspberry pull-apart bread in the cabinet, so I grab one of those too.

Then I make the drive out to Wildflower Ridge. Like every time I travel these roads, I assure myself I'll visit more regularly; spend more time with Violet, maybe hang out with my brother a bit, help on the farm on my days off. History shows I won't actually follow through, but I want to.

I would, if the place didn't remind me of Willow at every turn.

But she's gone back to the city now, another weekend trip over.

I park my ute and stomp up the porch steps, kicking my boots off at the door.

"Hey, Vi," I call as I make my way down the hall to the kitchen at the back of the house.

"Hey," she says from her seat at the kitchen table. She has watercolour paints and paper spread out in front of her, a paintbrush in hand. She gives me a smile and drops her brush into a jar of murky water. She spies the coffee in my hand and frowns. "Hunter, I said no coffee."

"And I didn't listen," I say. She grins and takes the cup from me.

"When do you ever?"

I hand over the bread. "I also brought you this."

She takes a peek inside the paper bag and groans. "Tilly is going to ruin us all working at that place. That girl can bake. Abi's looking at bringing her on as a wedding supplier."

"Yeah? You think she'd be keen?"

"Oh, yes. She's very excited. She's been wanting to establish herself a bit more, make something more of herself."

"I hope it works out for you both." I don't really understand the workings of the wedding and function venue here at Wildflower Ridge. By the time it was established my connection to the family was only through Violet and I've never bothered to find out more about that side of the business.

I pick up one of Violet's completed paintings, a bunch of

tiny blue flowers with yellow centres. Like everything Violet paints, it's stunning.

"What're these?" I ask, not sure why I need to know.

"Forget me nots," she says, her voice a little wistful. She shakes her head. "Now, what did you want to talk to me about?" She resumes her place at the table and I sit down opposite her.

"I need some financial advice."

Violet blinks at me. It's been years since I came to her about anything like this, probably not since Flynn turned eighteen and became self-sufficient.

"Kauri Creek Motors is for sale," I say. "Walter and I have previously talked about me taking it over when he retires, but with his health it's happening sooner than we expected. And worse, he's had another offer, one I can't compete with currently. His son is pushing him to take it."

"Oh, I'm sorry Hunter," Violet says, sitting back in her chair.

"I was hoping you could look over my numbers and see if I'm missing something?" I take a deep breath and grip the sides of the table, steeling myself to speak this part out into the universe. "Otherwise, there's the Torana."

Violet sucks in a breath. "You'd sell it?"

"I don't want to, but if I have to ..." I shrug. "I don't know if I'll still have a job if Walter sells to someone else. But that's a last resort, and I'd rather not mention it to Flynn yet."

"Of course." Violet has a crease between her brows and I can tell she doesn't like the idea. "Alright, well, let's see what we've got." She slides my file full of paperwork towards her. She spends a few minutes reading, occasionally making a mark on a page with a pencil. Eventually she drops her pencil and sits back in her chair.

"I can't see anything you've missed, or another way to make it work," she says. "I'm sorry."

My breath rushes out of me and I slump, propping my elbows on the table and resting my head in my hands.

Defeat washes over me. I guess that's it then. I have to give up and walk away.

"You know," Violet says, "there's one more person who might be able to help you. She might have a way around this that I'm not nearly smart enough to think of." She hands me back the file of papers. "She's in the office."

I scoop up the file. "Thanks Vi," I say, pushing out of my chair and heading for the office, my feet dragging. I don't know why she thinks Olivia might be able to help me. Finance isn't really her strong suit, but at this point I'll take any help I can get.

Except, when I pause in the doorway to the home office, it isn't Olivia sitting behind the desk in a sky blue hoodie with the top section of her hair pulled up in a messy bun.

It's Willow.

9

─────────

WILLOW

THE SOUND of something hitting the floor startles me from where I've been staring at my laptop screen, trying to figure out how to get my life back in order, and how to tell my mum I'm single again. I don't know why I've made it into a thing and haven't told her already. She's not going to judge me for it, but she *will* probably fuss and worry about me.

The sound from the doorway isn't the most startling thing about this moment though. It's that Hunter is standing in the doorway, a mess of papers scattered on the floor in front of him.

He's staring at me, a look of total shock on his face. My face probably has the exact same expression.

Why is he here *again*? Is he always here now?

"Hunter," I say eventually, breaking the shocked spell between us.

Hunter jerks, blinks and bends to pick up the papers he dropped. Straightening, he looks directly at me. "Willow." He takes a couple of steps towards me. "I didn't realise you were still here."

"Uh, yeah. Surprise!" I lift my hands and do some weird jazz hands gesture. What is wrong with me? I shove my hands under my thighs to prevent them doing anything else ridiculous. "Why are you here?"

He scowls and I realise how my words came across. It's not worth trying to talk myself out of it though.

"I needed some advice and your mum thought you might be able to help. I assumed that when she said 'she's in the office' she was talking about your sister. Not ... you."

I don't know if his final words are good or bad. Would he rather talk to Olivia?

"Um, well I don't know where Liv is right now. But I'm sure she'd be able to help."

"I don't actually think she could, but I do understand why your mum told me to ask you about it, now I know it's you."

"Oh, well ... okay then." I shrug, feeling hopelessly out of my depth. I don't even know what we're talking about, but Hunter's hazel eyes are fixed on me, his expression as serious as ever. He's wearing faded jeans and an old corduroy jacket with a sherpa collar. He looks incredible, especially as he crosses his arms and stares down at me. I wish I wasn't sitting here in a hoodie and pyjama booty shorts.

"You know what," he says, dropping his arms. "It doesn't matter." He turns for the door.

"Hunter, wait." My voice cracks over his name and I want to slap myself. Why does being around him make me this awkward?

It's been ten years since he told me he was in love with me.

Ten years since he broke my heart in the midst of tragedy.

I should be over this.

Pausing in the doorway, one hand on the wooden frame, Hunter looks back over his shoulder at me. His gaze trails over me in a familiar slow, torturous way. I pull my feet up onto the chair, hiding myself behind my knees, but when his eyes flash and darken I realise it's had the opposite effect. Damn booty shorts.

"What?"

"What do you need help with?" I ask, my voice quiet in the tense distance between us, the distance I've loathed since the day it started to grow.

He sighs and turns, crossing his arms as best he can while holding his file and leaning against the doorframe. "It's a financial thing."

I spread my hands. "Well, I'm your girl then." The words register a second too late. I plow on, trying to distract from them. "What is it? You know this is what I do."

"Yeah, I know." He steps back into the room and grabs the chair in the corner, dragging it over, then sits down beside me, placing his file in the middle of the desk. "My boss is selling the business. I'm trying to work out how I can afford to buy it." He taps the file. "This has all my numbers in it."

I drag it closer and open it, flicking through the pages in my lap while sitting cross-legged in the desk chair. The whole time I'm scanning the information I'm aware of Hunter's presence beside me, how close my bare knee is to his denim-clad one.

He's resting his elbows on his knees, his chin propped on his hands and I can feel his stare burning into me.

I reach the last page, then slowly lift my gaze to meet his. I shake my head and he squeezes his eyes closed, taking a slow breath before opening them again.

His expression is closed off. "Thanks anyway." His tone is gruff and goosebumps break out over my skin at the memory it triggers. The memory of the night he told me he wanted me, that he was in love with me.

He takes the file from my hand and moves to stand.

"Wait," I say, reaching out and wrapping my fingers around his wrist before I can think about it. "There must be something else. There's nothing in there about the money from your parents?"

"There isn't really money from Mum and Dad. It went on the house and living costs while Flynn was still at school. My apprentice wages didn't come close to covering our expenses."

"What about the house? Are there any other assets?"

"What *about* the house?" Hunter growls.

"It's freehold? You could remortgage it to get the funds needed to buy the business." I tap the file in his hands with the tip of my finger and sit back in my chair, a smile on my face. "That's the best way."

"I'm not remortgaging the house," Hunter snaps and I blink at him, startled by his vehemence. "It's my brother's home."

"I don't mean sell it. You just borrow against it," I say, voice quiet and soothing.

"I know what remortgaging means. I'm not a complete fucking dumbass. I'm not risking the house. It's Flynn's." He shoves out of his chair, towering over me again, jaw and fists clenched.

Someone else might find him intimidating when he's like this.

I don't. I know he's not going to hurt me, not physically at least. I don't think Hunter's ever hurt anyone like that.

I ache to reach out and touch him, but I keep my hands in my lap this time. We don't have the kind of relationship where I touch him anymore. "Have you talked to Flynn about this? Maybe he can buy you out of the house so you have the money to buy the business?"

"It's not Flynn's problem," he says. "Don't worry about it. I'll either figure something out or hope the new owner lets me keep my job."

He turns and strides from the room. I can hear him on the porch, stamping his feet into his boots. There's three crunches of gravel before I'm up out of the chair and racing after him.

This is the most time we've spent together in years, the biggest conversation we've had and I don't want it to end like this. I don't want another thing widening the divide between us.

For eighteen years of my life Hunter was my best friend, my other half, and every day since he broke my heart I've missed him.

I'm tired of fighting against myself when it comes to him. Tired of always biting my tongue to stop from accidentally slipping into conversation with him, or sitting on my hands so I don't reach out and touch him.

I thought staying away for all these years, keeping my walls up and distance between us, would dull the ache of missing him.

But I was wrong.

Right now I'm exhausted and emotionally screwed up from ending a relationship with a man I didn't even love, so fuck it.

Hunter might laugh in my face, or run for the hills, but I'm at least going to try.

By the time I reach the porch Hunter is already at his ute, opening the door. I throw myself down the steps and fly across the gravel driveway, barely feeling the sharp stones against my bare feet.

I'm not letting him leave me like this. Not again.

10

———

HUNTER

"NO," Willow's breathless voice says a moment before her body collides with mine.

She stumbles and my hands land on her waist, steadying her. Even through her cosy hoodie I can feel the curve of her hips and it takes everything in me to not drag my hand down her side to stroke the smooth skin of her thigh.

Those shorts are criminal. I bet if she turned around I'd be able to see the creases below her ass. It was not easy to concentrate on my financial woes while Willow was showing off all that leg in the office. It's probably why I was so harsh with her.

"Motherfucker these stones are sharp," she mutters, shifting from bare foot to bare foot, then forcing herself still and looking up at me. "I don't want you to go like this."

She shifts again and hisses.

I sigh. "Come here." My arms slide around her back and I scoop her off the ground, my hand landing on her ass as I pull her to me.

Fuck. I shouldn't be touching her. Not at all and definitely not like this. I close my eyes and will myself to be strong, to keep it together.

Willow gasps, then wraps her legs around my waist. Her fingers press against the back of my neck, her nails digging in just a tiny bit.

Fuck.

Fuuuuuuck. She feels so good. This wasn't what I had in mind when I picked her up. I don't know what I had in mind. Why did I think I'd ever be able to come back from touching her?

I turn and move towards my ute, lowering her down onto the driver's seat. She slowly unwraps her arms and legs from my body as I let her go. My hand skims down her leg and grips her ankle.

"Stop being mean to your feet," I scold her.

She lets out a breathy giggle. I should step back and give her some space, but I can't make myself move.

Then Willow leans forward and drops her head against my chest. My breath seizes as her fingers cling to the edges of my jacket, holding me there in the space between her bare legs.

My arms slide back around her, one hand cradling her head against me. I close my eyes and savour the sensation of having her back in my arms. I never thought this would happen again, not after what I did to her.

"What did you mean?" I whisper along her temple, my lips brushing against her hair.

"What?" she mumbles into the fleecy lining of my jacket.

"You said you didn't want me to go like this."

I shouldn't be asking her this. I shouldn't be pushing this moment to be over when I could happily stand here forever with her knees bracketing my hips and the scent of her in my nose.

She tilts her head back and looks up at me with watery eyes. God, the last time she looked at me like that was the day I broke her heart. I knew I was doing it at the time, but I knew in the end it would be worth it, for her anyway.

Willow sniffles. "I don't want you to go while you're mad at me." She bites her lip and a tear spills over her lashes to streak down her cheek. "I miss you, Hunter."

Her words shoot straight through my heart. I never thought I'd hear her say something like that again. I stare down into her gorgeous blue eyes—the colour of a perfect sky—and brush the tear from her cheek with the pad of my thumb. I tighten my arms around her and cradle her head against me as she turns her face away, a flicker of disappointment crossing her features as she does.

"I miss you too, Will," I murmur into her hair, her nickname sliding off my tongue like no time has passed since the last time I used it. The ache in my chest intensifies at the admission. "All the damn time."

Willow wraps her arms around my waist and squeezes me tightly enough to expel my breath. "Don't go yet. We can practise being friends again." She gives me another squeeze, then slowly releases her grip, sitting back to look up at me again. "Unless you have plans of course. You don't have to stay." Her cheeks turn pink.

"I don't have plans," I say. I finally force myself to take a step back, allowing her space. Whatever is happening here is not the kind of thing where her bare legs should be wrapped around my waist.

Willow wipes her cheeks with the back of her hand. "Do you want to come riding with me?"

I groan. "Horses? I won't be able to walk tomorrow. It's been years since I've been on one." I protest, but I know I'm going riding. I'll do anything she asks of me so long as I get to spend another minute in her presence.

"Sounds like you're overdue a ride then." The corner of her mouth curls up in a cheeky smile. "Paddy's probably missed you." She tugs the front of my jacket. "Come on. I haven't got my fill of this place yet."

The look she gives me is so hopeful that I can't say no to her, even if riding a horse is right at the bottom of my list of things I want to do.

"Fine," I grumble. "We'll go riding." I spin around so my back is to her. "Climb on. You need to find something to wear that's a little more suitable."

Willow giggles and barely hesitates before she climbs on my back. I kick the ute door closed and head back to the house, trying to think about anything but the bare skin of Willow's thighs against my palms as I piggyback her across the gravel. I set her down on the porch.

"You better be here when I get back," she says, pointing a finger at me. "No running away."

"I won't," I say, our eyes locking. "I promise."

She bites her lip, eyes on mine for a long moment, then she spins away and races into the house.

In that moment I feel it: the pressure in my cheeks as my lips tilt up into a smile.

IT TAKES Willow five minutes to get changed and meet me back on the porch wearing skin-tight, well-worn jeans, a warm jacket and her boots.

She's practically buzzing beside me as we walk down to the barn and horse paddocks. Willow keeps opening her mouth and drawing in a breath, like she's ready to say something, but never goes through with it. Meanwhile I stride along beside her, my mind entirely blank. After all these years I don't even know what to say to her.

We don't really speak while we're saddling Paddy and Scout, unless it's about getting the horses ready, mindless comments about which is the right bridle or could she use the dandy brush after me.

I don't know what to say to take the conversation deeper. We don't spend time alone anymore. Sure, we've talked over the years, we've even shared a joke or two, but always with someone else in the room and every time it felt like we were putting on a show. It didn't feel like *us*. Not since the conversation where I ruined everything.

Once the horses are tacked up, we swing up into the saddles and head down the main farm track, the horses walking companionably side by side.

The chilly autumn breeze curls around me and sneaks down

the collar of my jacket. I hunch my shoulders against the cold but take a moment to appreciate the clear skies and the fiery colours of the leaves. It's my favourite time of year, when the oppressive heat of summer is gone but we haven't hit the gloomy days of winter yet. The air is fresh but the colours are still vivid.

"I haven't been out here in ages," I say, words finally forming as I tilt my head back to feel the sun on my face. My muscles already ache from the riding, but I decide not to mention that.

"I came out with Liv yesterday, but it wasn't enough," Willow says. Her face is relaxed, a soft smile on her lips. She looks happy, at home.

I roll my next words around in my head, unsure how to ask what I want to know. "I'm surprised that you're still here," I say eventually. "I thought you would have gone home this morning."

Willow sighs, deep and long. The happiness fades from her face. "This is always home," she says, not really answering my question.

Fair enough, I guess. Sharing a couple of moments with her this weekend doesn't entitle me to details of her life.

She pulls Scout to an abrupt stop and turns to look directly at me, her face set. "I think this is the only place I'm calling home for a while," she says, then kicks Scout forward into a canter, leaving me, completely stunned, in her dust.

11

———

WILLOW

I ALWAYS THOUGHT I was a fairly sensible person. My parents never really had to worry about me as a teenager because I make smart choices.

Or I did.

Inviting Hunter to come riding with me is not one of them.

But as distracting as his thighs are astride a horse, and how captivating his hands are holding the reins, and how him squinting ever-so-slightly when the sun gets in his eyes makes me want to cup his face in my palms and smooth the tiny creases beside his eyes, it's nice to be with him again.

Scout and I race up the next hill and slow to a stop when we reach the crest, exhilaration thrumming through my veins. I'm never going to get tired of that feeling.

I glance back, expecting to see Hunter close behind, but Paddy is still strolling contentedly through the paddock. Hunter's either lost his nerve riding, or he's giving me some space after my little bombshell.

Why the hell did I come up with this harebrained idea to go riding with Hunter?

"You getting too old for this?" I call when he gets closer, adrenaline making me brave. "Can't handle the speed?" I grin at him and he scowls. My smile stretches wider.

"You're the same age as me, smart ass," he grumbles, halting Paddy beside Scout. The two horses reach out and snuffle at each other.

"Well, I'm never going to be too old for this," I say, arching my back and enjoying the sun on my face.

Hunter props his arms on the saddle pommel and leans on them. "Do you want to talk about it?" he asks, staring off into the distance.

I sigh. This is a conversation I should probably have with Mum, but I don't want her to be disappointed about the break up. I don't want her to worry, or to think I'm cut up over it.

I'm not. Not really. The relationship has been over for a really long time, but I didn't want to deal with the fallout from actually ending it. My glaring attraction to Hunter this weekend makes me wonder if I was ever really in it. Surely I've felt like this about Hunter all along, I just didn't let myself acknowledge it.

But right now, I'm feeling weak. And Hunter is the hottest man I've ever seen. I hate him a little for it.

"I haven't told Mum yet," I say, watching Hunter from the corner of my eye.

"Well, she obviously knows you're staying for longer than the weekend."

"Yeah, she knows that much. But not ... all the rest of it."

"You don't have to tell me, Will," he says and a little thrill passes through me at him using my nickname. The name only my family has ever called me. Him and Flynn are the only exceptions to that.

Hunter nudges Paddy's sides with his heels and the gelding starts forward again. Scout follows behind with little guidance from me.

I thought Hunter would push more than that. I thought he'd demand answers. I'm stunned he just ... let it go. I was about to tell him, too.

We work our way down the hill and I let the sway of Scout's gait wash away all of my stress and anxiety about my life and what the future looks like.

Without discussion, we head towards an old fallen tree at the bottom of the valley. When we reach it, we slide from the saddles and loop the reins over a branch to stop the horses wandering off. Not that I think they'd go far.

Hunter groans and I smile to myself. He's going to hurt on the ride home.

"Give me a boost," I say, placing my hands on the rough bark of the tree trunk. Hunter steps up behind me, grasps my raised foot and lifts me high enough that I can get my other leg over the log. I shuffle around until I've found a comfortable position and a moment later Hunter is climbing up beside me.

I don't know how we've fallen back into old patterns so easily, but I guess eighteen years of friendship isn't easily erased. Now we're together, it's like those ten years of separation never happened.

We're tucked away from the world down here. There's no

road in sight, no buildings. Only me, Hunter and the horses. It's a safe little cocoon away from reality.

"I don't know that I can go back," I whisper after we've been sitting in silence for a long minute. "To the city I mean. I miss this place, I miss my family. Maybe it's time I come home, or maybe it's time I finally do all that travelling I always wanted. I don't know, but the city has never truly felt like home."

Hunter rubs a hand over his hair. "What does whatshisface think about that?" His voice is gruff, his focus zeroed in on a random spot across the valley.

I snort. "You know his name is Mark." Hunter lifts one shoulder in a half-assed shrug. "And I don't really care, considering we aren't together anymore." I let out a shaky breath once the words are out. It feels so much more momentous telling Hunter than it did telling Olivia.

Hunter's head turns sharply, studying me with narrowed eyes. "Since when? I haven't heard about it."

I meet his eyes. "Why would you have heard about it? Do you keep tabs on me?" The thought shouldn't thrill me as much as it does. As much as I've missed him and longed for his friendship, I shouldn't be feeling this heady excitement about him.

"Your mum tends to keep me updated. She ... I don't think she realises how much it hurts." His voices trails off so I barely catch the last words. My jaw drops as they register. Hunter catches my eye and hurriedly continues. "Anyway, she hasn't told me about this development. Last I heard you were planning on marrying the guy."

"That's the part she doesn't know yet," I mutter, letting go of

Hunter's admission. I'm not sure how I'm supposed to feel about that. "I officially broke up with him on Tuesday. I packed up my stuff Wednesday and moved it into my friend's spare room. She cut all my hair off, then I drove here Thursday." I slump, exhausted from saying the words again, even though it's only the second time, no doubt of many. Slowly word will spread that I'm back and half the town knows I've been in a relationship for several years. They're all going to want to know where he is.

"I'm sorry, Will," Hunter says, his arm coming around me. He's hesitant at first but then the warm weight settles across my shoulders and I lean into him, his steadiness soothing something in me. It's like the moment earlier beside his ute, when I buried my face in his jacket while his big hands cradled my head. The scent of him in my nose and his unshakeable presence beside me just felt right.

Tears threaten, but I sniff them back and straighten my spine. "I'm not." I look Hunter dead in the eye. "He chose the dress and the shoes." I pause, letting my admission register. "He didn't really know me, not in the way it mattered, or if he did, he wanted me to be different. It's been over for a really long time, but I was scared of all the change. I'm not scared anymore."

Hunter's hand falls from my shoulder to my hip and he tugs me closer to him, so our thighs press together.

"You don't need to be scared of anything," he says against my temple, his lips brushing over my skin. Right when I think he's going to pull away he presses a soft kiss against my hair and tightens his arm around my body.

I curl into his side, resting my head against his shoulder.

This is a big change too, the way Hunter and I are together this weekend—maybe not all change needs to be scary.

12

HUNTER

THIS MOMENT IS ALMOST TOO much for me to bear.

It's so reminiscent of the days we'd spend out the back of the farm as teenagers, either on horses or motorbikes. We'd bring packets of chips and muesli bars or raid Mum's fresh baking for muffins and cupcakes, then we'd stay out here all day. I don't know what we did for most of that time, but we did spend a fair amount of it sitting like this, talking.

We sat like this—Willow tucked into my side with my arm around her—after her first boyfriend broke up with her when we were fifteen. I did something similar right after I turned seventeen and she found out the guy she really liked only wanted to get in her pants. I was ready to go smack his face in, but Willow dragged me out here instead.

After that day, she never mentioned another guy to me. I don't know if it was my threats of violence, or because she somehow figured out my feelings about her had changed from friends to something more, despite how hard I tried to hide it.

I don't know when the change happened, if it was one moment or a million tiny ones that built on each other, but one day I couldn't look at her without this desperate, longing ache taking over my chest.

I couldn't tell her then, because I knew she didn't feel the same and I wasn't going to risk losing my best friend.

I waited until I was sure, and my patience paid off.

My heart in my throat, I invited her out one night. It was nothing unusual, we spent most of our time together anyway, but for some reason I was convinced this time she'd say no.

Obviously she didn't, because to her it was simply another night hanging out with her friend.

I begged Dad to let me borrow the Torana. He wasn't going to let me. He wanted to drive it that night, but when I told him I was taking Willow out and it was *important*, he relented. Maybe he was as hopeful as I was about it. I'll never know because we didn't get a chance to talk about it.

I don't know why I was so desperate to have that car that night. Maybe if I hadn't been driving it, if I'd let Dad take it, everything would be different. But I needed the Torana for some weird confidence boost. Maybe because when Willow and I talked about our plans for the future we were sitting in that car while I polished the dash.

The night of what I hoped would be our first date, I picked Willow up. When she questioned me being allowed to drive the Torana, I kept my answers vague and she gave up. We drove up to the lookout and ate burgers at a picnic table there. I told her how as soon as we were done with school we should leave this tiny town and go see the world. She agreed. She was as excited about it as I was.

It wasn't the first time we'd talked about it and we'd both applied to university in Auckland as our first step out of Kauri Creek. It was when we started making plans together for our future that I realised Willow was feeling the same things I was. It was a subtle shift in the way she spoke, the way she looked at me and the way her touches lingered on my skin.

We made a list of places we wanted to go once we had our degrees, the things we could do. The whole world was laid out at our feet.

We climbed back into the car when the sun disappeared behind the horizon and the night began to cool. Stars appeared, but we stayed, talking as the last of the day faded.

"It's going to be amazing," Willow said, our conversation circling back to our travel plans again. "Why didn't we do this before uni?"

I laughed. "Because some smarty-pants won an epic scholarship."

I reached out to ruffle her hair, a casual move I've made a thousand times. Willow snatched my hand from the air, like *she'd* done a thousand times, but instead of her throwing it back at me like usual, she twined our fingers together. She rested our joined hands between us and I stared down at the way her delicate fingers fit with mine. I'd never seen something more perfect in my life.

Eventually, I dragged my eyes away from our hands and met Willow's gaze head on. She was staring at me, something unreadable in her expression.

This was the moment. The moment I'd been waiting for, because now I was sure.

I leaned closer and relief washed over me as she did the same. When I reached up and grazed my fingertips across her cheek she let out the tiniest gasp of shock, but didn't pull away. She didn't pull away when I slipped my hand into her hair, or cupped her face in my palm, or when I finally—FINALLY—brought my lips down on hers.

She melted into me and what I was expecting to be a soft, simple kiss to test the waters turned hard and fast and so, so damn hot.

She tasted like magic and happiness and all of my dreams coming true.

Willow moaned and clung to me, her hands caught in my hair as I pulled her closer.

"Wait, stop," I gasped, breaking the kiss but holding her face close to mine.

"What?" Willow whispered into the space between us.

"I have to say something first."

"You're going to stop this to *talk?*" Willow laughed.

"Shush. I planned it all."

Her eyes met mine and all the words I'd carefully thought out and stressed over for days, weeks, months, disappeared.

"I love you," I whispered. "I'm in love with you."

Willow's eyes—that perfect shade of blue—widened. "Take me home, Hunter." Her voice was so soft, so breathy, I almost didn't hear her. But then I did.

I jerked back, dropping my hands from her face, my face

burning. I turned towards the steering wheel and cranked the ignition.

Willow reached over and grasped my chin with her soft fingers. She turned my head so I was forced to meet her eyes. "Your home, Hunter. There are things I want to do with you that I cannot do in this car." She leaned over and pressed her mouth to mine, her tongue dragging across my lips. "Because I love you too. I have forever."

I drove her home, as fast as possible without speeding, because my dad would kill me if something happened to this car —or to either Willow or I.

When we finally made it back to town, I led her inside and we spent hours in my room, showing each other exactly how much we loved each other, and making plans for our future together, as a couple.

I'd never felt such pure, unadulterated joy. I wish it could have lasted longer, because before the night was over, so was any chance we had of being together.

Dragging my thoughts back to the present, away from the complicated, overwhelming feelings about that night, I shift on the log next to Willow, my ass and legs already beginning to ache from the saddle.

"I should probably head back," I say. "Got to organise my shit before work tomorrow."

The reality is I never want to leave this place, this moment, when I finally have Willow back in my arms after all these years.

But as easy as it's been to fall back into long lost familiarity, this isn't real life. At this point, with Willow tucked against my side, I'm pretty convinced this whole thing is a dream.

Willow straightens, pushing herself away from me with a hand on my thigh. I try not to react to the touch.

"Yeah, of course." She shuffles sideways to give me room to jump down. My feet hit the grass and I turn to help her down. My heart is in my throat as I offer my hand to her if she wants to take it, desperately hoping she'll reach for me.

She does, and when she jumps she lands right in front of me. If I took a deep breath I'd feel her chest against mine.

We hover there, millimetres between us. I need to step away, drop her hand and get out of her space, but I can't. I'm trapped here, under her spell.

I want to lean down and kiss her, feel her lips soft against mine, have her hands tangle in my shirt.

I've told myself a million times over the years that I'm past my feelings for Willow Austin. But I'm a filthy liar and this moment is proof.

She glances away and it feels like that moment all those years ago when she asked me to take her home and I thought it meant she didn't want me back.

Willow scuffs her boot in the dirt and the reality hits me. Now isn't then. It'll never be like that again, not because I lost my parents that night, which changed my whole life, but because of the way I had Willow's heart in my hands and instead of cradling it gently, keeping it close, I threw it away and shattered it instead.

13

WILLOW

I BROKE ALL my rules about Hunter in one afternoon.

Don't spend time alone with him, avoid eye contact as much as possible, stay away from any kind of bodily contact—especially skin-on-skin—and never, ever get close enough to smell him.

The rules were designed to protect myself and for a decade they have.

In a moment of weakness I broke every single one and spent hours with him alone.

And now I can't get him out of my head.

I keep thinking about the night he kissed me and told me he loved me. How sure he was of his feelings, how relieved I was that he brought it up so I didn't have to, how his hands felt on my body, how excited I was for the future, how my heart broke when he ended things between us before they even had a chance to start—though every time those particular memories surface I shove them away.

I think about the years that have passed and how every time I came home I'd make sure I only crossed paths with Hunter when I was prepared for it. I remember bringing Mark home early in our relationship. I thought I'd finally be free of the hold Hunter had on me.

But I was wrong.

He and Flynn came to dinner one night and Hunter scowled through the whole thing, saying nothing unless he was addressed directly. I was so on edge the entire time that later I snuck down to the barn, curled up in the hay bales, and cried.

After that day I knew Hunter Woods would haunt me forever.

I need to figure out what I'm doing with my life and get out of this town as soon as possible because I cannot live in a place where the ghosts of the past are real and right in front of me, tempting me into danger.

I thought about staying, about returning home and making my life here. But I can't do it. I need to leave.

I shake out the next sheet from the load of laundry I'm hanging out and toss it over the line at the back of Mum's garden. A gust of wind hits the sheet, blowing it up to smack me in the face.

My phone vibrates in my back pocket as I'm untangling myself. I pull it out to check the message, expecting to see Mark's name. He's been messaging and calling multiple times a day for nearly a week now. Apparently he didn't believe me when I said I was breaking up with him. Not until he got home from work the next day to find all of my stuff moved out of our flat.

The calls and messages hit a peak over the weekend when he went looking for me at Margot's place and she told him I wasn't there.

They've thankfully eased off in the days since, though I've still taken to leaving my phone at the other end of the house.

So, when I pull my phone out I'm expecting to see another message from Mark trying to convince me I'm being over-dramatic and what he did wasn't a completely self-absorbed asshole move. Personally I think I'm not being dramatic *enough*. But what I find isn't Mark's name. I almost drop my phone when it registers.

I have a message from Hunter.

HUNTER:

Hey. I have another idea about making up the shortfall in that budget. Can I run it past you sometime?

I stare down at the message. It's simple, to the point. Direct and clear. But I can't help wondering if he's using the finances as an excuse to see me again. Do I want that?

I don't want to go back to avoiding him like I have been. I enjoyed spending time with him on Sunday. He was my best friend for more than half my life for a reason.

My fingers feel shaky as I tap out my reply.

WILLOW:

Of course. I can come and meet you for lunch? Maybe tomorrow?

I take a deep breath. Lunch is a good idea. I can meet him at Sugar, we'll be in public, there will be a whole table between us.

Hunter replies before I can put my phone away.

HUNTER:

Sounds good. Does 12.30 at Sugar work?

WILLOW:

Perfect.

HUNTER:

See you then

I lock my phone and slide it into my pocket, pulling it out again almost immediately as another message comes through. I'm expecting an afterthought from Hunter and I can already feel my mouth curling into a smile as a warm fizzing feeling spreads through me.

MARK:

You're seriously going to end it all over this stupid issue?

The warm fizzy feeling dissipates.

I spin on my heel and stomp back to the house, kicking my boots off at the kitchen door, then slam it behind me as I step inside. Tears prick at my eyes, heat and pressure building.

I collide with a body standing inside the kitchen.

"You okay, Willow?" Strong arms wrap around me and a sob escapes. "Hey, what's wrong?"

Flynn tugs me against him and my arms automatically find their way around him.

"Fucking Mark," I mutter into Flynn's chest. God, I wish he wasn't here to greet me. I'd have been able to sneak off to my room to have a cry without witnesses.

"What do I need to do to him? How bad is it? Should I assemble the cavalry? We can ride at dawn."

My sobs turn to a choked laugh as I pull back and look up at Flynn. He's the total opposite of his brother; tall and lanky with a mop of red hair and a permanent grin on his face. He hasn't questioned why I'm still here, no one has. I don't know what Olivia has told them, but I appreciate them not asking me about it.

"It's not worth it," I mutter, swiping a few stray tears from my cheeks.

"Uh, if he made you cry then yeah, it is."

"It's really not, Flynn. He's completely irrelevant. It's just going to take some time for me to get used to that." I sigh and lean against Flynn. He hasn't dropped his arms from around my back, so I'll borrow his strength for as long as he'll let me. "And fuck, I miss my dad." My voice threatens to break again but I get the words out.

Flynn pulls me closer, guiding my head to rest against his chest. "I know," he murmurs. "I do too."

"Does it get better?" I ask.

"People say it gets better with time. My experience is it gets different with time. Better might not be the right word for me. I hate that they're gone—Mum, Dad, Henry—but I still love the life I have now. It's a weird thing to rationalise."

"Yeah, I kind of understand that," I say. "Maybe." A weird, almost bitter laugh escapes me. "Maybe not. I keep expecting to see him and he's not there. Every time it's like it just happened all over again."

Flynn's hand smooths my hair. "Yeah, well, we've all had

time to get used to not seeing him around here. You'll adjust. Eventually." He sighs, the sound soft and sad. "On that uplifting and positive note, are you sure I don't need to assemble the troops?"

I laugh again, but it's still not a happy sound. "You don't need to assemble the troops. Mark is an insignificant speck of muck on my boots. No more tears for him, he just caught me off guard."

I pull back from Flynn's hug and glance up into his face to find an unusually serious expression.

"Good," Flynn says. "No one should be making you cry. You let me know if it happens again."

"I will. Thank you, Flynn." I send a smile his way, then head for the hallway. "I'll see you around."

"Oh," he calls after me. "You should tell Hunter if whatshisname makes you cry again. He'd defend your honour."

The words follow me down the hall, echoing through my mind.

Would Hunter defend my honour? Stand up for me? Fight for me?

Maybe.

Would he be doing it for me though? Or some weird obligation he feels to my family or the past?

Maybe he wouldn't do anything at all.

Either which way, I have no idea what it would mean, so it's better not to wonder at all.

14

HUNTER

I RUSH DOWN THE STREET, pausing when Sugar comes into view.

I can see Willow through the windows along the storefront.

She's sitting at a corner table, tucked up against the back wall of the cafe. She's fiddling with a napkin, carefully shredding it into even strips. I take a moment to register that and what it means. She's nervous. About seeing me.

I push the door open, my eyes fixed on her. She glances up at the sound of the door and jolts when our eyes connect. I want to smile at her reaction. It's like she's shocked to see me when I'm who she's here to meet.

But I don't smile because I wonder if she thought I might not show up. That gives me pause.

Her face softens and a smile touches her lips as I reach the table.

"Hey," I say. "Have you ordered?"

She shakes her head, her loose hair swishing around her jaw. "I was waiting for you."

"What do you want?"

Willow stands and follows me to the counter where I order the bushman's brekkie and the largest coffee I can get from the ever-smiling Tilly Sheridan. This girl can rival my brother for her good moods.

Willow orders a BLAT and coke, then pulls an eftpos card out of the back pocket of her jeans.

"I got it," I say, placing my hand over hers and pushing it away from the machine.

"Aren't you supposed to be saving money?" she asks and I barely register the words because my mind is skipping over the fact that I'm touching her ... again.

"If I can't buy my friend lunch as a thank you for helping me then it doesn't seem worth it."

Willow hesitates, then relents, dropping her hand from under mine and putting her card away.

I swipe my own card and punch the buttons on the machine harder than necessary. I should feel good because she let me buy her lunch, but I don't because I'm pretty convinced she only allowed it to get her hand out of mine as soon as possible.

"Thanks guys," Tilly says, smile never faltering at mine and Willow's awkward interaction. "I'll bring it over soon."

I give her a nod, then follow Willow back to the table, sliding into the chair opposite her.

She immediately picks up the napkin and begins shredding it again. I watch her fingers, the nails painted a deep red, and wish I could fit mine between them.

This lunch was a very, very bad idea.

"I told Mum," Willow blurts. "About Mark."

"How'd she take the news?"

Willow shrugs. "Like I thought she would. Empathy, fussing, offering to take him out with her car."

That gets a laugh out of me. "And how do you feel now?"

"Fine." Willow sighs, then lifts her gaze to meet mine. "I really need things to not change for a while. I barely recognise my life anymore."

"It is a big change, Will," I say. "You've been with him for years." I know exactly how many years. I remember hearing about him for the first time. I remember meeting him and having to sit through a fucking dinner with him at Wildflower Ridge. I knew then that he wasn't right for Willow, but who was I to comment? "What are you doing about work?"

"I'm doing what I can remotely and taking some holiday time. But I need to figure that out. I can't stay here forever."

I want to tell her she can, that she should, but I'm saved from that by Tilly delivering our drinks to the table.

"Let me know if you need anything else," she says, beaming.

"Thanks, Tilly," Willow smiles back, the expression easy. I wish it felt that easy for me.

I redirect the conversation, asking her if Flynn's dog has driven her crazy yet.

She laughs and we slip into conversation the same way we did on Sunday afternoon. We talk about Flynn and Abi, Katie and Dallas, Olivia and Violet and Sadie. We talk about the people we went to school with and where they are now. Willow tells me about her life in the city, both of us carefully avoiding mentions of Mark.

It almost feels the same as years ago when we'd talk like this for hours on end. Almost.

The time flies by and my phone alarm interrupts Willow's hilarious story of her best friend Margot on a diabolical blind date. I'm glad I set the alarm, because I'd have talked right through my lunch break and for the entire afternoon if I didn't have the blaring reminder that I need to get back to work.

"Shit, I have to go," I say, silencing the alarm.

"Oh, we didn't even talk about what we were supposed to."

I blink at her, halfway out of my chair. I can't even think what we were supposed to be talking about. The money, the business, the car. That's right. I drop back into my seat. "Sorry, I dragged you all the way in here for nothing."

"I don't know about that. The food here is pretty good." She smiles at me, and I feel the corner of my mouth tip up at her teasing.

"Can we try again?" I ask. "Dinner? My shout."

Willow studies me for what feels like eternity. Surely it can't be this big of a decision. But maybe she doesn't want to spend time with me at all and I'm pushing her into a corner.

I stand, the chair scraping across the polished concrete floor of the cafe. "Don't worry about it. I don't think the idea would have worked anyway. I'll see you around."

I turn and stride for the door before she has a chance to respond. She was humouring me. She doesn't want to spend any more time with me than she has to. She's had plenty of opportunities over the years to do that, and she's avoided me for a decade.

I don't blame her. I don't want to spend time with myself either.

I reach the corner of the block before I hear my name being called. I turn to see Willow hurrying down the street after me, a scowl on her face.

"If you'd fucking wait a second," she snarks, stopping beside me, panting slightly. "Yes, we can do dinner. Tomorrow night. Let me know what time and I'll meet you at the hotel."

"You don't have to, Willow," I say.

"I know I don't have to. I want to." Her voice is still snappy. It's the way she used to speak to me when I pissed her off. I've missed it.

I rub a hand over my hair and sigh. "If you're sure."

"Yes, Hunter," she says, her voice softening. "I'm sure. I just ..." She huffs out a breath and looks everywhere but at me. "It's been ten years and it's taking some getting used to us being like this again." She gestures between us and finally meets my eyes again. "You get me?"

"Yeah, Willow. I get you."

15

———

WILLOW

I SIT in my car and stare at the front door of the Kauri Creek Hotel.

I don't know if Hunter is inside already and I can't decide if I want to be the first to arrive, like I was yesterday at lunch, or if I want to be a little late so I'm not sitting inside sweating that he's not going to show.

Instead, I'll sit out here in my car and worry that he's not going to show.

Hunter was so hot and cold at lunch. In some moments it was like we were eighteen again and nothing had ever come between us. We talked and laughed like it was second nature to have lunch together and hang out.

But then he'd close off and try to bail. When he invited me to dinner, I caught the glimmer of hope in his eyes before he locked his feelings back up.

That's why I came tonight.

Hunter called me his friend at lunch, and I want that. I

want our friendship back, and that look in his eye ... it told me he wants it too, even if he doesn't know how to say it.

I stretch up and check myself in the rearview mirror. Again. I swipe under my eyes in case any mascara has shifted in the two minutes since I last did this, then I check my teeth for lipstick. Again.

It's almost dark and the streetlights are on, so the street is shadowy and everything is more orange than it should be. I sigh and slump into my seat.

I spent the day working, trying to focus on my account reconciliations and not this dinner with Hunter. When I finished everything I could reasonably do for my actual job, I trawled through the Wildflower Ridge accounts, seeing where we can streamline processes and budgets to help Mum and Olivia.

When I'd done as much as I could there without Olivia's input, I went for a run. But even that wasn't enough to stop me thinking about tonight, or quell the jittery energy coursing through me.

I nearly offered to help Flynn repair a fence late this afternoon, but decided against it at the last minute and instead spent the time getting ready for a dinner that is definitely not a date, but for some reason I'm putting more effort into than any date I've ever been on, and that includes the night ten years ago that Hunter and I finally admitted our feelings for each other.

I spent over an hour choosing an outfit, then showered, washed my hair, and shaved areas of my body that really didn't need to be shaved for a friendly dinner with an old friend, especially when my legs are fully covered.

I close my eyes and take several long, slow breaths, finally managing to calm my racing heart a little.

Then, a tap on my car's window startles me so hard I shriek. I glance over, scrambling for something I can use as a weapon, to see Hunter's face looking at me through the glass.

I stop my scrambling and slouch into the seat again, pressing a hand to my racing heart.

Hunter opens the passenger door and pokes his head inside.

"Jesus fucking christ, Hunter," I snap. "You scared the shit out of me."

He chuckles, and for once he actually sounds legitimately amused. "Sorry, Will. I didn't mean to."

"Sure you fucking didn't," I grumble as I grab my bag and open my door, stepping out into the street. I lock the car behind me and fall into step beside Hunter as we head for the hotel.

It's the only place in town where you can dine in at this time of night and it's been that way my whole life. There's Sugar and a couple of questionable bakeries open during the day, but the Kauri Creek Hotel is the extent of the nightlife in this town. Well, except for the dodgy bar on the other side of town, but I wouldn't go there for a drink, let alone food.

We head inside the pub, Hunter holding the front door open for me. Passing the door into the bar, we follow the hallway to the back of the building where the restaurant is located.

It's nothing fancy, and the decor doesn't look like it's been changed in the last fifty years. But damn, it feels like home.

I scuff one of my boots across the faded carpet. "Do you remember the night Flynn snorted Fanta out his nose?"

Hunter huffs a laugh. "Like I'll ever forget that. He was trying to impress that girl. They had to replace the carpet after that."

"The last renovation this place has seen," I say.

"Sure is," Hunter replies. He indicates a table in the corner with a tilt of his head and when I nod, his hand lands on the small of my back, guiding me in that direction.

My breath catches at the touch, but I manage to suppress any other reaction I have to him. We've touched each other countless times throughout our lives. This simple, innocent touch shouldn't send me into a tailspin.

But it does.

Hunter's hand is barely on my back for a moment, through several layers of fabric, but all I can think about is what it would feel like against my bare skin.

Reaching the table I slip my denim jacket off and hang it over the back of my chair before sinking into the seat. Hunter sits across from me, his dark hazel eyes capturing mine in an instant. He glances away, then drags his gaze over me and I suppress a shiver at the intensity in his stare.

Dinner with a friend, I remind myself. That's all this is.

A waitress appears beside the table and breaks the moment of silent tension between us.

"Hi Hunter," she says, a shy smile on her glossy pink lips. "How are you?"

"Good, thanks." He barely looks at her.

"I've been keeping an eye on everything in my car, like you showed me."

His gaze flicks up to her again, then away again after barely a second. "That's good." He looks directly at me. "Do you want something to drink?"

"Ah, yeah. A gin and tonic, please." I smile at the waitress. She can't be more than twenty, with rich brown eyes and dark hair pulled back in a slick ponytail. She gives me a slightly wobbly smile and makes a note on her order pad.

"That's different," Hunter says to me, his brow drawn down. I shrug. It's what I always order. He just doesn't know adult me. "I'll have the beer on tap," Hunter says, glancing up to the waitress. "Thanks."

The girl makes another note. "Coming right up," she says, faking brightness, before spinning on her heel and scurrying away.

"Who's that?" I ask Hunter.

"I think it's Brian's daughter. He had me show her a few things on her car before she went to uni." His voice doesn't change when he talks about her and his gaze doesn't follow her as she retreats across the room.

"So, there's nothing going on there?" I ask, a teasing smile playing at my lips.

"What? With her? She's a kid."

I shrug. "She's actually an adult."

Hunter scowls. "No." He focusses on his menu.

"So it's all one sided then, huh? Poor girl."

Hunter sighs and drops his menu, leaning back in his chair and crossing his arms. "What are you talking about, Willow?"

I nod towards the waitress. "She's got a crush on you."

Hunter rolls his eyes. "Don't be ridiculous."

"She does."

"Well, it's not mutual," he grumbles.

"Is there someone else?" I ask before my brain can stop the words spilling from my mouth.

Hunter's head lifts in slow motion. When our gazes lock, his stare is even more intense than before. "I thought your mum would have kept you up to date on that," he says, his voice low.

I swallow and force through my sticky throat. "She hasn't."

"Must not have been anything to report," he says, those eyes burning into mine.

"Nothing?" I whisper. "No one."

Hunter shakes his head ever so slightly. "No one." His gaze dips, then meets mine again. "No one worth mentioning anyway," he says.

I shift in my seat, the power of his stare overwhelming me. My leg bumps against his, but he doesn't move it away. He presses it into mine.

He lifts his brows, a silent question.

I nod, because, yeah, I understand.

Hunter hasn't had a relationship since the brief moment in time that we were together ten years ago.

He holds my gaze for another moment, then nods and turns back to his menu, but his leg doesn't move at all.

16

———

HUNTER

WELL, that took a turn.

I don't know what I'm doing telling Willow about my dating history, or lack thereof.

I haven't been celibate since that night I spent with her. I've had plenty of experience of the physical aspects of a relationship, and for a time had a standing arrangement with someone. I wouldn't call it friends-with-benefits, because we weren't friends. She was older than me and picked me up on one of the nights I threw caution to the wind and drank at the bar across town.

I'd go there when I was feeling reckless and pissed off at the world.

She found me one night, drowning my sorrows and trying to get into fights over the pool tables.

She took me home and fucked my brains out, giving me an alternative way to manage my overwhelming feelings. After that night, when she called, I'd drop around to her place for another round. It probably wasn't healthy, but sometimes I needed a break from being my little brother's guardian and she offered that respite. She also taught me many, many things. Things all my partners since then have been very appreciative of.

But to tell Willow there's never been anyone serious, to imply that it's only ever been *her*, I don't know what I'm thinking.

It's true though. There only ever has been her.

I haven't wanted anyone else, not the way I wanted her.

The way I want her.

Present tense.

Because *fuck*.

She's sitting across from me in a soft creamy-coloured sweater with a low V-neckline, showing off the swell of her tits, and a skirt that barely reaches her mid-thigh. She's wearing tights and boots with it, so I can't even see her legs, but I'm rocking a semi regardless.

Her hair gleams under the soft overhead lights, the blunt cut accentuating her big blue eyes and lush, full lips. It's one of the best things I've ever seen in my life.

"What's good here these days?" she asks, eyes on her menu.

"I don't really know," I admit. "I don't come here very often. I think the last time was for Flynn's birthday last year."

"And let me guess," Willow says, a smile tugging at those delectable lips. "It was under duress."

"Obviously."

She laughs and the sound is like magic. I want to bottle it and hold it close to my chest, never let it go.

But the reality is I do have to let her go, because her life isn't in Kauri Creek anymore. She has a job and friends to go back to in Auckland.

And the other brutal reality is that she isn't mine to keep here anyway. I had my shot and I blew it. Maybe if I'd handled everything differently back then, I'd have a chance now.

But I didn't, and I don't.

"Roulette it is then," Willow says, referencing our stupid childhood game, and I glance up to see her smirking at me.

"Do we have to?" I groan. "I'm not over that seafood pasta I had to eat that time."

Willow's laugh is loud this time, drawing the attention of a group of diners across the room. "Those poor little octopuses. Octopi? I can never figure out what the right way to say that is."

"I don't care. One octopus in my dinner was too much, let alone multiple." I shudder, remembering their tiny tentacles.

Willow scans the menu again. "Well, you're safe today, no octopus mentioned on this menu."

"Fine. But if I get something gross we're sharing yours."

"Deal," Willow says, before closing her eyes and waving her finger through the air. She presses it against the menu and opens her eyes. "Mmm, stuffed chicken breast for me. What're you having, Hunt?"

Hunt. She hasn't called me that in a long, long time. No one has. Except Katie, who does it purely to piss me off. It works too. The only people who've ever gotten away with it were my parents and Willow.

I close my eyes and stab at the menu with my pointer finger, then crack open my eyes to peer at what I've chosen. Lamb pot pie. I can live with that.

Willow waves over the waitress she claims has a crush on me and orders our meals.

I don't even remember the girl's name, but I pay more attention this time, and yeah, she's sending me way too many simpering looks.

Fuck. It's not like I've ever done anything to ingratiate her towards me. I treated her like I do anyone else I work with. Polite, but detached, because I cannot be bothered with people ninety-nine percent of the time.

My brother and the Austin family are the only exceptions.

The waitress sends me another smile before she leaves us. When I return my focus to Willow, she's smirking.

"Shut up," I say before she has a chance to say anything.

She raises her hands, palms towards me in a surrender gesture, but I can read the look on her face clear as day. She told me so.

I expect her to continue teasing me, but when she resumes conversation it's not about the waitress, or my lack of dating history. Instead she brings up the first time we played menu roulette, when she couldn't make a decision about what to order at a dinner we had for some occasion, I can't even remember what it was now. I do remember sitting at the end of the table, across the corner from Willow, whose hair was in two long braids.

Our conversation meanders from there, a long, nostalgic trip down memory lane as we recount stories from our childhood, many of which happened in this room.

We barely break conversation when our food is delivered. We got lucky and both meals are edible. In fact they're pretty damn good for a small town hotel in the back blocks of nowhere.

As the waitress, whose name still eludes me, clears our plates she offers the dessert menu.

"Yes, please," Willow says, eyeing me across the table as though I'm going to say no.

She hasn't realised yet that I'll never say no to her about anything.

Once she has a menu in hand, Willow scans it, chewing on her bottom lip as she reads. Then she sighs and drops the laminated card on the table.

"I really wish they did decent ice cream," she says, propping her chin on her hand. "I could go for a basic scoop right now."

"I have some at home," I say before the words register. I've invited her to my place. It's bad enough being with Willow in public. But she wants to be friends again, so I'm going to have to deal with it.

Willow narrows her eyes at me. "It's hokey pokey isn't it?"

"Uh, yeah," I say. "Because it's clearly superior."

Willow laughs. It doesn't matter how many times I hear it, it's like injecting joy directly into my bloodstream.

"Sounds great, Hunt. Let's go."

Willow pays for dinner, insisting on it because I paid for lunch yesterday, and dessert tonight by supplying the ice cream. I let her, because I know it doesn't matter how much I argue, Willow will win.

This time.

I'll make up for it somehow.

We head out into the cool night air, shrugging into our jackets as we head down the block to my flat.

There's a keypad on the door to the upstairs apartment and I punch in the combination, then hold the door open for Willow. I follow her inside and up the dark, narrow staircase which opens out into my tiny kitchen and living area at the top.

"Well, this is cheerful, isn't it?" Willow mocks as she steps into the space.

"It doesn't need to be cheerful. It's a place to live and it's all I need." I sound like a grouchy bastard, but what else is new.

I drop my phone and wallet onto the kitchen bench as Willow discards her jacket, draping it over a stool at the island bench, then I pull the ice cream from the freezer, silently hoping it hasn't gone icy. I crack the lid off the container and let out a breath of relief.

Willow peers over my shoulder, her proximity sending a bolt of awareness through me. I catch a whiff of her perfume or shampoo or something and I want to turn and inhale the smell.

"I see you're still uptight about scooping ice cream," she says, indicating the clean straight lines a spoon has made through the dessert.

I roll my eyes and hand her a spoon, trying not to react when her fingers brush mine, leaving behind a burning sensation. "Just eat, you menace."

She digs a huge hole in the middle of the ice cream, lifting the spoon to her mouth with a smirk. "Whatever you say, Hunter," she says before slipping the spoon into her mouth.

I try not to watch the movement of her lips sliding over the ice cream, or the way her tongue slips out and licks the dessert from her lips. I really, really try.

Willow finishes her spoonful with a satisfied hum, then digs another hole in my tub, purposefully pushing my buttons, but I'm too distracted to react, especially when she lifts the spoon to my mouth.

"Want some?" she asks.

I open my mouth, still a little dumbstruck from watching her eat, but instead of feeding me, Willow flicks the spoon up and smooshes ice cream against the tip of my nose.

I hiss. "Fuck, Willow." She cackles and backs away from me. "I see you haven't grown up at all in the last few years," I growl, stalking towards her.

She cackles again, the laugh loud in the tiny, mostly bare space. She tries to flee to the other side of the island bench, but I'm too fast.

I lunge for her, my hands snagging her around the waist, the fabric of her sweater soft under my palms. I spin her around and back her up against the bench, holding her in place with one hand and reaching for her discarded spoon with the other.

"You want to play, huh?" I growl, holding the spoon an inch from the tip of her nose.

She squirms, giggles and tries to fend me off. Every time her gaze lands on my face another laugh bursts out of her and I realise I still have ice cream on my nose.

I wrap my arm around her, holding her in place. "Hold still, Will," I murmur.

"No, you'll get me."

"That's kind of the point." I creep the spoon closer and she shrieks, and squirms harder. At the very last second, I drop the spoon to land against her bottom lip, instead of smearing ice cream on her nose.

Willow gasps, going still in my arms. The moment registers and her eyes widen slightly, then her tongue darts out and swipes across the ice cream heaped on the end of the spoon. I slip the utensil into her mouth and her lips close around it, sucking it clean, her eyes never leaving mine.

Willow swallows, licks her lips, then drops her gaze to my mouth. She reaches up and swipes the tip of her finger across my nose.

"You got a little something," she whispers, holding up the finger.

It would take the barest movement for me to lean forward and suck it into my mouth.

With that thought I realise how close we're standing. I've boxed Willow in, my body pressing up against hers. My arm is still wrapped around her, fingers splayed across her back.

The spoon clatters against the bench top and Willow startles, glancing down to where our hips are aligned and I stagger backwards, hoping she didn't feel what I fear she did.

"I—I should go," Willow says, her voice choked. "Drive back to the Ridge."

I press my back into the fridge, holding myself back from crossing the kitchen and doing what I really want to do, which is find out what hokey pokey ice cream tastes like on Willow's tongue. "Yeah, um, yeah. Sure."

"I'll see you later," she says, then spins on her heel and disappears down the stairs, leaving me alone in my kitchen, my heart heavy and my cock rock hard and aching.

17

WILLOW

IT'S A FUCKING miracle I don't fall face first down Hunter's stairs. I virtually sprint from his apartment and down the narrow, dimly-lit staircase.

At the bottom of the stairs I pause, taking a few deep breaths to calm my racing heart.

What the hell just happened?

I don't know why I attacked him with ice cream. It's definitely something I would have done when we were kids.

But we aren't kids anymore.

We're adults.

Adults who are trying to find some kind of friendship after all this time.

But he kept staring at me with that intense expression on his face and his words from dinner kept echoing through my mind. *No one worth mentioning.*

Between that, the feel of his leg against mine all through dinner, and his absolute ambivalence to the waitress being completely smitten with him, just like when he was in high school and girls would flirt with him, I needed to lighten the mood. Hence the ice cream assault.

I should have known he'd come after me. Only, it never occurred to me what that would look like. Or feel like.

Because having Hunter's big, solid body pressing me into the bench, his hips pinning me in place, was fucking hot. It makes me dizzy just to think about it.

Remembering the rock hard bulge in his pants makes me a little more than dizzy. I feel a hot flush crawl across my cheeks and I push through the door, out into the night. The door slams behind me with resounding finality. Whatever happened in that apartment needs to stay there, behind that closed door.

I hiss at the cold night air hitting my skin, but stride down the street, hoping some distance from Hunter's place will help me think more clearly.

I knew attacking him with ice cream would piss him off, who wouldn't be pissed off with having frozen dessert smeared on their face?

But instead, those few moments seemed to be the most fun I've seen Hunter have since I've been back. For years actually.

Mark would have lost his shit with me if I'd ever done that to him, then he would have sulked about it.

Not Hunter though, and somehow I instinctively knew that, but what I was hoping to achieve by doing it I have no idea.

But the feel of those big, calloused hands on me ... that was a bonus I definitely didn't expect. Same with seeing his expression up close as he watched me lick the spoon clean. I didn't try to make it sexy or anything, but the way Hunter was looking at me made me think that maybe I did.

And the way his dick reacted.

Shit, shit, shit. Did we screw everything up? Ruin this attempt at friendship already?

I reach my car and lean against the side in a pool of light from a streetlamp.

Some distance from Hunter's intense stare helps. My heart slows, the feeling of panic that washed over me when I felt his erection ebbs.

Now I have to think clearly.

I shiver and realise why I'm so cold. I left my jacket behind. I could go back for it, Hunter and I could have a conversation and clear the air, put everything on the table, and move past this. I can't let another ten years go by without him in my life. Plus, again, we didn't talk about his loan situation.

Decided, I straighten and head back down the street. I hesitate at the front door. Should I knock or let myself in?

I didn't mean to watch him enter his entry code, but I did and the number is seared in my brain. I'll save him the trip down the stairs, if he could even hear me knocking at all, and punch in the familiar numbers, the door latch clicking open.

I'm refusing to think about what it means that he chose my birthday as the code. Maybe he didn't choose it and it's pure coincidence.

Or maybe he did.

Hopefully when we have this conversation I'll understand.

I climb the stairs slowly, taking my time and some deep breaths. "Hunt," I say as I reach the top of the stairs, then freeze.

Hunter is sprawled across his couch, his button-down shirt undone to expose the well-muscled planes of his chest and abs. One hand is splayed against the couch beside him, the other is wrapped around his hard, thick cock.

My lungs seize, breath frozen in my throat and I immediately forget everything I've ever known.

I should leave. Right now. I need to go, but then Hunter groans and pumps his fist up and down his shaft and I'm trapped in the moment, unable to step away.

My gaze rakes over him. That sinfully hot body, those big hands, the expression on his face, an equal mix of torture and pleasure. His eyes are closed, his brows drawn down and lips slightly parted. His tongue darts out and wets his bottom lip as he lets out a breathy sound.

"Fuuuck," he mumbles, jerking his hand faster. His hips flex, pushing his cock through his fist. "Fuck, yes," he moans in a voice that sends bolts of electricity through me. Wetness pools in my underwear. I press my thighs together, eyes still fixed on Hunter.

I need to leave but my feet are glued to the floor. I can't move. I can't breathe. I can't think anything except that this is the hottest thing I've seen in my life.

I thought it was hot seeing him walk down the street, or riding a horse, or sitting across the dinner table from me.

But this. This is something else. He's all bare skin and muscles and fucking sexy moans.

The throbbing between my legs is becoming unbearable and I need to go, need to stop watching him. It's fucking creepy and

I need to stop, but then he reaches his free hand down to cup his balls and the other speeds up, his strokes hard and fast.

"Fuck, yes," he mutters. "Oh, god. Willow."

A final pump as my name passes his lips and Hunter tenses, coming across his stomach.

Oh shit.

This is bad.

This is worse than us both knowing I got him hard earlier. This is worse than me knowing he hasn't had a serious relationship since our attempt at one. This is worse than anything else that could have possibly happened.

Because I watched Hunter jerk off and come.

Over my name.

Over me.

I thought shit was awkward before, but it's about to get a thousand times worse.

How the fuck am I ever going to look him in the eye again?

Especially because I didn't want to watch, I wanted to go over there and do it for him.

I wanted to feel the weight of that thick cock as I wrapped my fingers around it. I wanted to taste it, to feel it stretch my lips. I wanted to climb in his lap and sink down onto it and get a close up view of the expression on his face as he came.

Hunter is still sprawled on his couch, one hand cupping his dick, the other covering his eyes.

"Fuck," he says. "Fuck, *fuck*."

Those aren't breathy, turned on moans. That's his normal voice. Any moment now he's going to get up from the couch and see me standing here, staring at the cum streaked across his stomach like a complete perv.

I turn and flee, racing down the stairs as fast as I can for the second time tonight, this time trying not to make a sound. I push through the door and this time the cold barely registers as I scurry down the street to my car. I throw myself inside, turn on the engine and pull out onto the road. I need to get as far away from Hunter as possible.

And I really need to get home so I can release this throbbing, building pressure between my thighs.

18

HUNTER

A NOISE BRINGS me out of my post-jerk off stupor. It sounded suspiciously like someone on my front stairs. A moment later the door slams and I jolt off the couch.

Someone was here? Someone saw that?

I peer out the window and see a small figure hurrying down the street. Short dark hair, a cream sweater, a skirt I just came to the thought of.

Fuck.

Willow.

Did she see me? Did she hear me?

I'm not totally sure because I was lost in a haze, right on the brink of orgasm, but I think I said her name, out loud.

I really thought things couldn't get worse tonight, but apparently I was wrong. I shouldn't be surprised. This is my luck when it comes to Willow.

I don't understand though, because I definitely heard the

door close right after she sprinted from my kitchen after the debacle with the ice cream.

Why did she come back, and how did she get in the door?

I groan. She must have seen my code when I put it in earlier. It's hardly a number she'll forget.

And she called my name as she came up the stairs. I heard it, but assumed it was my imagination playing tricks on me. Because I didn't think Willow would come back. I thought she'd felt my hard dick pressing up against her and fled. I figured that was the end of whatever this attempt at friendship was.

Which would have been a shame. Because I've been having a great time with her, even if my chest still aches every time I think of what could have been between us. Teasing her over the ice cream, threatening to get her back for smooshing it on my face, it's the most fun I've had in years.

Being with Willow, around Willow, makes everything better.

I thought I'd ruined it, but then she came back.

I want to know why. I *need* to know.

But after seeing what she saw, after watching me come while saying her name, will she ever want to speak to me again? I'm such a fucking moron. I knew it couldn't work out.

I'm in the past for Willow Austin.

She has a whole future ahead of her, and I'm not a part of it. This town isn't a part of it. She's here for a short time and then she's going back to her real life, leaving me behind.

Again.

I head for the bathroom and turn the shower on, shedding my shirt, jeans and underwear, and tossing them into the corner of the room. I step under the hot spray, letting it wash away the mess on my stomach and wishing it could wash away the mess that is the rest of my life.

When the water runs cold I turn off the shower with more force than necessary. I dry myself roughly, then collapse into my bed, hoping for sleep.

It doesn't come.

THERE SHOULD BE some exception made for having to go to work when you epically fucked up trying to befriend the love of your life again.

Because working after no sleep and with thoughts of Willow playing on a constant loop in my head is shit.

I'm making a bunch of stupid mistakes today, from double booking a service that the office administrator had to fix for me, to almost using the wrong type of oil in a vehicle. An apprentice pointed it out to me, luckily before I'd started pouring, and all he got for his troubles was me snapping at him for leaving his tools out. Turns out they were my tools.

Walter taps me on the shoulder mid-afternoon and suggests I take a break, for the rest of the day. I try to protest, pointing out how much work we have on, but he shakes his head.

"You're no good like this anyway," he says. "You sick or something?"

I shake my head. "Didn't sleep. At all."

Walter slaps me on the back. "Take the rest of the day.

We're almost wrapped up anyway. Get some rest, come back tomorrow."

"Alright," I concede. "Thanks."

"No worries, Hunter. See you tomorrow."

I clock out and trudge up the stairs to my flat, taking in the barren space. Sure there's a little bit of furniture here, but nothing that lets anyone know that I actually live here. I have a single photo of my parents, Flynn and I in my bedroom, but nothing else.

My eyes catch on a denim jacket tossed over one of the stools at my bench. Willow's. That must be why she came back last night.

I'll have a shower, rinse off the workshop grime, then take it out to her at Wildflower Ridge. At least out there her family will be around and it'll be way less likely to get weird. Maybe I'll drop the jacket with Violet and avoid seeing Willow altogether.

I step under the scalding hot shower spray and scrub away the grease, dirt and sweat of the day. I try really hard not to think about it, but my mind keeps coming back to last night when Willow stood there and—possibly, probably—watched me jerk off.

I feel like I should be embarrassed, or feel ashamed for being caught out, but the reality is, the thought is fucking hot. My only worry is how it's going to affect our friendship, but when I'm not thinking about that part, the idea of Willow standing in the doorway, her gaze trailing over me as I jerked myself to thoughts of her ... yeah, that's downright fire.

My cock thickens and hardens and I brace a hand against the shower wall as I wrap my other hand around my shaft. It's not going to hurt anything now to get off over her again. Last night was far from the first time, and the image my mind is conjuring of her—eyes on me, cheeks flushed, wanting to cross the room and take matters into her own hands—is a brand new fantasy.

It doesn't matter that she was probably horrified and disgusted. I'm still pretending.

It doesn't take long and when I'm done I finish my shower, then dress and grab Willow's jacket. I shoot my bed a longing look, but I know I won't sleep until after I've seen Willow.

I'll return the jacket and make sure we're fine.

We have to be.

I'm going to fix the mess I made, then I'll come home to sleep.

And hopefully this time I'll actually be able to.

19

———

WILLOW

MY MOTHER IS GOING to have to invest in a flour mill at the rate I'm baking this week.

I pull a tray of muffins out of the oven and slide it onto a cooling rack, then turn back to the mixer on the bench, currently beating a batch of cookie dough.

My sister and her friends are gathered around the kitchen table, making plans for Friday night. I smile to myself as I pour chocolate chips into the cookie dough. I love watching Olivia, Flynn and Katie together. They have the kind of friendship anyone would want, that bond that goes beyond what's on the surface.

They'll fight for each other, go to bat for each other, and celebrate every tiny moment. Ride or die friends, and I *love* that for my sister.

I try not to think about the person who I thought was that for me. Because then I think about what he looks like coming, and what my name sounds like on this lips in that moment.

Then I think about what would have happened if he'd known I was there, or what would have happened if I'd crossed the room to him, or maybe what would have happened if I hadn't run out of the room in the first place. Would he have kissed me? Run his hands over my body? Slowly stripped me out of my clothes? Or maybe he would have ripped them off in the heat of passion?

Too many questions I can't answer, but all of them are inappropriate to be thinking in my mother's kitchen with my sister and friends behind me.

"Look who I found," Mum says, interrupting my wild, downright filthy thoughts. I turn, wondering who's come to visit. Random drop-ins aren't unusual here at Wildflower Ridge, but I'm definitely not expecting to see the man standing beside my mum, clutching my denim jacket in his fist.

"Hunt!" Katie cries. "Good to see you."

Hunter scowls at her, which only makes her grin wider, then he looks to Flynn.

"What're you all doing here? Shouldn't you be working?"

Flynn rolls his eyes, but his smile never slips. "Smoko time, brother," he says. "Shouldn't you be working too?"

Hunter shrugs. "Finished up early." He crosses the room, his eyes finally meeting mine as he reaches me. "You left this behind," he says, voice low, before dropping his gaze again.

I take the jacket and set it on the end of the bench.

Why is he being weird? He's not the one who walked in on his friend getting off.

Unless, *shit*! Does he know I was there? Not good. Not good at all.

"Thanks," I manage to croak out and he nods, then pours himself a coffee.

"Do you want one?" he asks Violet, then me.

"I'm good," I say. "I need to finish these." I indicate the cookies I'm now rolling into balls and placing on trays. Hunter nods and I expect him to go and sit at the table, but he leans against the bench near me, watching as I work.

"Mum," Olivia says at the table behind me. "You can watch Sadie on Friday, right? There's a band playing at the hotel."

"Oh, sorry. I had plans with Riss," Mum replies, referring to Clarissa Sheridan, the owner of the neighbouring farm and her best friend since Hunter and Flynn's mum Isla died.

"Well, there goes that idea," Katie says. She sounds a little disappointed, but not particularly upset over it.

"But I can cancel," Mum says hurriedly. "We can reschedule."

"No way," Katie says, with Flynn echoing the sentiment right after. These two are essentially Sadie's step-parents and I've never seen such a close-knit and cohesive co-parenting unit as Sadie's family.

"You go have your fun," Flynn says with a wink. "We'll figure something out, or we might have to stay home." He mock gasps in despair and the others, including Mum, laugh.

"I'll watch Sadie," I say over my shoulder. "You can all go and have your fun."

"Really? Are you sure?" Katie asks.

"Of course. We'll grab takeaways and watch movies and eat seven million cookies." I gesture at the tray in front of me. "We'll have a blast."

"She'll help you bake the cookies if you want," Katie says. "She's getting pretty good."

"You could hang out with them too, right Hunter?" Flynn pipes up. "Maybe bring the takeaways out to them?" He has a smirk on his face that looks far more suspicious than usual.

"Uh." Hunter shuffles his feet and readjusts his position leaning against the bench, then shoots a glance in my direction before quickly looking away again. "Yeah, I could do that."

"You can?" I ask, dumbfounded. I was expecting him to duck that suggestion.

"Yeah." His voice is gruff and he reaches out to swipe a chunk of cookie dough from the edge of the bowl. "Might need those seven million cookies just for me though." He bites the cookie dough from his finger and my knees go weak as his tongue slips out, licking his finger clean.

"Sadie and I will get right on it," I say, voice breathy as I blink at him, wondering what that tongue would taste like, would feel like.

"Well, that's settled then." Olivia claps her hands and I jerk back to the present. In the kitchen, surrounded by my family. "Thanks, Will," Olivia says.

"No problem," I say, focussing on my little cookie dough balls and not the looming presence of Hunter beside me. "We'll have a great time."

"Right, well I better get back to work before my hard-ass boss starts cracking that whip again." Flynn winks at my sister, puts his coffee mug in the dishwasher, then heads down the hall, Katie following behind him.

"I'm the best boss you've ever had," Olivia shouts after him.

"You're the only boss I've ever had," he calls back, laughter in his tone. "See ya, Livvie. Don't let the paperwork break you."

Olivia lets out a groan. "Thanks for the reminder," she grumbles, then turns to me. "You're not in need of the office are you?"

I shake my head. "Nope, besides, it's your office, Liv. You can use it whenever you need it."

"I better get back to it then. I have a thousand terrible CVs to go through." She shoots a scowl in my direction. "I don't know why you're making me employ someone else."

"Because you need more hands and the budget is available. Think about it, maybe you'll get a break."

"Ugh, fine. I'm holding you to that though." She grabs one of the barely-cooled muffins and stomps down the hall. A moment later twangy, beat-driven country music blasts from the office.

Mum sighs, her gaze following my sister.

"Is she okay?" I ask, sinking into a chair at the table.

Mum nods, shakes her head, shrugs. "I don't know. She's not saying much, but I know this isn't exactly how she saw things going."

I reach out and squeeze Mum's hand. "It's not how any of us saw things going."

"Ain't that the truth." She smiles, but it's laced with sadness. "You sure you're okay for Friday with Sadie?"

"Of course. Uncle Hunter's going to help me out." I glance over my shoulder to where he's standing, sending him a teasing smile. He's already looking at me, his gaze heavy and when our eyes meet, something flashes in his expression.

Over the years there have been so many times when I thought I caught him looking, staring, watching me, but he'd always glance away and I was never sure. In the past few days though, he's stopped turning away, and today there's something else there. Something that causes goosebumps to spread down my spine and heat to race to my cheeks and other places.

"I sure will," he says in that deep, slightly rough voice. The one I want to hear him say my name in over and over. "I should get going. I'll see you later."

"See you," I say, my breath catching.

Mum says goodbye too, but I barely register it because I'm too captivated by Hunter's hands, his forearms, his thighs in the jeans he's wearing.

"You'd better finish those cookies," Mum says, snapping my attention away from the empty doorway. "Hunter's going to need all the sugar to get through an evening with Sadie."

"What? She's not that bad. I thought she was pretty great."

"She is great. Fantastic kid. But Hunter is ... well, he's Hunter. I'm surprised he offered."

"He didn't exactly offer," I say.

"Yeah, but he still could have said no." She's giving me a look. One that lets me know she's well aware there's more to the story than I've let on. "You must have had a good catch up last night."

"Yeah, it was nice." I force myself to only think of the dinner portion of the evening. "It's been too long since we've had a chance to catch up properly," I add as though that isn't entirely my fault.

"It has," Mum agrees. "It's nice to see you two together again. It never seemed right when you went your separate ways."

"Yeah ..." I trail off, thinking about what could have been, what could have happened if Hunter's parents hadn't died the night he told me he loved me.

It was the perfect night—a date at the lookout, time spent alone at his place, the drive back to Wildflower Ridge, our fingers tangled together.

It was the perfect night until Hunter dropped me home and my parents were waiting up for us. At first I thought we were somehow in trouble, but it was worse than that.

I don't remember too many details, mostly the echoey, underwater feeling I got, like the words Dad was saying weren't actually real.

I remember Hunter sinking onto the couch beside Flynn whose cheeks were blotchy and red and stained with tears.

Hunter didn't cry. He didn't cry that day, or any of the days that followed, not even at the funeral. The only time I saw him close to breaking was the day after the funeral when he told me he couldn't leave Kauri Creek.

I understood it. He couldn't leave Flynn. I was sad, but I could handle it.

But then he told me it was over between us, that it could never happen, that I needed to move on. He told me I was naive for believing we ever had a chance, that he had to be realistic and his reality was Kauri Creek.

He got all of it out without breaking down. He shattered my heart without a waver in his voice.

The only time the cracks showed was when he said I shouldn't wait for him because he wouldn't be waiting for me. His voice splintered then, the agony in his eyes plain to someone who knew him as well as I did.

But still, Hunter didn't cry.

I cried more than enough for the both of us.

20

HUNTER

ONE DAY my brother is going to get himself into more trouble than he knows how to deal with.

I can't believe he threw me under the bus like that and now I'm babysitting. I don't think I've ever babysat anyone aside from Flynn and Olivia before, back before my parents died.

If he wasn't my little brother I'd give the shit-stirrer a piece of my mind. But Flynn gets away with everything. It's a good thing he never actually gave me any trouble when he was a teenager, because I would have handled it terribly.

I step onto the Wildflower Ridge porch and a moment later the front door flies open.

"Uncle Hunter!" Sadie cries, bouncing on the spot.

I'm exhausted already.

Sadie launches herself at me and I barely manage to keep a hold of our dinner while she wraps her arms around my waist. I awkwardly pat her on the shoulder and breathe a sigh of relief when she lets me go.

"Everyone's in the kitchen," she says, taking my hand and leading me through the house like I don't know where I'm going.

"Uncle Hunter is here," Sadie announces to the room, somehow raising her voice to be heard over the pounding music.

I hesitate in the doorway, taking in the chaos in front of me. I wasn't expecting so many people to be here.

"Sup, Hunt," Katie calls, nabbing a cookie off a cooling rack on the kitchen table. I grit my teeth because I know correcting her will only give her the satisfaction she's after.

Flynn and Olivia are across the room and don't acknowledge my arrival. It looks like Olivia is trying to teach Flynn line dancing steps, which I know he's learned before. Abi is sitting at the table watching and laughing her head off at them. I like that Flynn found someone who doesn't turn into a simpering mess around him. I've seen it happen way too often with relationships. Abi's a tough cookie though and, while I've been wary of her being right for Flynn, the more I watch them interact, the more sure I am about the relationship.

"We should go," Dallas shouts over the music and Sadie drops my hand to launch herself at her dad. She goes from his arms, to Abi's then to Katie's and Olivia's. Finally she says goodbye to my brother with a giant hug, a ruffle of his hair and finger guns. He does the same back, the pure happiness on his face evident.

I watch them stupidly, realising that when she calls me Uncle Hunter, she's right.

I know my brother isn't actually her stepdad—yet—but seeing them like this, even after seeing them together over and over, it's finally hitting home. Flynn has his own family now.

It shouldn't, but it makes me feel superfluous.

Once everyone leaves, Willow turns the music down, making me realise I'm suddenly alone with her. I don't know how to handle this. I've been back and forth and round and round over the past few days and am no closer to a decision. Do I bring it up and we talk about what she saw like grown ups, or do I pretend it never happened and we try to carry on like we have been?

Willow collapses into a chair, giving me a tired smile. "Hey, Hunter," she says, eyes not quite meeting mine. "Please tell me that's food in there?" She points to the paper-wrapped parcel in my hand.

"Sure is," I say, dropping it on the table and opening it up. "Fish and chips, plus a couple of hotdogs. I wasn't sure what Sadie would like, and I wasn't sure if you still preferred a hotdog to fish."

She grins. "I will *always* prefer a hotdog to fish. Hey, Sadie," she says as Sadie comes back into the room, I assume after waving off her many parents. "Grab the tomato sauce out of the fridge, please."

Sadie skips to the fridge, gets the bottle, then skips to the table, her eyes lighting up at the sight of the food. "Yummy! What can I have?"

"Whatever you want," I say, impressed she bothered to ask. I thought kids just grabbed whatever they want. Though I should know better. It's not like I haven't been around Sadie for a while now. She's a good kid. I shouldn't lump her in with all the horror stories I hear.

"Can I have a hotdog, please?" She's looking up at me, hope

in her eyes, but she's still looking uncertain.

"Sure. You want sauce?" Sadie nods and I take the sauce bottle from her hand and pour some onto the paper, then drag her hotdog through it. "Go hard, kid." I slide into the seat across the corner from Sadie and glance up to find Willow watching me, her lush bottom lip caught between her teeth.

She catches my gaze and jerks, yanking her eyes away. She looks guilty, and worried, maybe anxious. I can't quite place the expression. Catching Willow in moments like that isn't unusual though, so I shrug it off. I don't even allow myself to consider that she might be thinking about what she saw, and that maybe she liked it. Definitely not.

We eat dinner at the kitchen table, then head through to the lounge with a plate of cookies, where Willow puts on some kids' movie for Sadie. It's actually not too bad and I find myself laughing in more places than I would have expected.

When the credits roll I'm ready for Sadie to head off to bed, but she turns pleading eyes on Willow.

"Will you do my hair? Please?"

Willow smiles. "Sure. Go put your pjs on first and brush your teeth, then bring me your hairbrush."

Sadie races from the room and I hear her footsteps pounding up the stairs.

"Does she ever slow down?" I ask as Willow sprawls back on the couch.

"Eventually," she says, sounding weary. "Thank you for coming and hanging out with us. And for dinner."

"It's fine," I say. "It's not as bad as I was expecting."

Willow laughs and reaches out a foot to kick me in the

thigh. "How bad did you expect it to be? You're spending time with *me* after all."

Her eyes glimmer with humour–that is, until my hand comes down on her ankle, fingers brushing the bare skin between her leggings and socks. The second our skin connects, Willow's eyes darken and she inhales a sharp breath. Our eyes gazes clash and there's something in her expression, something I can't describe, but it makes me want to push the limits. I drag the pad of my finger up the inside of her ankle.

She drops her gaze, focussing on my hand on her skin and I take a moment to drink in the sight of her sprawled across the couch like this.

She's wearing her sky blue hoodie again, the one that highlights the colour of her eyes and she's paired it with a pair of black exercise tights that emphasise the delectable curve of her ass. I've spent all night resisting the urge to reach out and cup it in my palms. I'm desperate to know what it feels like, and now, seeing her like this, one foot on the floor, the other stretched across the couch, it makes me want to kneel between her spread thighs and do far more than just squeeze her fucking delicious ass.

Willow lets out a breathy sigh and I deliberately drag my finger back down to her foot, then wrap my hand around her leg, holding firm.

"Hunter," she whispers, and I realise that, while I've been staring at the way her leggings mould to her body, she's been watching me stare.

I make an incoherent grunting sound, because my throat is

like sandpaper, my tongue thick in my mouth and words won't come, no matter how hard I try to get them out.

"I—"

"I'm ready," Sadie says, bouncing back into the room, hairbrush in hand.

Willow startles, jerking her foot out of my grasp and bolting upright. She turns to Sadie, plastering a smile on her face. "Come here then," she says, patting the front of the couch cushion where she's sitting.

Sadie plonks herself down between Willow's knees and hands over the brush.

I sit there, watching as Willow removes the hair tie from Sadie's existing ponytail, then carefully begins brushing the tangles from her blonde curls.

My hand feels empty now that it's not curled around Willow's leg. I flex my fingers, wishing I could reach out and touch her again, wishing I could hold her.

Instead I push to my feet and retreat to the kitchen, pretending to tidy up even though there's no mess left over from dinner.

I want Willow with every fibre of my being. I want her in every way possible.

But I'm starting to wish she'd stuck to keeping her distance from me, because spending this time with her ... it's going to break me when she goes back to her life in the city.

I watched her walk away from me once, but I couldn't let it break me, not then.

I don't know if I'm strong enough to do it again.

21

———

WILLOW

I TIE off Sadie's braid and pat her on the shoulder.

"Time for bed now," I say as Sadie scrambles off the cushion and spins to throw herself into my arms.

"Thanks, Willow," she says, squeezing tight. "Where's Uncle Hunter?"

"Kitchen I think, why?"

She looks at me like I've suggested she wash her hair with horse poo. "Because I have to say goodnight," she says, then flounces across the room, disappearing into the kitchen.

I push myself off the couch and follow her, wanting to see how this is going to go. I reach the kitchen doorway as Sadie throws herself into an unsuspecting Hunter's arms.

He manages to catch her and his startled eyes meet mine over Sadie's head.

"G'night, Uncle Hunter," Sadie says. "Thanks for coming." Then she drops back to the floor, gives him a wave and heads back towards me. "Will you read me a story?"

"Yeah, sure. You head up and choose one. I'll be right there."

Once Sadie has disappeared up the stairs I lean against the doorframe. "Thanks for coming," I say, watching as Hunter folds his arms across his chest and leans back against the kitchen bench. "I should be alright now though if you want to head off."

He clenches his jaw. I can see it flexing, even all the way across the room. His head tilts as he studies me and his gaze trails down my body, from my face down to the socks on my feet and back up again.

I try not to fidget under his gaze and press my shoulder into the timber doorframe to stop myself.

His expression reminds me of that moment on the couch before Sadie rudely interrupted us, completely unaware of what she was interrupting. Hunter had looked at me like he wanted to devour me, his grip on my ankle a steady anchor as his heavy stare set me on fire, making the world tilt and spin.

"You want me to go?" he asks, his voice that deep, gravelly rasp that makes my insides turn to jelly.

"I ..." I shrug. "If you want to go you can," I say. "Otherwise I'll be back down in a few minutes."

"Okay," Hunter says, not moving from his position.

"O-okay," I stammer, then turn on my heel and follow Sadie up to the guest room we have set up especially for her, even though she barely needs it anymore now that she has a four parent family.

I read Sadie her story, straining my ears the entire time, listening for Hunter's ute to start up and head down the driveway. We're on the backside of the house though, so I'm pretty sure I wouldn't be able to hear it.

Once the story is done, I tuck Sadie in, turn on her galaxy night light—which is so cool I've considered stealing it for my own room—and say goodnight.

She mumbles her reply, already on her way to sleep.

I slip into the bathroom before heading back downstairs, staring at myself in the mirror for a long moment.

Hunter will have left, and that's fine. It's probably for the best actually, because I'm not sure I'm ready to face whatever has happened between us the past few days. Having Sadie as a buffer has been great. Maybe I need to seriously consider reverting to my old ways and avoiding any one-on-one time with Hunter.

The thought makes me sad and I scowl at myself in the mirror. Surely I can handle being alone with a man.

A hot, hot, hot man with glorious muscles and who's generous with his time and kind and who knows me in a way that no one else does.

A man who people assume is grumpy and sullen, but I know better. I've seen the softness behind that hard exterior, I've seen him peel it back and expose his heart. I've seen him face tragedy head on and be there for his brother, over and over, even when Flynn didn't realise the extent of what Hunter was sacrificing. And Hunter wouldn't want Flynn to know. He'd never want Flynn to feel guilty about the choices he had to make.

I sigh and head down the stairs, stopping in the lounge to pick up the blanket Sadie had been snuggling under.

I'm midway through folding it when Hunter's voice startles me.

"You thought I'd left didn't you?"

I drop the blanket in fright and spin around, my heart racing. Hunter is leaning against the doorframe, much like I was earlier, his arms folded across his chest again, making his biceps flex and stretch the sleeves of his well-worn grey t-shirt. He's wearing black sweatpants and the whole combination makes him look huggable, and fuckable. Completely and utterly fuckable.

God, have I always had this burning desire for him? Or has it only kicked off since the other night when I watched him jerk off over me? After I felt that thick, hard cock pressing into me as he pinned me against the bench at his place?

Whenever it happened, there's no denying anymore that Hunter Woods is the hottest fucking man I've ever laid eyes on, and I want him.

Badly.

Desperately.

"Yeah," I whisper, bending down to pick up the soft fleece blanket again.

"I figured we should probably talk about some things," he says, still leaning casually against the doorframe. His voice though, it's anything but casual. It matches the intense expression on his face.

"Yeah?" I whisper again, my voice catching in my throat. "Like what?"

"That financial stuff we were supposed to go over days ago for one," he says and I nod. I would laugh at how useless we've been at actually reviewing that really important situation, but Hunter's gaze has me trapped. "And," he continues, "I think we need to talk about the other night."

"The other night?" I feel my cheeks heat. Does he mean how close we got with our ice cream fight? Or does he know I witnessed him coating his abs with cum while saying my name? Fuck. Either conversation is one I don't want to deal with.

Hunter pushes off the wall and stalks towards me, eyes locked on mine, gaze penetrating. "The other night," he confirms. "At my place."

He stops his prowling when he's right in front of me and I'm forced to tilt my head back to look up at him.

"What about it?" My voice is thick, the words barely audible.

"You came back."

I gulp, feeling like there's a boulder stuck in my throat as I swallow. I nod.

"You saw me?" he asks and I nod again.

His eyes slam closed and he takes a deep breath, then pins me with another dark stare. "How much?"

"Enough," I whisper, heart hammering, wondering where this could be going. Is he angry? Is he disgusted that I stood there and watched?

I lick my lips and he follows the movement.

"Did you stay and watch, or did you catch a glimpse and leave again?"

"I—" I clear my throat and try again. "I stayed. I watched." I lift my chin, meeting his gaze square on.

He hums and takes the blanket from my hands, our fingertips brushing as he pries the soft fabric from my clenched fingers. Once it's free, he tosses it on the couch and takes another step forward.

I want to stand my ground but find my feet moving back of their own accord. Hunter follows my movements, stalking closer as I stumble backwards.

"Willow," he says, tilting his head in that assessing way of his. "Did you like what you saw?"

My back comes up against the wall and Hunter stops a breath away, not touching me, but it wouldn't take much to eliminate the tiny amount of space. One big breath should do it.

"Yes," I say, my voice clear, sure, because yeah, I liked what a saw. I liked it a whole fucking lot. I liked the way his thighs spread, how his hips thrust forward, pushing his cock through his fist. I liked the way his abs flexed and the veins on his forearms stood out. I liked the expression on his face as he came and the way his cum painted those fucking glorious abs while my name was on his lips.

Hunter groans and closes the gap between our bodies, fitting his over mine. He presses his cheek to my temple, his ragged breathing heavy beside my ear.

"I liked what I heard too," I murmur against his neck, my lips barely touching his skin as I speak. I inhale his scent as I suck in a deep breath and push my hips forward, seeking his.

"Fuck, Willow," he moans as he jerks his body forward, his dick straining against his sweatpants and pressing into my belly.

"Yeah, that," I say, feeling my fingertips dig into the wallpaper of the lounge wall. Hesitantly, I lift one hand and trail it over his hip, up his side to settle on his waist, my fingers grasping at the fabric of his t-shirt. When Hunter doesn't react, except for a brief fluttering of his eyelids, I lift my other hand and drag it along the line of his jaw. My fingernails graze the flushed skin of his neck and collarbone before tangling themselves in the neckline of his t-shirt.

He groans as his hips thrust against me again, seeking friction. I want to reach down and wrap my hand around his shaft and relive the other night with me as an active participant this time, but I have no idea what's going on here and I'm too scared to cross yet another line when I don't know if we'll be able to come back from what we've already done.

"I want you so bad," Hunter moans, his breath caressing the shell of my ear and making me shiver. "So fucking bad, Willow. You have no idea."

"Yeah, I actually think I do." I grind my hips against him and he helps me out by sliding his thigh between mine. I whimper. "I need you," I say, my voice a desperate whine as we rut against each other, pressed up against the lounge wall.

Hunter pulls his head back and stares down at me. His pupils are blown wide and he's panting. He clenches his jaw and finally lifts his hands, one landing right below my hip, on the curve of my ass. He takes a fistful of my flesh and squeezes tight. His other hand cups the side of my neck, his thumb dragging over my parted lips.

"You need me," he says, and I nod. He leans closer, watching intently as his thumb catches my bottom lip and drags it down. He continues tugging down, applying pressure to my chin and I give into the feeling, letting my mouth drop open. Hunter dips his thumb inside and I scrape my teeth along it before sinking them into his flesh.

"The question though," he says, an intimidating growl in his tone, "is do you want me?"

I can't tell where he's putting the emphasis on that sentence, but it doesn't matter. Because the answer is yes. I *want* him. I want *him*.

He leans in even closer. Our bodies are flush from our toes right through to our shoulders, his bigger, more solid body covering mine, pinning me against the wall.

There's no place I'd rather be.

Our mouths are so close, but Hunter holds back. When I lean forward to kiss him, to finally feel his mouth on mine after all these years, he draws back and I whimper, the sound wrecked and needy.

"Do you want me, Willow?" he asks again, rolling his hips to press that mouthwatering cock against me again.

"Yes." The single word is a hoarse, broken moan.

Hunter rolls his hips again, still keeping his mouth just out of reach as he watches my reaction to his movement.

"Thank fuck for—" he starts, but whatever he was saying is cut off by the sound of the front door.

Hunter flies backwards so fast I'm worried he's going to trip over the coffee table. He scrambles and picks up the blanket we discarded on the couch.

Shit, shit, shit.

I push away from the wall, making for the coffee table to pretend like I'm casually picking up the cookie plate and that I definitely haven't been dry humping against the wall with my childhood best friend and one time lover.

A moment later Mum walks into the room, a smile on her face, utterly oblivious to what she's interrupted.

"Hey, you two," she says. "How was your night?"

"It was good," I say. "Sadie was no trouble."

"Yeah, she was great," Hunter says. "Great night." He plasters a smile on his face that makes both Mum and I do a double take. Way to not make things weird Hunter, I think as I shoot him a look when Mum takes the plate from my hand and heads for the kitchen.

"I better head off," Hunter says. "That kid wore me out."

Mum laughs. "She does that. I definitely can't keep up. Thanks, Hunter."

"No problem," he says, then turns to me, an expression I can't decipher on his face. "I'll see you later."

Then he turns tail and flees for the door, leaving me in the middle of the lounge, my blood still thrumming and my underwear soaking.

22

HUNTER

WELL, that was mature.

I'm not even sure what was the worst part; calling Willow out for watching me jerk off, grinding against her with her pressed up against the wall and virtually begging for her to tell me she wants me, or bailing the second her mum got home.

The interruption was probably a good thing, considering we had a kid in the house and I was about to come in my pants.

I drive all the way home with my windows down, the cold night air blasting me in the face, trying to cool myself down.

Stupid, stupid, stupid.

But fuuuck.

I've had some hot sex in my life but me and Willow against a wall, dry humping ... nothing has been better than that.

Nothing has been better than her staring up at me with those perfect sky eyes and letting her mouth drop open with the slightest coaxing from me.

Nothing has been better than hearing her moan and

whimper and whine in my ear as I dig my fingers into her delicious fucking ass.

Nothing has been better than her telling me she liked what she saw when she watched me jerk off, or hearing her say she needs me, *wants* me.

I groan and readjust in my seat, trying to ease the aching in my pants. At least they're sweatpants and not jeans.

I park in my usual spot and punch in the code to my front door. My phone vibrates in my pocket as I reach the top of the stairs and toss my keys onto the side table I keep there solely for that purpose.

WILLOW:

Thanks for your help tonight. I appreciate how hard it was for you.

I blink at the message, wondering if she's being coy or if she actually thinks me spending time with her while babysitting is difficult.

I still haven't decided when a photo comes through. Willow is lying on her bed, propped up by pillows. Only half her face is in the frame, but I can make out the line of her shoulder, even in the dim lighting of the photo. Her bare shoulder, except for a single strap bisecting the expanse of skin. The strap leads down to the bottom of the frame where I can make out the swell of her breast and the barest edge of dark coloured lace.

Holy fucking shit.

What is this? How am I supposed to reply?

A moment later another message pops up on my screen.

WILLOW:

Are you home yet?

HUNTER:

Just walked in the door

Thank fuck she asked me a question I can actually answer. I'm studying the photo again, drooling over the tease of her gorgeous tits, when her next message comes through.

WILLOW:

Sweet dreams Hunter. I'll be thinking of you

And before I have a chance to decipher the meaning behind that one, another photo.

Even though the lighting in the picture is dim, I can clearly make out the curve of her hip, bare legs sprawled comfortably across her sheets, a slip of dark-coloured satin covering her hips and enough that I can't see her pussy. And lying across her lower belly, clear as day against the midnight-coloured satin is a hot pink sex toy.

Fuck, fuck, fuck.

Holy shit. I'd just got my dick to go down but in an instant it's hard again. I plunge my hand into my sweatpants and fist my cock, hitting the call button with my other hand.

The phone rings, and rings, before Willow's sweet voice comes on the line telling me to leave a message. It's gone to voicemail. *Voicemail.* I hang up and immediately call again. Voicemail.

I groan and slam the hang up button so hard I'm surprised my screen doesn't crack.

I head through to my bedroom, shucking off my hoodie, t-shirt and sweats before I collapse onto my bed.

HUNTER:

What. The. Fuck. Willow. Answer the damn phone.

I watch my screen, waiting for a reply as I slowly drag my fist along my cock. I lie in the dark, my imagination running rampant with thoughts of what she's doing to herself right now. Is it a vibe, or a dildo? Is she running it over her pussy, teasing her clit, or fucking herself with it, sliding it in and out of her tight, wet cunt?

I want to see it. I want to watch her pleasuring herself. I want to listen to every sound she makes and I want to watch her face as she comes, that thick toy buried inside her.

God, I can't believe after all these years I'm thinking about her like this. Sure, I've had these kind of thoughts before, but tonight it feels like I have permission.

HUNTER:

Willow, please. Answer the phone.

She never does.

I CAN'T BELIEVE I have to work today. I should be driving directly to Wildflower Ridge and cornering Willow, asking her what the fuck she was doing to me last night.

She completely ruined my sleep again, first because I forced myself to stay awake, deluding myself into thinking she'd answer my calls. When I finally gave up, got myself off and passed out, images of her plagued my dreams.

I'm barely better off than the other night when I didn't sleep at all.

I have no idea what's going on between Willow and me, but if I don't sort it out soon I'm never going to have a decent sleep again.

She's clearly into me. Physically, at least. That much is obvious after last night, even to me. But is that all it is? Did she just like what she saw the other night and want to let off some steam? Does she want a rebound from whatshisname?

My mind strays to the possibility that she actually wants me for more than a hookup, but I reject that possibility before I let myself look at it too long.

That can't be an option.

She's already given me her heart once, she's not going to risk it again, not after I so thoroughly broke it the first time.

But I had to, I remind myself. I couldn't let Willow stay here with me. I couldn't let her wait for me, because she would have been waiting forever. I knew it then and things aren't different now.

There's a whole world out there for her to experience, a whole life for her to live.

I'm not a part of that, not a part of her future. I understand that and I'm going to make myself be okay about it.

But, in the meantime, if Willow Austin wants my body, it's hers.

My heart has been the whole time anyway.

I sigh and tighten the last bolt on the oil filter I'm replacing on Tilly Sheridan's little Toyota. It was old when her parents bought it for her brothers when they turned sixteen, but years later it's still in excellent condition.

"Yo, Hunter," a voice calls and I slide out from under the vehicle.

"Yeah?" I answer.

"Some chick is here to see you."

"Some chick?" I echo, wondering if it might be Willow, hoping that it is.

"Yeah," Nikau, one of the workshop apprentices says, rounding the bonnet of Tilly's car. He makes a chopping motion at the side of his neck. "Brown hair about this long, smokin' hot."

I leap to my feet. Willow is *here*. I grab a rag and wipe as much of the grease off my hands as possible.

"Dude, take a breath," Nikau laughs and pats me on the shoulder.

"Don't hassle him about that one," Paul says, peering through the grimy window between the workshop and office. Paul has been a mechanic here even longer than me. "Willow Austin, right?" he asks me.

I nod, taking a steadying breath and wondering why he's telling Nikau not to hassle me about her. Do other people know about my feelings for her? I can't imagine how they would.

"Well, are you going to get the girl, or stand there staring at your hands all day?" Paul asks.

"Right, yeah." I spin on my heel and head for the office where Willow is waiting, Nikau and Paul's laughter echoing behind me.

I step through the door and my gaze immediately lands on Willow. She's facing out the window, staring at the street with her arms crossed against her chest. The door clicks quietly as it closes behind me and Willow turns.

God, she looks incredible. Tight jeans and a leather jacket with a tight white t-shirt. My gaze gets snagged on the swell of her tits and the obvious outline of her bra beneath the shirt, but I force my eyes to keep moving.

Neither of us have said anything yet, and I haven't even managed to meet her eyes, but when I do, I realise there's something not right in her expression.

"Hunter," she whispers. Her voice cracks and breaks, tears spilling down her cheeks.

Shit. I can't touch her right now to offer comfort because I'm filthy and covered in oil, grease and grime.

Willow presses her fingers over her eyes. "I'm sorry," she mumbles. "I didn't know where else to go."

"It's fine," I say. "You can always come to me." I reach around behind the reception desk and fish out the box of tissues always kept there, holding them out to her.

"What happened?" My heart is racing, every breath getting stuck in my throat.

"Mark is here," Willow says, her voice meek.

Now I can't decide if I want to hold her close and wrap her up in my arms, or if I want to go and hunt the bastard down for making my girl cry.

I catch myself. She's not my girl, no matter how much I want her to be.

"I should go." Willow wipes her cheeks with a tissue. "Sorry to bother you," she says, her voice breaking again and another swell of tears filling her eyes.

"Go upstairs," I say. "Wait for me there. I'll finish up here as soon as I can." I glance at the clock. "Only another hour or so. I'll be as fast as possible."

"It's—it's okay," Willow mumbles, voice still clearly shaking. "I'll leave you to your day."

"Willow," I say, stepping closer, but forcing my hands to stay at my sides. "The second I walk out of here I'm coming to find you. I was planning to anyway, before this. Please, can you wait for me?"

Willow stares up at me with glassy blue eyes and bites her lip.

God, the things I want to do to this woman.

But now is not the time.

I guess Mark's sudden arrival means I don't get to make Willow pay for what she did to me last night, but at this point I don't care. She came to me when she needed someone.

Me.

I'm not taking that lightly, and as much as I want to go and find Mark and run him out of town, Willow is my whole focus right now.

Willow nods slowly, letting out a long breath with a shaky smile. "Okay."

"Make yourself at home," I say, lifting my hand to brush a tear away with my thumb. I catch myself at the last minute, noticing the grease staining my fingernails. I drop my hand and Willow watches the movement, a crease between her brows.

"My hands are filthy," I say. "Give me an hour."

"Okay," Willow whispers again.

"Good. There's plenty of ice cream." I watch Willow's cheeks turn pink and remember what that ice cream had caused earlier in the week. "You know the door code," I say, then turn and flee back into the workshop before I can do anything stupid like kiss her.

23

WILLOW

I SPEND the next hour snooping through Hunter's apartment.

Well, not the entire hour, it's not a big place and I'm not snooping too hard. I don't want to come across evidence of other women in his life, so I keep it superficial. Once I've opened every cupboard in his kitchen and studied the contents of his bathroom drawer (a spare toothbrush, a new tube of toothpaste, some old hair product that he clearly no longer needs and two new bars of soap), I raid his freezer and collapse onto the couch with the tub of ice cream and a spoon.

I should be all grown up about it and use a bowl, but I can't be fucked, and eating directly out of the tub is cathartic in its own way.

The last twenty-four hours has been a whirlwind of emotions, starting with utter lust from Hunter's body pinning me against the wall. So much lust that after he left I texted him a picture of my vibrator. Watching his name light up my phone screen over and over while I got myself off was the hottest thing that's ever happened in my life.

I should have answered his calls, then who knows how hot my night might have been, but after I sent the photo I couldn't quite bring myself to pick up the call.

I don't know how I'd cope with hearing his deep voice talking about sex and then ever look him in the eye again.

I'd been worried about it this morning when I woke up, even through my post-exceptional-orgasm bliss. I knew Hunter would hit me up about it, like he hit me up about watching him jerk himself off on this very couch.

The thought of it causes a twinge in my core. Maybe I could repay the favour. I suck ice cream off my spoon and take a moment to imagine it, me laid out on Hunter's couch touching myself when he walks in the door after work. I should have bought the vibe.

Then, I remember why I'm here.

God, I went from truly blissed out, looking forward to the repercussions of taunting Hunter, to being slapped in the face with the repercussions of my other recent actions.

I came into town this morning to pick up some groceries for Mum, along with a few other bits and pieces for the farm, then I was planning to visit Hunter, once I knew he was done with work.

But, as I passed Sugar, I glanced in the giant front window, wondering which delicious pastry would be Hunter's favourite, and there he was.

Mark.

Here in Kauri Creek.

He was sitting in the corner of the cafe, in the same spot I waited for Hunter the other day. I stood and stared for way too long, cataloguing his carefully styled hair, the crisp button up shirt with the cuffs firmly buttoned at his wrists and his hands, one wrapped around a coffee cup, the other holding his phone.

It's impossible not to compare it all to Hunter's 'don't give a fuck' buzzcut, his disdain for dress shirts and my appreciation for that fact that when he does wear one, the sleeves are always rolled, exposing strong forearms. He never buttons the shirt all the way up either, so a glimpse of sculpted muscle and chest hair is always a guarantee. Hunter's hands are calloused and always a bit rough, with grease staining his nails.

I've never wanted to feel hands on my body more.

Thankfully, Mark was staring down his phone and didn't see me standing, mouth agape in the window.

The moment my wits came back, I fled. Chocolate custard danishes would have to wait. I raced around the corner, grateful my car was parked off the main street so it wasn't immediately noticeable.

Why is Mark here?

Well, I suppose I know why he's here. To see me. But with no warning?

I didn't even notice when my feet carried me right past my car and into the office of Kauri Creek Motors. I'd numbly asked to see Hunter, but it wasn't until he was right in front of me that the reality hit.

Hunter doesn't make me feel small.

Mark does.

He'd take decisions out of my hands under the guise of romance. And I hated it.

Like him turning up in Kauri Creek when it's obvious that I don't want to talk to him. He'll probably think it's some grand gesture and I should fall at his feet then follow him home like a simpering little puppy.

I dig another spoonful of ice cream out of the tub and savour the flavour of it on my tongue.

I guess it's telling that I haven't missed Mark at all since I fled the house we'd shared. I haven't wanted to go back once.

Meanwhile, when I think of Hunter, the longing and desire are overwhelming.

He's such a grump—he was always a little serious, even before his parents died, and it's only got worse over the years—but earlier, downstairs when he'd asked me to stay and wait for him ... the softness in his expression, the tenderness in his eyes ... god I want to see that all the time.

I think back to the other night, giggling in this room, attacking each other with ice cream. It's the first time I've seen Hunter truly laugh in years. I want to make him do that more often.

And I want that growly, always-too-serious man to devour me, sink his fingers into my flesh the way he did last night when he grabbed my ass and ground his cock against me. I can't believe I wasted so many years with Mark, who never turned me on the way Hunter does.

I wasted so many years being with a man who makes me feel insignificant. Why did I do that when a man like Hunter Woods exists?

Not that I even know what this is between us. Some hot hook up before I go back to Auckland?

Is that what I even want to do anymore? Do I want to go back to the city and the daily grind? Sure, farm life is a daily grind too, but it's different. At least down here I can see the stars at night and inhale clean air. It smells like cow shit half the time but it's still better than city smog.

I've enjoyed being home. I've enjoyed hanging out with Mum and Olivia, plus all the extra crew around the farm. I love watching Flynn be an actual grown up and dad to little Sadie and watching Katie completely settled in her new family.

I like that Flynn's puppy, Jett, is always under my feet and there's always a horse ready to ride.

I like being able to drop into Sugar and say hello to the people I've known my whole life.

And most of all, I like seeing Hunter again and spending time with him like we used to.

If I stay, could that continue?

I'd have to quit my job. As good as they've been about me working remotely for the moment, it's not sustainable long-term. And I'd never find a comparable job here. I'd have to take a considerable pay cut and resign myself to working as an office girl in some small town farming related business. Maybe Hunter could employ me to manage the KC Motors accounts once he takes over the business, though I'm pretty sure their current office manager would have something to say about that.

I sigh and slump back onto the couch, shovelling another spoonful of ice cream into my mouth. I wish I was wearing sweats and a cosy hoodie, not these jeans, as hot as they are.

Eating ice cream on Hunter's couch while having an emotional crisis wasn't on my agenda for the day.

Getting Hunter to peel these sinfully tight jeans off my body was, but I really do wish they were more comfortable.

At least now I'm certain I made the right decision about Mark. I was always pretty sure it was right, but now there isn't the slightest doubt. He's not the man for me.

My phone rings and I glance down at it where it lays on the couch beside me.

Mark's name lights up the screen and for the first time since I left him, I pick up the phone and answer it.

"Hi, Mark," I say, keeping my voice flat and neutral.

"Willow," he says, relief evident in his tone. "Where are you?"

"I'm in Kauri Creek," I say, being vague on purpose.

"Me too."

"Okay," I say. "Why?"

Mark huffs a disgruntled sound. "I'm at the farm. Your sister said you're not here. She on her period or something? She's been a right bitch."

I make a sound that sort of sounds like a laugh, but the harsh noise is anything but amused. "Tell me you didn't. Tell me I misheard you."

"What?" Mark asks, completely oblivious.

"Don't talk about my sister like that," I bark. "Don't talk about any woman like that."

Mark sighs. "Where are you, Willow? How long until you come back to the farm?"

"I'm not sure," I reply. "How long will you be there for? I'll be a little longer than that."

"Willow." Mark's voice changes as his anger grows. "I'm not fucking around. I came all this way to see you."

"It's not my fault you didn't bother to check if I wanted to see you. To which the answer is no, Mark."

"Oh, come on, Willow. You're not even going to give us a chance to work this out?"

"There's nothing to work out. The relationship is over. You're welcome to wait at the farm, but I don't know when I'll be home."

Mark grunts. "You're being a bit dramatic, don't you think? You're going to throw it all away?"

I can hear voices in the background, a blast of chatter and a wild laugh that must belong to Flynn.

Mark makes another frustrated noise. "Are you with the mechanic? The one you assured me nothing was going on with? Have you been fucking him every time you come back to visit your mum? Is that why you stopped bringing me?"

"No, Mark," I say, willing my voice to stay steady. "You chose to stop coming with me, another reason our relationship is over."

"If I leave today, that's it. We're done," Mark says.

"Good," I shriek, finally losing it as his accusations echo through my head. "That's what I want. I don't understand why you can't get that when I tell you to your face, move out, leave town and refuse to answer your calls."

He makes a huffing sound. "Fine. I'm done. You couldn't even be a grown up and talk to me about it, so fuck you. Good luck with your dumbass mechanic. You better hope he's a good fuck, because that's all a guy like him has to offer."

The line goes dead before I have a chance to retort. But a red haze has settled over my eyes. I throw my phone as hard as I can, aiming it at the couch cushions so it doesn't damage Hunter's apartment.

It misses completely and bounces off the wall, leaving behind a hole in the plasterboard.

Fuck my life.

I grab the device and throw it at the floor, following it up with a banshee screech.

Footsteps pound up the stairs and Hunter appears.

"Willow." He steps towards me. I can barely make him out through my tear-filled eyes. "Hey, it's okay," the blurry image of Hunter says. "Give me two seconds to clean up."

I give a short nod and Hunter disappears into the bathroom.

My rage builds. How fucking dare Mark imply I've been cheating on him this whole time? How dare he imply Hunter is worthless?

The walls of the flat feel like they're closing in, pressing in on me. I need to get outside—fresh air, the open sky, grass and trees. That'll calm me down. Maybe. What I know for sure is that I can't be in this room any longer.

I shoot a plea towards the bathroom door Hunter closed behind him a moment ago. A plea for what I'm not sure; for him to understand, to follow me maybe, to not hate me at the very least.

Then I head for the stairs.

24

___

HUNTER

I SCRUB AT MY HANDS, willing the grease to come off faster. I washed them downstairs with our industrial grade cleanser, but I always feel like I need to do them again when I get home.

Then, I strip off my sweat-stained work clothes that somehow still get filthy even under a pair of overalls. I pull on sweats and t-shirt and step back into the living area of the apartment.

Willow is gone.

The only evidence she's been here is a half-eaten, slightly melted tub of ice cream on the couch and a hole in the wall above it. I'm assuming that was the first bang I heard as I opened my downstairs door. She must have thrown her phone at the wall first, then the floor, which I witnessed as I came up the stairs.

God, what happened?

I snap the lid back on the ice cream and shove it into the freezer, tossing her spoon into the sink to be dealt with later, then I grab a hoodie and race down the stairs, pushing through the heavy door into the street as I pull the sweatshirt over my head.

I contemplate my options. Would she have headed towards town or away?

Away. Definitely away.

I know Willow, and when she's upset, she needs open spaces.

I turn and stride down the footpath, crossing the street at the end of the block, my eyes constantly scanning. They snag on a familiar car and I breathe a sigh of relief.

She hasn't driven then. I can still find her.

There's a park the next street over with a small children's playground and I head in that direction, not really knowing why.

Thunder booms and for the first time I notice the heavy black clouds rolling across the sky. A gust of wind stirs up brittle, dry leaves and the first raindrops splatter against the concrete footpath.

As I reach the park I pass a mother hurrying her small children back to their car, the toddler screaming under her arm as she drags the resistant older child behind her. She looks frazzled and exhausted.

I suppress my shudder at the idea of children, then think of Sadie.

Maybe not all of them are so bad.

I wonder for a moment if Willow wants them, then push the thought from my mind. It's completely irrelevant to me, especially when she's just run out of my place in tears after throwing her phone so hard she made a hole in the wall.

The rain is coming down heavily now and I'm already feeling the chill down my spine as droplets soak through my hoodie. I scan the park, hoping, hoping, hoping.

There's a lone figure sitting on the swings.

Jackpot.

My strides easily cover the ground between us and the next thing I know I'm kneeling in front of the swing, blinking up at Willow through the rain.

Her fingers are wrapped around the swing chains, knuckles white. I place my hands below hers, but close enough my index fingers hook over her pinkies.

"Willow," I breathe as she lifts her gaze to meet mine. Her normally clear blue irises are red-rimmed and dull. Tears are still running over her cheeks, mingling with the pouring rain. Her hair is plastered to her scalp, sticking to her cheeks.

I smooth the wet strands back from her face and she leans into the touch, allowing me to cradle her head in my palm.

"Kitten," I whisper. The sound is barely audible over the splattering of rain colliding with the ground. "What happened?"

"Mark." Willow sniffs, then drags her soaked sleeve across her face. When she clasps the chain again, her hand is resting directly on top of mine. She doesn't pull away. "I'm so *angry* ... I can't talk about it right now."

"That's okay." I smooth my hand over her hair again, then slowly slide my arm around her. Her fingers tighten on my hand, then release as she wraps her arms around my torso, dragging me into her.

She clings to me, her body shaking with sobs while I cradle her head and make soothing noises into her hair, my knees aching from the bark-covered ground.

"I'm sorry I ran out on you," she whispers against the fabric of my hoodie.

"It's okay," I reply, dragging a comforting hand up and down her spine. "I know you. As long as it's him you're pissed at and not me."

Willow laughs softly, still holding me close. "Don't worry, it's all him." She heaves a sigh. "He came to see me," she says eventually, pulling back so we're eye-to-eye.

I hold my breath. Is she upset because she wants to see him? Because she's not ready to go through with ending their relationship?

"We don't have to talk about it," I say.

"I told him to fuck off," she says, a wicked gleam sparking in her eyes.

"Fuck yes you did." I grin back at her and her gaze drops to my lips. She slowly drags her focus back and meets my stare head on.

"You should smile more, Hunter," she says.

I grunt. "Probably. Generally don't have a lot to smile about though."

"I've seen you smile more this week than I have in years."

Her hands are resting on my shoulders, her thumb brushing against my neck, from the hinge of my jaw to the neckline of my soaked hoodie.

I press my fists into the swing seat on either side of Willow's hips, curling my fingers tight against my palms to stop myself reaching out to caress her curves.

Her lashes are clumping together, from the rain or the tears I'm not sure. She watches me intently and the scrutiny is making me uncomfortable. How can I tell her why I've been smiling more? How do I tell her that the amount of times I smile in a day is in direct proportion to how much time I spend with her?

I shrug. "Guess I've had something to smile about this week."

I drop my gaze, avoiding her stare and instead noticing the spread of goosebumps across her neck and cleavage. Fuck, her tits look incredible in that tight, white shirt, especially now it's soaked through and I can make out the details of her bra beneath. I drop my gaze lower, so I'm staring at her denim-clad knees. That feels a whole lot safer. And less pervy.

She's sitting here with tears on her cheeks and I'm admiring her body. I need to get a grip.

Willow hooks her thumb under my chin and presses firmly. I want to slip away from her touch, avoid the head-on stare I know is coming.

But at the same time, I don't want Willow to ever stop touching me and I never want to disappoint her again, so I allow her to tilt my chin up and meet her eyes.

"I thought this was going to be one of the shittiest weeks

ever," she says, her voice deliciously soft, matching the tenderness of her fingers dragging over my skin. "But I've had a lot to smile about too."

Willow's hand drifts from my shoulder, the pads of her fingertips leaving a trail of burning fire and goosebumps in their wake.

She strokes down the length of my jaw and my entire body shudders at the contact.

I've spent so many years holding myself back around her, first when we were young and I knew she didn't feel the same way about me as I did her, then in the aftermath of my parents' deaths.

I knew that night that things would never be the same; the night Henry Austin perched on the edge of their living room coffee table—Flynn and I sitting wide-eyed and dread-filled across from him—and told us we were parent-less. Orphans.

I knew immediately I wasn't going off to uni with Willow, even though I'd already promised I'd follow her anywhere, so long as she wanted me to.

Willow sat next to me that night, so close it was impossible to tell where one of us ended and the other began. Her nails dug into my bicep as she clung to me, her grip squeezing tighter and tighter the more her dad talked.

She cried. Flynn cried. Violet and Henry both cried.

I didn't.

I sat there, stony-faced, and watched my future burn.

Then I pried Willow's fingers from my skin and never let myself touch her the way I wanted to again.

Until this week.

Willow's gentle hands cup my face, her eyes soft on mine.

I let go.

I let go of all the heartbreak and pain and what ifs.

I close the distance between us and press my lips to hers.

She tastes exactly the same as she did the first time I kissed her: like magic and happiness and all of my dreams coming true.

25

WILLOW

HUNTER IS KISSING ME.

His lips are soft on mine, almost hesitant, but he's kissing me.

His hands that have been carefully avoiding touching me settle on my hips and tug me forward, pulling the whole swing toward him. My knees fall open, bracketing Hunter's torso as he drags me closer.

I melt into his touch, into his kiss.

The scruff on his jaw is coarse under my palms as I cradle his face. I wrap one hand around the back of his neck right as he breaks the kiss.

We didn't even get to open mouths and tongues and the desperate moans I know I'll be making any minute now.

"Willow," he breathes, voice choked and uncertain.

I answer him by digging my nails into the back of his neck and dragging his mouth back to mine.

That first kiss was perfection. Soft, gentle, tender and

loving. The perfect first kiss after all this time. It lets me know everything I need to. Hunter is still that same sweet man I've known my whole life, even with his hardy exterior.

I want more of those kisses. So many more.

But after last night, I need something else right now.

Pressing my lips to his, I drag my tongue across his mouth and let out a tiny moan when he lets me in. Our tongues tangle and I take what I need from him, deepening the kiss as I cling to him.

I wrap my hand in the front of Hunter's hoodie and try to drag him closer, but instead of invading my space and wrapping his arms around me, deepening the kiss like I want and need, he pulls back. Away.

"Willow," he gasps. He smooths a hand over my sodden hair, then pushes to his feet, stepping away, and not taking me with him.

The swing sways morosely as I sit here, stunned.

"I shouldn't have done that." His voice is ruined as he stops and spins back to face me.

"What?" My voice is a brittle croak. Doesn't he want me? I was so sure yesterday that he did, but maybe it's not like I thought. Maybe I've got it all wrong because I'm so caught up in our history.

"Come on. You need to get out of the rain," he says, his usual stony expression back on his face. He gestures in the direction of his place, then turns and starts trudging in that direction.

"Hunter!" I push to my feet and chase after him. He can't kiss me like that then shut me out. We've spent years dancing around this. It's obvious we both still want each other, especially after last night.

I grab for Hunter's arm, but instead of stopping him in his tracks like I was hoping, he carries on walking. He doesn't pause when we near my car and I take it as a sign that he wants me to follow him.

He punches in his door code—my damn birthday—with such violence I'm surprised he doesn't break the keypad, then he holds the door open and ushers me inside.

He steps in behind me, pulling the door closed, then brushes past me and heads upstairs, not saying a damn word.

I'm left blinking in the stairwell as his broad shoulders and hot ass disappear through into the apartment.

I race up the stairs. "What the fuck, Hunter?"

He pauses in the doorway to his bedroom, looking back over his shoulder at me. "Give me a sec." His eyes narrow on me. "Don't leave this time."

I huff. I should leave. It would serve him right.

A moment later, Hunter is back, a bundle of clothes in his hands. "Here." He passes them to me. "Bathroom's in there," he says, indicating the other room. "There's fresh towels in the cupboard if you need one." Then he disappears back into his bedroom, closing the door behind him with a soft click.

I stare at the closed door, then down at the soft, dry clothes. I shiver again. I'm cold to my bones and getting out of these wet jeans does sound like a fantastic idea.

In the bathroom, I peel off my sodden clothes, fighting to get the jeans down my legs. My underwear is soaked, and not in a fun way, but going without doesn't feel right at the moment, not when Hunter clearly doesn't want to take things further. Which is a shame because the silky matching set I'm wearing is to die for. I would have liked to watch him strip it from my body.

I grab a towel to wrap my dripping hair in, then pull on a pair of soft sweatpants, a navy blue t-shirt and a dark grey hoodie, studying myself in the bathroom mirror when I'm done.

What am I doing here? What are Hunter and I playing at? Whatever it is, it feels like a dangerous game. I had my rules for a reason, and they kept me safe.

But, if I'd stuck to them I wouldn't have had that kiss out there in the rain.

It was a great kiss. Fucking perfect actually.

And Hunter ended it.

After pushing me against a wall last night and grinding his hard dick against me, then begging to know what I was up to with my vibrator.

He's the one who kissed me, damnit.

I shake the towel from where it's wrapped securely on my head, give my hair a rough dry, then throw the towel on the floor with my pile of wet clothes.

I throw the bathroom door open and storm into the main area of the flat. Hunter is leaning against the kitchen bench, also wearing dry clothes and looking at something on his phone.

"What the fuck, Hunter?"

His eyes meet mine. The open vulnerability I'd seen in the playground is gone, the heated lust from last night is nowhere to be seen. Instead he's wearing the same closed off expression he's had around me for the past decade.

He sighs and runs a hand over his hair. "I'm sorry, Willow."

"You're sorry?" My voice raises to a shriek as all the warring, conflicting emotions raise to the surface.

"I shouldn't have kissed you."

"Well not if you're going to regret it three seconds after it happens. What was last night then? You regret that too? Or is it okay to dry hump me against a wall but you draw the line at kissing?" I'm well aware I'm screeching at him, but I can't stop myself.

Hunter's expression finally breaks from that infuriating, closed off one to a look of confusion.

"It was a fucking good kiss," I yell. "And you fucking ruined it."

"Willow." Hunter's hands come down on my shoulders. "Willow," he says again. His thumbs brush against the side of my neck. "My timing was shit. I'm sorry for that." He takes a deep breath, then tilts his head back and closes his eyes for a moment before leaning in and resting his forehead against mine. "I'm not sorry for kissing you. I could never be sorry for that."

Oh. My hands loop around his forearms and we stand for a long moment, foreheads pressed together, staring into each other's eyes, hands anchoring each other.

"You're right," he says. "It was a fucking excellent kiss. But you're upset. You were out there crying over whatshisname and you deserved better than what I did." He lifts his head and presses a kiss to my forehead. His lips linger for a long, sweet moment before he breaks contact. "That said, I think you should head home now."

I jerk back and blink up at him. He's kicking me out?

I really want to stay, to hang out, maybe grab dinner

together later. I want to stay and show him I'm not upset over Mark. I want to forget about this afternoon and get back to where we left off last night.

But Hunter doesn't want that. He wants me to go.

"Yeah." I clear my throat. "I should head home and make sure Olivia doesn't need help hiding a body or something."

Hunter laughs, though his expression is sad. "You think she's taken care of your problem, huh?"

I shrug. "Wouldn't put it past her. Last I heard she showed him where Jett's water bowl was and told him they don't let dogs in the house, then Katie whistled for Jett and he followed them inside, leaving Mark on the porch."

Hunter laughs again, this time the sound real. It lights up his eyes and curves his mouth in a tantalising way. I want to kiss him again.

Which is exactly why I need to leave right now.

My life is a mess and Hunter can obviously see that. It's understandable that he doesn't want to be caught up in it all.

"Thank you, Hunter," I say. "For being here. Sorry I screamed at you." I glance behind me. "And sorry about the wall."

"Don't worry about the wall," he says, stepping back and finally dropping his hands from my shoulders. I miss the contact immediately. He's barely a metre away, but it still feels like too far. "And I'm always here for you, even if you want to scream at me."

I give him a tight smile, wanting more from whatever is going on between us.

Hunter leans back against the bench, increasing the

distance between us even further, so I collect my sodden clothes from the bathroom floor, take the umbrella he's offering me, and head back out into the rain.

I have no idea where things stand with Hunter. I'm desperate to feel his touch again, to kiss him again, to have his mouth and hands explore my body, and explore his. I thought he wanted the same. This morning I was sure of it.

I climb into my car and head back to Wildflower Ridge, hoping that Mark is long gone, and Hunter's change of heart truly is only a timing thing, not that it's particularly reassuring.

It's not like we've ever had good timing before.

HUNTER

THE SECOND THE door closes behind Willow I regret her leaving.

I don't want her to go. I never want her to go.

But I'm doing the right thing. I'm sure of that.

If she'd stayed, I'd have done something else insane, like pick her up, wrap her legs around my waist and carry her to my bed. I'd have peeled my clothes right back off her body.

'Cause god damn, she looked good in them.

But I didn't want Willow to do something reckless today, then have second thoughts about it later. I couldn't handle it if whatever happens between us is something she regrets.

It'd be bad enough if she decides she doesn't want to do anything with me at all, if we went back to the way things have been for all these years, but to have her, then lose her because my timing is shitty ... I wouldn't recover from that one. Not again.

She's confused about me suggesting she leave, and I understand that. We both thought today was going to go differently than it actually did.

Fuck, if Olivia hasn't taken care of whatshisname—Mark—then maybe I should. The absolute loser ruined my chance. At least I have another one, unlike him.

With that smug thought, I deal with my drenched clothes that I dumped on the bedroom floor while Willow was in the bathroom earlier.

I still get Willow in my life, I still have a chance to be a part of hers. We have a chance at this. I just couldn't have her in my space tonight because I knew being alone with her would lead to trouble.

But that doesn't mean I can't spend time with her if we're around other people.

I briefly wonder how many people will be around Violet's kitchen table tonight. Will it only be the three Austin women? Or will everyone else be there as well?

Do I want to go out there for dinner if it's going to be a big, noisy affair?

Yes.

Because Willow will be there, and for her, I can endure pretty much anything, even a decade of pretending like I haven't loved her my entire life.

THE LINE of vehicles parked outside the main house at Wildflower Ridge is, well, kind of intimidating.

I spent the rest of the afternoon cleaning my flat because,

now that Willow knows the code, it needs to be kept tidy at all times in case she drops by. Then I went to the gym and smashed out a workout, channelling all my pent up frustration into lifting.

After a long, hot shower and deliberating over what to wear—a rare occurrence in my life—I climbed into my ute and drove out to the Ridge.

I park, then take a deep breath and head for the front door. I don't bother knocking. I never have and I doubt they'd hear me over the music and commotion coming from the kitchen.

I lean against the kitchen doorframe and take in the chaos. Violet, Dallas and Abi are clearly trying to make dinner, but my idiot brother, his friends and Sadie are in the middle of a jousting match.

Something twinges in my chest at the sight. We used to do this all the time when we were little. Our dads would piggyback us across the kitchen while we pretended to knock our opponent off. Once, Dad shattered one of Violet's mixing bowls so they kicked us outside and we continued the game out on the back lawn using pool noodles as lances.

I didn't know they still did it. I haven't seen it, or heard it mentioned in years, not since before my parents passed.

Katie is carrying Olivia, who's scolding her 'horse' for misbehaviour, which is only causing Katie to be even more ridiculous. Flynn is playing horse to Sadie, who's giggling so hard at the two women I'm surprised she hasn't fallen off.

Not that Flynn would let that happen. He loves that kid. He did even before he met Abi, when it was just Sadie and Dallas in Kauri Creek. I sometimes wonder if he picked Abi partly because the kid came as part of the deal.

Abi leans against the wall beside me, as if my thoughts of her summoned her presence.

"Hey, Hunter," she says softly.

"Hey," I reply.

"I wanted to ask you …" She trails off, then fidgets with the end of her long dark ponytail.

"Yeah?" I'm curious where this is going to go.

"Well, two things." She squares her shoulders, like she's trying to find the courage. "My car needs a service."

Oh, here we go. The mates rates plea. I love my job, but the amount of people who assume I'll want to spend my free time servicing their shitty cars for cheap drives me nuts.

"Do I need to book it in, or can I just turn up at the workshop?" Abi continues and it takes me a moment to register that she's asking about work. Well, that's a surprise.

"Uh, well if you need it for a specific time, best to book it in."

Abi smiles up at me. "Thanks. The other thing was about Flynn's birthday."

Shit. That's coming up soon. I haven't even thought about it. We don't usually do much for our birthdays, but Violet likes to cook us a special dinner or something.

I nod for Abi to continue when her words trail off again.

She sighs and leans back against the wall beside me, watching Flynn from across the room. "I was thinking about booking the hotel and having a party for him."

"A party?"

"Yeah. He kind of mentioned he hasn't had one in a long time."

"He's never wanted one," I say, hostility sneaking into my voice. I tried to organise a party for Flynn's sixteenth birthday, his eighteenth and his twenty-first, and the most he'd ever wanted was a dinner, like every other year.

Abi chews on her lip, eyes still on my brother. "That doesn't make sense to me," she says softly. "Flynn not wanting a party."

"I know, but I tried," I say. "He never wanted one."

Abi deflates a little and I feel bad for her. "I know you did," she says. "He really likes parties, I don't understand why he's always said he doesn't want one."

I shrug. Parties have never been my thing, but I would have had them for Flynn, because Abi's right, he loves a party.

"But we can try again," I say. "He's only twenty-five once. Maybe it'll be different this time."

"You think so?" Abi peers up at me, a spark of hope in her eyes.

"Maybe this year he won't feel like he's completely alone. This year he has a family to celebrate with."

"You're his family too, and you've always been here," she says, her hand landing on my forearm and giving a soft squeeze.

"I'm not quite the same as you though," I say. I wish I could have been enough for him, but I know I wasn't, as much as I've always tried to pretend like I was. "I think the party is a good idea. Let me know what you need from me."

Abi smiles. "We won't let him out of it this year."

We. I like the way she included me in that.

"Thanks, Abi," I say, trying to keep my voice even and not

show the emotions swirling around inside me. Everything's stirred up tonight, from Willow, from the jousting, from thinking about my little brother turning twenty-five and how this woman is standing here looking at him like he hung the moon and stars and crafted rainbows with his bare hands.

He's not even doing anything particularly special, just holding Sadie on his hip and doing some kind of ridiculous dance while she giggles maniacally. But the way he's looking at that little girl is pretty close to how Abi is looking at him, and his smile is absolutely huge. I appreciate everyone in this room for making that happen.

"Willow's upstairs in her room I think," Abi says quietly. "If you're looking for her."

Then she pushes away from the wall and heads back to the bench where she picks up a knife and starts slicing tomatoes.

I guess I'm not subtle then.

I slip out of the room, thankful Flynn and Katie haven't noticed me and made a fuss of my arrival.

I climb the familiar stairs, turn left at the top and head towards Willow's bedroom.

The door is wide open and I take in the sight before me.

The room looks pretty much the same as it did a decade ago. Pale blue walls, a flowery duvet—though the one on her bed now is different than the one she had as a teenager—and photos stuck up all over her mirror and wardrobe doors. I wonder how many of those photos have me in them, or if she threw all of those ones away after I told her we could never be anything more than friends.

Willow is sprawled across her bed, wearing a soft-looking

pair of jeans and my hoodie. Mine. Her laptop and a notebook are on the bed beside her, but she's discarded them and instead is staring at the ceiling, muttering to herself as she plays with the drawstrings on the hoodie.

My hoodie.

She's obviously changed since she got home, because those are definitely not the pants she was wearing when she left me, but she put my hoodie back on.

I knock lightly on the doorframe and Willow startles, shooting upright and nearly knocking her laptop to the floor.

"Hunter," she says. "What're you doing here?"

I lift one shoulder. "Wanted to hang out with you."

She narrows her eyes at me. "You told me I should leave."

"My place wasn't a good idea."

She rolls off the bed and to her feet. "And you think this," she points to the floor, indicating the cacophony from the kitchen below, "is a better idea?"

I shrug again. "I can go if you want me to."

"Don't you dare. If I have to deal with our siblings, so do you. I'll just—" She cuts off and lifts the hem of the hoodie, starting to pull it off.

I catch the fabric and tug it back down. "Leave it. Don't change it."

Willow meets my eyes and some kind of electric frisson passes between us. "Okay."

She slips her hand into mine, lacing our fingers together, anchoring me without even knowing the power in her touch. Willow leads me downstairs, the tiniest smile curving her delicious pink mouth. At the kitchen doorway, she squeezes my hand, then lets go before stepping inside.

I take a deep breath and follow her into the room. I can put up with anything for Willow, even Katie and her shit stirring, which I know is definitely coming with Willow wearing my hoodie.

My hoodie.

Mine.

27

———

WILLOW

THANKFULLY THE MUSIC has been turned down by the time we get to the kitchen, but that only emphasises the shocked silence that follows Hunter entering the kitchen behind me.

Olivia, Katie and Flynn all stare at him like he's grown an extra head, even Mum looks startled. Abi just smiles and continues tossing the salad.

Sadie breaks the tension.

"Uncle Hunter's here!" she shouts, then races across the room and flings herself into his arms. The others share glances between them, then resume their earlier activities.

Hunter does well, barely flinching as he catches the little girl.

Sadie hugs him tight, and I feel a little pang of jealousy, which is ridiculous. Hunter barely tolerates Sadie's presence at the best of times.

Meanwhile, he tells me to leave his house, then a few hours

later turns up at mine. Does he simply not want to be alone with me?

I'm not sure how I feel about that. Does he want to stay friends and nothing else? Is he worried about being caught up in my catastrophe of a life?

He said he wasn't sorry for kissing me, only the timing of it, so does that mean he wants more, just not right now?

But then why ask me to leave earlier?

I can't make it make sense.

I've been going around in circles all afternoon, finally coming to the conclusion that he didn't want us to be anything more than friends. With that, I turned my attention to sorting out my life because, regardless of whether Hunter wants me or not, there are things I need to handle.

And now Hunter is here, which, based on everyone's reactions, is unusual. This is the problem with only coming home for fleeting visits over the years; I don't know what's normal.

Hunter holds Sadie to him, waiting patiently until she's finished her hug.

"Hi," she says when she finally releases her death grip around his neck.

"Hey, kid," Hunter says. "You should take up rugby with a tackle like that."

Sadie thinks for a moment, then shakes her head. "If I play rugby, Dad will make me give up riding. He says I can't do it all." She rolls her eyes dramatically, like she can't believe her dad is such a downer.

"You know, he's right," Hunter says. I watch on, dumbstruck as he actively continues the conversation. "If you're out there playing rugby then you won't have as much time to spend with Scout, then she might miss you."

"Do you ride?" Sadie asks him.

"Sometimes. Not very often. I went riding with Willow last weekend, but before that it'd been a long time."

"You can come riding with me if you want," Sadie says, then wriggles free of Hunter's hold and races back across the room.

"Thanks, kid. Appreciate it," Hunter murmurs, his eyes following her, the teeniest, tiniest smile gracing his mouth.

We serve ourselves dinner, then gather around the table. No one mentions seating arrangements, but I don't think it's an accident that no one sits in the seat to my right, especially not when Hunter slides into the empty space.

I love this feeling. As much as I made out to Hunter that dinner was going to be a drag, I actually love being surrounded by family. I love the noise and the chaos and the random conversations we have, usually started by Sadie, but sometimes from Flynn or Katie.

I love watching Olivia with her best friends. Some of the pressure of running this whole place is lifted when she's sitting at the dinner table with them.

I love watching Dallas and Abi slot right into the mix, even though they're new around here, especially Abi.

And I love watching the smiles on my mum's face. She was meant to be surrounded by people to love. It always worried me when I was in Auckland that Mum and Olivia would be sitting at this giant table, just the two of them, heartbreak and grief heavy in the air.

But being back here for an extended period of time I'm realising that isn't the case at all. In fact, it's very rare that they'd have dinner with only the two of them. There's always someone around. There's always love and laughter in this house. It settles something in me, knowing that they'll be okay. They have each other, and this whole family. I thought I might feel like a little bit of an outsider considering how close everyone else is, but they've absorbed me into their bubble, and Hunter too, on the days he shows his face.

I'm startled from my musings when Hunter leans forward, his big hand landing on my thigh.

"Could you pass the sauce?" he asks, deep voice low in my ear.

I blink at him, struggling to comprehend his words with the way his palm feels on my leg. He drags his thumb along the side seam of my jeans and my brain blinks offline for a second.

"Sauce," I say, voice thick. "Yes." I reach for it, passing it to Hunter without meeting his eyes.

Hunter withdraws his hand to use his cutlery and I want to whimper and drag it back, but I manage to refrain from completely losing my mind over his simple touch.

Dinner passes in a flurry of chatter and laughter, but I can't focus on any of it. Because Hunter is beside me, occasionally brushing my arm with his in a purely casual move that doesn't feel at all casual to me. I don't even know if he's doing it on purpose.

He takes part in the conversation, even engaging with Katie, which even I know is out of the ordinary. She's driven him crazy on purpose for years. But there's no teasing in her voice tonight, and she acts like it's completely normal for them to have a conversation.

Everyone is acting like this whole thing is normal, even though I know they're aware there's something going on.

Olivia noticed my hoodie and gave me a long, knowing look. I ignored her, because while she clearly thinks she knows what is going on here, she doesn't. How could she? I don't even know.

Once we've finished eating, we clear the dishes, but settle back at the table, the conversation still flowing.

As Hunter takes his place again after loading the dishwasher, his seat seems closer than before. Close enough for his knee to bump against mine. He stretches his arm out, resting it along the back of my chair, and I almost pass out from the shock of it. His thumb brushes against my shoulder, once, twice, three times. It's not an accidental touch.

He carries on conversations with everyone at the table, and I'm struck dumb because Hunter is dragging his thumb up and down my shoulder.

I want to leap up from this table and drag him from the room, demanding to know what the hell he's playing at. But there's no way to get out of this without drawing everyone's attention, and I'm not ready for that, not until I know what's going on here.

So I sit back and lean into the touch, pressing my leg back against his for good measure.

"Right," Flynn says eventually. "We should go." He glances at Abi and they share a heated look.

"Us too," Katie adds, glancing at Sadie, who is valiantly trying to stay awake while curled up in her dad's lap.

"I'm surprised you all made it this long," Mum says. "I thought the headaches from last night were going to be a lot worse than they are."

Olivia makes a pfft noise. "We're responsible grown ups now, mother."

"Speak for yourself," Flynn says, reaching out to ruffle my sister's hair. She bats his hand away and they start to playfully scuffle.

"Yep, real mature," Dallas says, while Abi grabs Flynn's flailing hands out of the air.

"Take me home," she says and Flynn stops his assault on my sister immediately.

"Yep. Okay. Bye, everyone," he calls, halfway out the door and dragging Abi with him before he even has the words out.

Hunter makes a huffing sound beside me and I turn to him, savouring the increased contact as my shoulder presses into his arm.

"What?" I ask, arching an eyebrow.

Hunter shrugs. "It's so weird, seeing him like that." He's silent for a really long time, while Dallas and Katie say good night and carry Sadie back across the paddock to their cottage. "He's so happy," Hunter says eventually, his voice so low only I can hear it. There's a trace of pride in his tone, along with a whole lot of sadness and maybe a touch of longing.

"I'm heading to bed," Mum says, her voice soft like she's sorry for interrupting. "You two good here?"

"Yeah," I say. "We're good."

"Alright. Love you. See you tomorrow." She leaves the

kitchen and I realise we're alone. I have no idea where Olivia has disappeared to.

"Want to sit on the porch?" I ask, wanting it way too much. "Or do you need to head back?"

"The porch sounds good," Hunter says, brushing the flat of his palm against my back as he rises from his seat.

I collect a blanket from the couch in the lounge, then follow Hunter outside. It's a cold night, the chill immediately seeping through even the warm fabric of the hoodie. I settle into the swinging chair and tug the blanket over me.

Hunter takes the spot next to me, so close our bodies are pressed together. For the body heat.

I lean into him, like I can't get enough. Which is true. I can't.

"Flynn is happy," I say. "He seems really settled, in a way I haven't seen from him before."

Hunter sighs and runs his hand over his hair, before looping his arm around me and tucking me into his side. I snuggle in, even though a tiny voice in the back of my mind is screaming at me that I should be more careful.

"Yeah. He is. You're right."

"Why do you sound so ... sad about it?"

"Not sad exactly," he murmurs. "I just wish Mum and Dad had gotten to see it. Wish they'd been able to meet Abi and Sadie. Fuck, they never even got to meet Katie. There's so much of his life that they missed, that he's missed having them here for." His voice sounds wrecked.

"He has you though," I point out.

"I'm hardly the same."

He sounds so resigned, and I'm fully aware he's mentioned wishing his parents had a chance to see Flynn's life, not his.

"You did what you could," I say. "You did *everything* you could."

Hunter's arm tightens around me and I wrap mine across his stomach, holding him close.

"Sometimes," he says, "I think I should have left him here with your parents. I think they would have done better than me." He releases a shuddering breath. "I wish I hadn't had to give everything up, especially because I screwed it all up with Flynn anyway. I fucked up my entire life, and his." He pulls back slightly and I turn my head to look at him. His expression is wrecked. "Maybe if I hadn't tried to be the fucking hero everyone would have been better off. I wouldn't have hurt the most important people to me." His voice cracks and a stray tear spills down his cheek.

I reach up and swipe the tear away, cupping his cheek with my palm. "Flynn wanted to stay with you."

Hunter snorts and shakes his head.

"No, listen," I say, refusing to let him look away from me. "I heard my dad talking to him. Dad asked Flynn what he wanted and Flynn said he wanted to stay with you. He asked for it. Do you think my parents would have fought so hard for you to stay together if Flynn didn't want it? If they didn't believe *you* were the right choice?"

"Well, they were wrong. I failed."

"No, you didn't. Look at him now. I know things have been tough, for both of you. But Flynn is here, happy, because of what you did for him. I promise you, you didn't fail."

28

HUNTER

WILLOW'S small hand is so warm on my face. She's holding me here, forcing eye contact and I never want it to end.

The bloody tears that keep filling my eyes could end though. They could fuck right off.

I repeat her words back to myself, over and over inside my head.

You didn't fail, you didn't fail, you didn't fail.

I feel like I did. I failed Flynn, I failed Willow and my parents. Everyone that matters.

Willow has that look in her eye though, the stubborn one that shows she's prepared for whatever I'm going to reply with. Whatever I say next, she'll have an answer for. She's adamant. I wish I had that kind of confidence in myself.

"I hurt you though," I whisper, finding the one thing she can't refute. Of all the things I've done in my life, hurting Willow is the only one I truly regret.

Her gaze doesn't waver. "Yes," she says, her voice barely

audible. "I was hurt, but I understand why it happened. I understand why you did what you did, why you said what you said."

"You should hate me. I can't believe you still give me the time of day."

"I could never hate you, Hunter. Never. You didn't have a choice." She slips her hand from my face and for a second I'm disappointed the contact is over, but then she wraps her palm around my nape, fingers splayed over the back of my head and everything is right in the world again.

"I did. Not about staying, I didn't have a choice about that. But I had a choice about how I handled things with you. I made the wrong one. I'm sorry," I whisper as Willow brings our foreheads together. "I'm so damn sorry for everything that happened with us."

"For everything?" Willow asks, eyes closed as she holds our faces a breath apart. God, it would be so easy to close the minuscule distance and brush my lips over hers.

"Not everything. That night, before I brought you home ... it's still the greatest night of my life."

Willow exhales in a heavy rush, her warm breath fanning over my cheek. "Me too."

Two simple words and everything—*everything*—in my heart settles.

"Come here." I slip my free hand under the blanket, sliding it under Willow's legs so I can hook them over my lap, turning her on the seat so she's facing me. She lets out a tiny gasp at the movement, but doesn't pull away, even as I spread my hand across her thigh. She leans into my touch.

I draw back, just enough that I can see her face clearly. A moment later her eyes flutter open to meet mine questioningly.

Eyes the colour of a perfect sky.

A handful of freckles sprinkled across her nose.

Plump, edible lips made for kissing.

I want to devour her.

But I've waited ten years for this chance, and I'm not going to blow it by rushing. This time I'll get my timing right. This time, I'll do better.

Willow's lips part as she tilts her chin up, offering me that delectable mouth. All I have to do is lean in and take it.

I move closer and brush a kiss over her cheek, then do the same to the other. Willow's breath hitches. I press a soft, soft kiss to her forehead, each temple, the tip of her nose. I drop my mouth lower and ghost a kiss over the corner of her lips.

She lets out the tiniest whimper and her hand grips my bicep, nails digging into my flesh.

"Hunter," she whines, chasing my mouth with hers, but I never let her get close enough.

"Hush, kitten," I whisper, my hand finding its way into her hair, the silky strands slipping through my fingers. "I've waited ten years, I'm not going to rush this."

Willow pulls back, her eyes assessing and I wonder what I've said to trigger such a reaction. I've probably said too much, telling her I've waited ten years is probably not the low key vibe I should have gone for.

"Kitten?" she asks.

"Huh?"

"You called me kitten. Why?"

"Oh, because you've got claws." I grin down at her, then lift the sleeve of my t-shirt to show her the marks her nails left in my skin.

She gasps and trails a finger over the tiny crescent shapes. "I'm sorry."

"I'm not." I lean in so my lips are brushing her ear and whisper, "I'm looking forward to another day, when I have you alone, and I get to see what those nails can really do."

Willow's breath stops for a moment, before she draws in a shuddering one. Her fingers curl around my nape and I feel the sting of her nails digging in again. "Careful what you wish for," she says, looking up at me with a sweet, sweet smile on her lips.

"Bring it on." I drag my hand down the length of her thigh, the denim of her jeans soft beneath my palm. My other hand is still in her hair and I claim a fistful.

Willow hums at the pressure on her scalp, leaning into it, and shifts so her knees fall open. It's not a lot of space, and we're both still tucked under the blanket, but I accept her invitation and run my fingernail back up the inner seam of her jeans.

"I'm a big fan of these," I murmur as she squirms under my featherlight touch. She makes a little huffing sound. "Also a really big fan of the hoodie you're wearing tonight."

I lean in and brush a kiss against the corner of her mouth, then another, and another, until I've drawn a line of tantalising kisses along the edge of her jaw.

"I should hope you like it," she gasps, "since it's yours."

"Mm." I drag my open mouth down the deliciously soft skin of her neck. "Not anymore. It never looked that good on me." I bury my face in the curve of her neck, seeking the spot where it meets her shoulder, nudging the fabric of the hood out of the way as I go. When I find the place I'm searching for, I sink my teeth in.

Willow moans and the sound goes directly to my dick. It's been hard since we started whatever it is we're doing out here on the porch swing, but now it's aching, throbbing and desperate.

I need to end this now, before we go too far and I blow my chance, or my load.

I drag my tongue up Willow's neck, savouring the taste of her, and desperate for more. She squirms again and the movement brings my fingertips in contact with her pussy. I press down and Willow tips her head back, exposing her throat.

"Fuck me," I whisper, my voice rough and hoarse.

"Yes," she moans.

I withdraw my hand and her lust-drenched noise turns frustrated.

"Not tonight, kitten. When I finally get to have you again I don't want there to be any interruptions."

"Everyone's asleep," she mutters.

"Well, we wouldn't want to wake them, would we?" My mouth tips up at the corners as I take in her desperate expression. I tilt her chin using my thumb and forefinger, and lean in close. "I don't want it to be some quiet, hurried thing. I want to take my time with you, and I want you to scream my name as loud as you like when I'm buried inside you."

I ghost my lips over hers as she lets out a shuddering breath.

"Good night, Will. Sweet dreams." Another brush of my

lips against hers, then I untangle myself from her, stand and head down the porch steps to my ute.

I don't pause, I don't look back, because if I do I know I'll go back to her. I'll rush this and I refuse to take that risk. I'm not gambling my chance with her. I want this time with her to be perfect and a hushed, hurried romp now isn't enough.

The last thing I hear before I climb into my ute is Willow's low, furious voice.

"You're a right fucking asshole, Hunter Woods."

"Whatever you say, kitten. I'll see you soon."

29

WILLOW

I AM CONSTANTLY HORNY, and it gets worse the more time I spend around Hunter.

I need him so desperately. I need him to strip the clothes from my body, touch every part of me, then fuck my brains out, if we're putting it mildly.

God, the man is the king of the tease.

I understand why he didn't want to follow through tonight, but fuuuuck, his hand in my hair, his mouth on my neck, his fingers between my legs.

I need that.

I need more than that.

He knows it, too. After he edged me until I was ready to start begging for his dick, his hands, his mouth, *anything* to make me come, he disappeared off into the night.

But I know how long it takes to drive from Wildflower Ridge to his place, and he texts me the as soon as he walks through his front door.

HUNTER:

How many times has our pink friend made you come?

Tonight, I mean.

WILLOW:

Wouldn't you like to know.

Even though he can't see me, heat flares across my cheeks. The fact that he knew I immediately went inside and pulled out my vibe is too much.

HUNTER:

Please, Willow. Please.

WILLOW:

Ooh, like the sound of you begging.

HUNTER:

I'd do pretty much anything at this point.
Begging's the least of it.

WILLOW:

Maybe you shouldn't have left. You could have counted for yourself.

HUNTER:

You wanna put on a show for me, kitten?

WILLOW:

You'd like that?

HUNTER:

You've seen mine. Fair's fair.

And FUCK YES. Obviously. Fucking hell, yes.

WILLOW:

Yeah, you got a picture though.

A few moments later a picture comes through.

It's shadowy and shows Hunter lying back on his bed, one arm propped behind his head, showing off his flexed bicep. I can make out the dips and grooves of his chiseled torso. Smooth, strong lines, and the edge of the tattoo I know exists, but have never actually seen. I only know about it because Olivia told me he got one. The photo stops below his bellybutton, right before it becomes indecent, but Jesus Christ on a cracker. Turns out I might have another round in me after all. I thought I was spent, but seeing Hunter's hard body ... shit, I want him.

I have no idea what any of this means. We still haven't actually talked about what we're doing, or if either of us want a relationship out of this.

Every so often he'll say something that makes me think he does, that this is what he wants for our future, a shot at a life together. A redo for the life we had planned.

But things are so different now. I don't even know what I want to do with my own life, how am I supposed to tangle his up with my disaster?

When I was with Mark I was happy to settle down. I have a good job that I enjoy, he had a good job, we'd made a home together. We probably would have got married, bought a house and had kids. The whole white picket fence thing, because that's what was expected we do.

But before Mark, before Hunter's parents died, that was never the plan—not for the immediate future anyway.

Hunter and I were supposed to go to university, then travel. We wanted to see the world.

But after Trent and Isla died and Hunter had to stay behind when I left Kauri Creek everything changed.

Does he still want to travel? If he's looking at buying the mechanic's business, I'd say no. That's a pretty permanent thing, indicating he's intending to stay in Kauri Creek long-term.

But will those plans change if something happens between us?

My phone vibrates in my hand and I turn my attention back to it, dragging my attention away from the photo to read Hunter's next message.

HUNTER:

Will that do, kitten?

WILLOW:

I'd rather the real thing.

HUNTER:

Me too, but you've had a day. We've got time.

WILLOW:

Tomorrow?

Please say yes

HUNTER:

Not tomorrow. Patience, kitten.

WILLOW:

Some night this week?

HUNTER:

I'm working late all week. But I'll message you.

Goodnight, Willow.

I pout. The bastard. He's killing me. He's pretty much dismissed me for the whole week. How am I supposed to get through life when all I can think about is the way Hunter pressed his palm against my pussy for a bare second before *leaving?*

I tug at my silky pyjamas, dragging the neckline low, then push my tits up so they're almost spilling out the top. I hold my phone up, pout again and snap a photo.

I send it, then add a message below.

WILLOW:

Sweet dreams baby

If he's going to tease me ... well, two can play at that game.

MUM'S alone in the kitchen when I head downstairs the next morning. It's surprising because it's not exactly early.

I needed the sleep in though, because I did not get to sleep early.

I'm surprised Olivia isn't around, or Katie, or Flynn. Or any of the others who hang around this place more than their own homes. I love it for Mum though, that she has all these people around to take care of, and who will take care of her when she needs it.

"Hunter head home last night?" she asks as I slide into the seat opposite her, coffee in hand.

"Yeah." I hope the heat I'm feeling on my cheeks isn't totally obvious to her.

"He's been around a lot lately." She takes a sip of her own coffee, looking completely innocent, but I'm not sure I trust that face.

I shrug and silence falls between us. It's not exactly awkward and I know Mum won't push a conversation on me that I'm not ready to have, but maybe I'm finally ready to talk about what happened.

"Do you ever think about how things would be different if Trent and Isla hadn't died?"

"All the time," Mum whispers. "Flynn wouldn't have spent so many years with a broken heart, Hunter would have got the life he wanted … you would have had the life you wanted, with Hunter."

I glance up sharply, meeting Mum's eyes, the same colour blue as my own.

We don't need to say anything, she simply smiles a motherly, knowing smile and it's all right there between us. She knows Hunter and I were more to each other than just friends.

"I loved him so much," I whisper, my eyes burning with tears.

"I know you did."

"Everything was perfect. He loved me back, we were going to be together." My voice cracks and a tear spills down my cheek. Mum's hand wraps around mine and squeezes tight. "He told me that night, and by the time he brought me home his parents were gone and so was our chance."

"Oh, honey." Mum stands, rounds the table and sits beside me, pulling me into a hug. Her arms wrap tightly around my back as my single tear turns into a flood. "I'm so sorry."

She holds me tight until my sobs subside into mild sniffling and I pull back. She wipes the tears from my cheeks.

"He broke my heart," I whisper. "But his whole life was

shattered so I couldn't even hate him for it. He did what he had to do, and I lost him."

"You never lost him, Willow. He's still right here, and I don't know for certain, but I'm pretty sure he's always been yours."

I sniff, wipe my cheeks again and straighten. "You think so?"

"Yeah, I really do, but you know, there's one way to find out."

"I know. But that's so much scarier than everything else I've done recently. I think it's easier not knowing for sure, because what happens if he's honest with me, and it isn't what I want to hear?"

"Then you'll cry, and after that, you'll pick yourself up and keeping moving forward. It's the only way, Willow. We have to keep moving, even when everything feels broken."

She would know. She lost her two best friends and then her husband—the love of her life. And yet here she is, still moving forward, pouring love into me and Olivia, Katie and Flynn and Hunter, Dallas and Abi and Sadie.

I sniff and wipe my cheeks with my sleeve, saved from answering my the sound of the front door and chatter coming down the hallway.

Olivia, Katie and Abi stop abruptly when they see Mum and I sitting at the table, Mum's arm still snug around my shoulders.

"Are you okay?" Olivia asks.

"Yeah, I'm fine," I reply, my voice thick and raspy.

"Is this about shithead Mark?" Katie asks, pouring coffee for the three of them, then joining us at the table.

"No." The word bubbles out of me on a laugh. "Not Mark."

"Hunter then," Olivia says, way too knowingly. How does she know anything about Hunter?

"What?" I splutter.

"He was here really late last night," she says with a shrug. "You've been almost inseparable the last week, even though you've barely given the poor guy the time of day for years. Got to admit though, I'm surprised he made you cry."

"Do we need to add him to the hit list?" Katie asks and Abi chokes on a mouthful of coffee.

"You have a hit list?"

Katie nods, a wicked gleam in her eye, and I wouldn't doubt her for a second.

"Hunter doesn't need to go on a hit list," I say with a sigh.

"Didn't think so," Katie replies. "He's way too in love with you to ever hurt you."

It's my turn to choke on my coffee. "What now?" I croak.

"It's true," Olivia says, like this isn't news to any of them. "Even Abi knows it."

I turn to the newest member of the Wildflower Ridge family and she nods.

"I've only ever seen that man smile when he's in your presence."

"Bullshit. He smiles all the time." Admittedly, not enough in my opinion, but he still smiles often.

Abi shakes her head. "Literally only when you're around. I swear it. Even Flynn's noticed. *Flynn.*"

"That idiot of a man still forgets Abi's in love with him, yet he's always known about Hunter being in love with you," Olivia adds.

I stare blankly at the three of them, words having deserted me. I try to say something, but nothing happens and I shake my head instead.

"Do you want to be with Hunter?" Abi asks quietly and I shake my head, shrug, nod, shrug again, then drop my head to the surface of the table.

"I don't know," I moan. "Yes, but also ... there's a lot of history."

"I knew it!" Olivia cries. "You hooked up in high school didn't you? I can't believe you didn't tell me."

"It's more complicated than that," I mutter.

"I know how to uncomplicate things," Katie says. "Dancing at the hotel, this week. A night out will do you wonders. Maybe Hunter will even join us."

I snort a laugh. "Even I know that's unlikely."

Katie shrugs. "You never know. And a night out worked rather well for both me and Abi in our love lives, so maybe it's your turn."

"I'd like a turn too please," Olivia says, which spins Katie off into a tangent about other eligible men in Kauri Creek. Of which there are few.

I glance over at Mum, who's stayed quiet during my conversation with the other women.

"It can't hurt," she whispers. "It'll be fun at the very least."

30

HUNTER

I MAY HAVE some regrets about teasing and taunting Willow.

Because she's turned the tables on me and is doing it right back.

I haven't seen her all week and I've had a near-constant boner. It's torture.

I wish I'd been lying to her when I said I was working late this week, but I wasn't and by the time I finish work each evening, I barely have enough energy to shower the grime off, eat some food and collapse into bed. I do get to start slightly later in the mornings, which is nice, but it's not enough time to head out to Wildflower Ridge and see Willow.

So I'm stuck with text messages and barely decent photos of her body in slinky lingerie.

But the time and space is probably a good thing. When I'm not thinking with my dick, it's definitely a good thing.

Willow needs time to process the break up of her last relationship and, while she told Mark to piss off when he turned up in Kauri Creek, she still cried over him. You don't cry over someone if there's no feelings involved. I doubt she's still in love with him, not with the things she's said, but the anger is still raw for her, the break up of a long term relationship still fresh.

The space and time between us is a good thing, though I'm not sure how much longer I can endure it.

Abi drops her car in for its service on Thursday morning and updates me on the plans for Flynn's birthday party. She's always been a little standoffish around me, which is probably my fault because I don't think I made a great first impression. Or second impression.

But I was worried about my brother, worried he was lonely and latching onto the first person he found, worried he was getting in too deep with a single mother who had a history of letting people down.

But I was wrong, and I can admit that. Abi has been good for Flynn. He's settled in a way I haven't seen from him in years, and he loves Sadie more than anything on this earth. An instant family might not work for everyone, but it did for Flynn. Having his best friend as Sadie's stepmum probably helps. It's a weird dynamic, which is another reason I was so worried about it, but whatever issues Abi had in the past seem to be firmly left behind.

My brother is the happiest he's ever been, and for that I'm grateful to her.

I finish scanning the proposed guest list Abi insisted I check before she starts inviting people, even though I really don't have an opinion on the matter.

"Looks good," I say, handing Abi back her phone.

"Okay. I'll send some invites out."

"You floated this with Flynn yet?" I ask, curious how she's playing it with my brother. While Flynn loves people, he sometimes gets flighty around important dates and occasions. I know why, but it doesn't mean I like it happening. I'm worried Abi's going to go to all this effort and Flynn's going to let her down, which is something I never thought I'd worry about.

Abi makes a noncommittal humming noise. "It's a work in progress," she says. "Thanks for your input. If someone could let me know when my car is ready?"

"Yeah, sure, of course."

Abi turns and heads for the door, but I call out to her before she can disappear onto the street.

"Abi. Thank you," I blurt out and she stops, turning to look at me over one shoulder, her dark hair in a sleek ponytail. "Thank you for doing this for him, and for everything else you've done for him. You make him really happy and I— I ... well, just thank you. I hope he doesn't let you down."

Abi turns to face me fully, then slowly approaches, like she's worried if she moves too fast I'll startle and run. It's not too far from the truth.

"Flynn's never going to let me down," she says softly. "Not with something like this. I love him and I want him to be happy. If a big party isn't going to make him happy, then that's okay. I'll cancel it."

"For what it's worth, I think he'll love it. And you do make him happy." I run my hand over my hair. "I'm sorry I was an asshole to you."

She blinks at me a few times, like those were the last words she was ever expecting me to say.

"You weren't an asshole," she says, voice quiet but resolute. It's reassuring. "You were wary of me, and worried about your little brother. I get it, especially with my history. You're all he's had for a really long time."

"It's not that I'm all he's had. We both know he's had a lot more support than only me. Thank fuck, because I screwed him up enough. Violet and Henry kept him together through everything, he's got Olivia and Katie." I sigh and drop my gaze, because the last part is hard to admit and I can hardly believe I'm going to say this out loud, especially to Abi, but somehow, she seems to be able to see the situation with clear eyes, maybe because she's so new to it. "It's more that he's all I have. He's all I've got left," I whisper, my voice shaky as I stare at the tips of my scuffed old workbooks. It's probably time for a new pair.

I'm startled when a soft hand lands on my arm, and even more shocked when Abi slides it over my shoulder and pulls me into a hug.

"I'm probably really dirty," I mumble.

"I don't care," she replies, squeezing me tight. "He's not all you have, Hunter. I promise you that."

She lets me go after another long moment and I try to recall the last time someone other than Willow was that close to me. Once released from Abi's hold, I sink into the office chair and rub both hands over my face, then prop my elbows on my knees and my chin on my hands, finally making eye contact again as she starts listing names.

"Flynn, Violet, Olivia, Katie—"

I snort and Abi pins me with a look.

"Yes, Katie. I know she winds you up, but if you think she wouldn't go to bat for you at the drop of a hat you're wrong. There's also Dallas and me. Hell, even Sadie." She crosses her arms over her chest and stares down at me, then says one word with so much certainty I feel it in my bones. "Willow."

"I don't—things with Willow are ..." I trail off because I have zero words to describe my relationship with Willow, or that we haven't had one for ten years.

Abi smirks down at me. "Yeah, I know. But she's on your list, okay? I promise."

Her phone chimes before I have a chance to reply and Abi pulls it from her pocket, reading the screen and letting out a whispered curse.

"Everything okay?" I ask, glad for the distraction from her analysis of my life.

"Yeah, just drama with the caterer for an event on Saturday. He's incredibly unreliable but I haven't got another option in this damn small town."

"I'm surprised you have anyone at all," I say. I've never heard of a catering company in the area.

"Yeah, well he's barely a caterer, but it's all I've got. Sorry, I need to go and deal with this."

"Yeah, of course. I'll let you know when your car's ready. And again, thank you."

"Anytime, Hunter. I mean it," Abi says, then turns and pushes through the office door, her phone already to her ear as she switches into business mode.

I pull my own phone out of my pocket and open my string

of messages with Willow. At the top of the screen is the bottom edge of the last photo she sent me last night before she went to sleep. She's looking cosy and relaxed in her bed, a small smile on her lips, hair mussed by the pillows and the strap of that damn silky top falling down her shoulder. It's probably the most demure photo she's sent me, with barely a hint of cleavage, a stark difference to the one she sent a couple of nights ago where I could clearly make out the hard point of her nipples against the fabric as she scooped her tits up with her hand like she was offering them to me.

But the photo she sent last night, I think it's my favourite.

I study it again for a moment before I return my attention to the last message she sent me. It came through this morning as I leaned against my kitchen bench eating a bowl of Weet-bix.

WILLOW:

Good morning, Hunter. Hope you have a great day.

A string of happy, sunny, smiley emojis followed it.

If anyone else looked at the message they wouldn't see anything special about it. But to me it's everything, because it means she woke up this morning and thought of me.

My chest warms at the thought and I tap out a message.

HUNTER:

Can I see you tomorrow? I finish work at five.

Her reply doesn't come through for an hour.

WILLOW:

Sorry, I can't. Have plans.

I stare down at my phone when the message finally comes through. I want to demand answers. What's she doing? Who's she doing it with? Why did she make plans when she knew I'd be available?

I push all the questions aside. She doesn't answer to me. She doesn't answer to anyone but herself.

HUNTER:

Okay. I hope you have a good time.

This time she doesn't reply, but half an hour later I get a message from Flynn. I almost throw my phone in my haste to read the message and there's a massive spike of disappointment that rips through my chest when I realise it's only my brother asking me to hang out tomorrow night. Though the fact he's available gives me a little glimmer of hope. The request itself is a little unusual, we don't have the type of relationship where we simply hang out, but maybe Abi told him I was having a break-down or something. She's obviously passed on something about our conversation.

But if Flynn wants to see me, it means Abi is busy. Maybe Willow has plans with the other women and that's why she can't come and see me tomorrow. If that's the case I hope they have fun, even if it means I don't get to touch Willow yet.

Since I have nothing better to do with my life than wait for Willow, I reply to my brother and agree to meet him at the hotel tomorrow night.

31

———

WILLOW

I'M STILL REELING from the discovery that apparently *everyone* knows Hunter is in love with me.

I'm not sure I believe it to that extent.

Like, I can understand that we weren't subtle about our feelings for each other as teenagers, but for everyone to so firmly believe Hunter Woods is in love with me, and has been this whole time?

Surely not. It doesn't seem possible. I would have noticed.

Maybe.

Maybe if I hadn't been avoiding him as much as humanely possible because I was feeling rejected and heartbroken and so, so conflicted over those feelings.

Hunter didn't have a choice but to stay in Kauri Creek and I *know* that. And logically I understood what he was trying to do when he broke up with me.

But it didn't hurt any less. It didn't leave me any less devastated to know he'd done it out of necessity.

I sigh and swipe another coat of mascara over my lashes, then lean back to study my face in the mirror.

The other girls insisted on full glam for tonight, which seems ridiculous when we're going to the Kauri Creek Hotel. Most people in this town wouldn't know what glam was if it smacked them in the face with a brick.

But they were adamant, so here I am, attempting to style my choppy little bob into something that constitutes glamorous.

"Are you done in there yet?" Olivia calls through the door.

I flick the bathroom door lock open and turn the handle, revealing my sister, who is dressed to the nines.

"Woah. That's a lot of sequins."

Olivia glances down at herself, then makes a show of rolling her eyes. "My friends are obsessed with them. This is Katie's dress."

"It looks great," I say, because it does. The deep pink is a gorgeous colour on her and the dress hugs her in all the right places, showing off plenty of her toned legs without being indecent.

"What are you wearing?" Olivia ignores my compliment and gestures at me, before pulling a bottle of instant tan out of the cupboard under the vanity and starting to apply it to her legs. I'm currently wearing a ratty old tank top and a pair of bike shorts well past their best days.

"I have this red velvet dress," I say, suddenly unsure of my choice.

Olivia's brow creases. "I don't think I've seen it?"

I shake my head. "I've never worn it." I watch as my sister

rubs the lotion into her legs. "I was going to wear tights. Aren't you going to freeze?"

"I'll wear a jacket. That way it'll at least tone down the sequins."

I laugh. "Why are you wearing it if you don't like it?"

"I do like it. On Katie. I made a comment about it once and apparently she hasn't forgotten." Olivia sighs, washes her hands, then perches on the side of the bath. "She's trying to help."

"Help with what?" I ask, sitting beside her.

Olivia shrugs. "Making me feel better about life, I guess. Making sure I'm still included even though I'm suddenly the fifth wheel." She smooths a hand over the sequins. "I'd have loved this dress once upon a time, but I don't really feel like a sequins person anymore." She peers at me sideways. "Do you get me?"

I reach out and wrap my arms around her, because yeah, I get it. "You'll find that sparkle again, Liv," I whisper.

"I miss Dad so much." Five choked words and my heart breaks for her.

I love my dad and I miss him every damn day, but Olivia was *with* him every day. For her the loss must be tenfold. Plus she's had so much more work and responsibility thrown on her while trying to process her grief.

I smooth her hair, blinking back the tears and hoping the mascara I just applied isn't about to run all over my face. "I know you do."

Olivia sucks down a huge breath and pulls away from my hug, blinking rapidly. "Nope. Not ruining my make up tonight.

I cannot be bothered redoing it." She stands, then pulls me to my feet. "Come on, let's go get your man."

"I don't know that it's like that," I say, nerves suddenly flittering through me. I'm very aware that I'm wearing my best set of underwear—a delicate, lacy black set that's not entirely comfortable but makes me feel like some kind of sex goddess.

Like the dress, I've never actually worn it.

"Go get dressed," Olivia says, giving my shoulder a shove. "Katie will be here any second."

As if on cue, the front door opens and Katie, Dallas and Sadie enter, their easy conversation filtering up the stairs.

Olivia heads downstairs, where I can hear Katie squealing over the dress, while I head to my room and peel off my tank top and shorts, staring down the red dress that's hanging on my wardrobe door.

I catch sight of myself in the full length mirror in the corner of my room and a wicked plan comes to mind. It's been a couple of days since I dangled something in front of Hunter.

I flick off the overhead lights, plunging the room into shadow, then angle my body so I can capture a picture of the way the lace panties curve across my hip. There's a tease of asscheek and my entire back in the shot.

Without thinking too hard about me sending more erotic pictures to a man I'm not even sure I have a chance with, I send it through to Hunter.

WILLOW:

I'll be thinking of you tonight when I'm with the girls. Will you be thinking of me?

I wait a few moments for a response, but nothing comes through, so I turn the lights on again and pull the dress off its hanger.

I'll see Hunter later. I know I will, because he's probably at the Hotel right now, meeting Flynn. This whole evening has been engineered for me and Hunter.

I'm not sure how I feel about everyone being in on the plan. It's a little embarrassing to be honest. Do they think I'm that incapable of getting my shit together that I need four other people to set us up to spend time together?

Even though I know I could have simply turned up at Hunter's place tonight.

I could have replied, 'yes, I'd love to hang out. Let's get dinner' to his text message, instead of my stupidly vague response about having plans.

I tug the dress into place and smooth the skirt down, then pull out the shoes I was intending to wear with it: a pair of black, closed toe heels with a cute t-bar strap.

I think of Hunter and leave out the tights.

Shoes in hand, I head downstairs, completely unsurprised when Katie lets out a piercing wolf whistle as I enter the kitchen.

"Hot damn, Willow," she cries. "You look fantastic."

"No tights?" Olivia asks. "Won't you get cold?" She's got a cheeky smile on her face, her whole demeanour lifted now she's with her best friend.

"Long sleeves," I say, indicating the dress. The simple scoop neck and long sleeves are offset by the incredibly short, flared skirt. I should definitely be wearing tights.

"Mmhmm," Olivia hums. "Sure. That'll make all the difference."

I poke out my tongue at her.

"Here, eat something," Mum says, interrupting our light-hearted bickering. She thrusts a plate of pasta into my hands and I take a seat at the table.

Dallas is right across from me, wearing a well-worn hoodie. Definitely not going out clothes.

"You not coming?" I ask, surprised. I thought he was in on this scheme too.

He shakes his head. "Girls' night. Leaving those two to it tonight." He gestures towards where Katie and Olivia are giggling together. "God help you all. They probably shouldn't be left unsupervised."

I laugh. "There's only so much trouble someone can get into in Kauri Creek. They'll be fine."

"If there's trouble, Katie will find it."

"I hope you mean that as a compliment," Katie says, sliding into Dallas's lap even though there's several empty chairs at the table.

"Of course," he replies, brushing a kiss over her exposed collarbone.

"Isn't Flynn coming, where does he fit into girls' night?" I ask.

"Well he's the decoy, then he'll be making those big moon eyes at Abi for the rest of the night," Katie says, leaning into Dallas with such casual affection.

"It's not fair," Sadie pipes up. "I'm a girl but not allowed to go to girls' night," she says with a frustrated little pout.

"This one's for big girls, Lady Sadie. But we'll do an all ages one soon," Katie replies, smoothing her hand over Sadie's hair.

"We need to get this show on the road," Olivia says, staring down at her phone. "Flynn reckons he can only keep Hunter there for so long."

Katie leans into Dallas for a lingering kiss, then hugs Sadie goodbye. I stack my plate in the dishwasher and slip my feet into my shoes, then we head outside and pile into Olivia's ute.

As I settle into the backseat the nerves hit me. They've been lingering all day, flittering in and out, but now they hit me like a solid wall.

This could be it. This could be the night that changes everything.

32

HUNTER

I'VE BEEN SET UP.

First, Willow sent me a photo of her ass in the sexiest underwear I've seen in my life, causing an instant boner while waiting for Flynn to arrive.

Then, my brother played me like a fiddle.

He did a damn good job of it too. I truly didn't think he was capable of this level of deceit, but I was wrong.

We met fifteen minutes ago, ordered a beer and slid into a booth at the back of the pub. We're still fairly early so there was space, but once the music kicks up soon it'll fill up.

At the moment it's an odd mix of the old drunks who're always here, guys who've finished work for the week but clearly don't want to go home to their families yet, a few couples on dates and a trickle of the ones who're coming in for a night of partying.

A fairly standard Friday night at the Kauri Creek Hotel.

My brother is sitting across from me, telling me a story about

Jett, his border collie puppy, having his first meeting with a Hereford cow.

It's a funny story, and the way he's telling it, fully invested in the tale, should be holding my interest, except movement at the door behind him has caught my eye.

A flash of pink sparkles. Four women.

They're all dressed up to the nines, which really isn't necessary for this place, where half the guys are still in work clothes. But I kind of love that these girls don't give a shit and wear what they want anyway.

They all look fantastic, but my focus zeros in on one.

A deep red dress hugs her body so tightly that I can see every delectable curve of her. At her waist, the skirt flares out so it swishes around her thighs. Her bare thighs. And, thanks to the photo from earlier, I also know what's underneath that skirt.

Jesus Christ.

Flynn notices my distraction and glances over his shoulder. "Oh, the girls are here," he says innocently.

"Like you didn't know they were coming," I grumble. "You can cut the bullshit, Flynn."

He cracks up laughing. "Come on, are you not happy to see them?"

I narrow my eyes at him. "So this is why you insisted on coming here. What's going on?"

I mean, I know what's going on, but I want to make him admit it. I don't know how they know about me and Willow, or how *much* they know, but it's clear Flynn's aware of *something*.

"Nothing," Flynn shrugs.

"You think I'm going to believe that you didn't know Abi

and your two best friends were going to be here tonight? Zero chance."

"Just giving my big bro a helping hand," Flynn smirks.

"I don't need a helping hand," I mutter as the women cross the room and head for the bar. I know they saw us, even if they all pretend like they didn't. Willow's gaze skitters right over me, and my chest twinges painfully when it carries on around the room.

It's the same feeling I got when Violet told me Willow had a boyfriend in the city, the same feeling as when she mentioned they'd moved in together, the same feeling as every time I've seen Willow since my parents died and she avoided me.

"Sure you don't."

"I don't," I insist. "I've got everything under control."

"So there *is* something going on with you and Willow? Like other than you pining after her for your whole life?"

I open my mouth to snap back at him, but his words stop me in my tracks and I end up blinking at him.

"You were hardly subtle, Hunter," Flynn says, his smirk fading as he realises he's hit a nerve. He sighs and rubs a hand over the back of his neck. It's so reminiscent of Dad that this time the pain in my chest has nothing to do with Willow.

"I don't know what you're talking about," I mumble, but the words are about as believable as me saying I'd like to be a ballerina.

"You've been in love with her for years," Flynn says, voice unusually serious. "Even I can see it, and that's saying something." He gives a self-deprecating little chuckle. "Now's your chance."

"It's ... it's complicated," I say. I've never admitted these things. Not out loud. Not to anybody. But I keep talking. "This isn't our first attempt."

Flynn's eyes fly wide. "Wasn't actually expecting you to admit anything to me," he says with another laugh. I'm not sure how that tidbit of information makes me feel. Does Flynn think I don't talk to him specifically? Or does he realise I don't talk to *anyone?*

I run a hand over my hair, then take a long pull of my beer. I'm exhausted by this whole night. I don't want to talk to Flynn about Willow. I want to cross the room, take Willow's hand and lead her right out of this pub. I want to take her straight to my place and get first-hand experience of those lace panties.

"We're working stuff out," I say to Flynn. "We don't need the help." I glance across the room to where Willow, Olivia, Katie and Abi are laughing over a round of drinks. "But it's nice to see Willow having fun. She's had a shitty couple of weeks. So, whatever this whole set up was for, thanks for giving her a chance to have a good time."

Flynn nods. "Just don't leave it too long and miss your shot," he says. "And don't freak the fuck out and almost lose her entirely. That's a shitty option, trust me."

"You did that with Abi?" I ask and Flynn nods, a self depre-cating smile on his face. "You got through it though," I say.

I don't know a lot about Flynn's relationship with Abi, or how they got together, except him insisting they were only friends, even though I caught her leaving his place early one morning, wearing his clothes.

But I do know that they love each other and they're happy so, for once, I'm going to let that little bit of joy into my life too.

"You two are good together," I continue. "I like her."

Flynn blinks at me. Apparently I've stunned him stupid by admitting I don't think Abi is awful. Cool. This is all proving what a great brother I am.

Awkward tension expands between us. We don't hang out like this. I should have known there was something else going on. I assumed Abi had told him I was having a mental break-down or something and he was checking on me, even though it's not something we *do*.

And I regret that.

He's my brother and we don't even hang out unless it's out at Wildflower Ridge for some kind of event.

We're saved from further awkwardness by Katie. I never thought I'd be grateful for her blustering into a conversation.

"Hunt! Fancy seeing you here," she says as she leads the group to our booth.

Flynn and I slide along our seats as the women pile in, Abi next to Flynn, Katie next to her. Willow slides in beside me and Olivia perches on the end.

"Hey," Willow says softly.

"Hey, kitten," I murmur, my mouth close to her ear so only she can hear the nickname. "I've got a bone to pick with you later."

She giggles. "Did you say a boner?"

A laugh bursts out of me, startling myself and everyone around us. I wait until they all get over their shock and return to whatever it is they're talking about before I lean in close Willow again, inhaling her scent as I do.

"Same difference," I say, gently placing my hand on her thigh.

She shifts in her seat, pressing her leg against mine. I skim my fingers up her bare skin and she shudders against me. I glance around the table. No one is paying attention to us. My hand slips under Willow's skirt and I hear her suck in a breath. I splay my hand over her leg, my pinky finger reaching all the way to the top of her thigh, so it's brushing against the lace edge of her underwear.

Willow's hand wraps around my forearm and I feel the sting of her nails biting. "Yep," Willow breathes. "You definitely said boner."

I chuckle again, quiet enough this time that I don't draw attention. "And what if I did?" I ask. "You going to recreate that photo for me in real life?"

I flick the edge of her panties with my finger and Willow shivers.

She gives a tiny shrug. "It's girl's night," she murmurs. "I'm here with the girls."

"You might be here with them, but you'll be leaving with me."

Willow lets out the tiniest sound, a breath of a whimper, then her nails drag down my forearm. She tugs my hand out from under her skirt, but before the disappointment can hit, she laces her fingers through mine and lays our entwined hands in her lap.

She leans into me, then turns her attention back to the group.

"I like your necklace," I whisper as she pretends to follow the conversation. Her only response is to squeeze my hand tightly. But I don't need her to say anything, because it's the necklace I gave her years ago; the tiny gold flower with a sparkling red gem in the middle. The one I've seen her wear since she's been home, well before we started whatever this thing between us is.

That itself is answer enough and I now know for certain.

Tonight, Willow is coming home with me.

33

———

WILLOW

BAD IDEA. This whole charade was a bad, bad idea.

Not wearing tights: bad idea.

The photos and text flirting I've been doing with Hunter: bad idea.

Because now I'm sitting at a table with the memory of his hand ghosting over my bare thigh while he carries on a conversation with Flynn like he didn't just have his hand up my skirt.

I think I might die if I don't get his hands on me soon. Like properly on me, in places too indecent for a pub.

And he's one hundred percent correct in his assumption that I'll be leaving with him.

Thank fuck he only lives a block away so when we do leave we don't have far to go until his hands are back under my skirt and I finally get to get a proper look at his abs. I want to lick them, and also something else while I'm down there.

I try to concentrate on the conversation around me, but nothing is registering in my brain. It's too hard to focus with

Hunter's muscled thigh next to mine. He slipped his hand out of mine a few minutes ago, now keeping both of them above the table, and it's driving me mad.

Repeatedly smoothing my skirt down and willing Hunter to notice, I completely tune out to what Katie, Olivia and Abi are talking about, just occasionally nodding and smiling. I'm pretty sure they know I'm not focussing on them, but they're letting it slide.

The other women all slip out of the booth and yep, I really did tune out. Olivia grabs my hand and pulls me after her. I glance back at Hunter, but he's laser focussed on Flynn and barely notices me being dragged off to the dance floor.

There's only one couple on it, Mr. and Mrs. Henderson, who I'm pretty sure come down to the Hotel every Friday night for dinner and a turn around the dance floor. They've been doing it for as long as I can remember, and I'd thought they were old back then.

The wooden floor in the corner of the room we call the dance floor is permanently sticky and a bit dingy, but the music is loud, the lighting dim except for the flashing rainbow disco lights.

I fall into the beat, resisting the urge to continually look Hunter's way.

Katie sashays closer and wraps an arm around my waist, leaning in close. "I knew he was down bad, but I didn't realise it was this bad," she says into my ear to be heard above the music. She spins me in her arms, holding my back against her chest as we sway.

It gives me a direct line of sight to where Flynn and Hunter are sitting in the booth, watching us. Well, Flynn's watching Abi, and Hunter's eyes are firmly fixed on me.

I expect him to jerk his gaze away and pretend he wasn't watching, but he doesn't. He looks and lets me know he's looking. His gaze is hot and heavy when it meets mine and I don't know if it's a conscious move on his part, but even from across the room I can see him drag his tongue along his bottom lip.

I want to go to him, right now, and beg him to leave.

Fuck girls' night.

I want to fuck Hunter.

I need to.

More than I've needed anything in my life.

This tension between us is at breaking point, wavering on a hair-trigger.

Katie spins me back to face her and I blink, returning to reality. I'd forgotten she was there, even though her arm was wrapped around my waist the entire time.

"Not yet, make him wait for it. Make him work for it," she says and I groan, dropping my head to her shoulder.

"But that means I have to wait," I mutter and Katie laughs. "You don't understand," I say, lifting my head to meet her grey eyes straight on. "We didn't need the help, we just needed the right timing. It should have happened last week but Mark showed up."

Katie pulls a face. "Ugh, no offence to you, but I hate that guy."

I laugh. "I don't, but I want to put him in the past and move on."

Katie twirls me, sending my skirt flaring out, then pulls me back into her, wrapping her arms around me. It's not a dance hold, it's a hug.

"That's the best way to be," she says, squeezing tight. "It's nice to have you home for a bit, Willow."

"It's nice to be home." And it is, but I still don't know what that means for my future plans. I don't know what this thing with Hunter means either. Yes, I'm completely desperate for him, but is it going to be a fast—hopefully filthy—fling, and then we go back to the way things were before? I hope not, but I don't really know what's on offer here.

Katie and I stay wrapped up in each other for a few more moments, as we sway awkwardly to a song that's really not intended for slow dancing.

When Katie pulls back, Hunter is right beside us, his hand raised like he's about to tap her on the shoulder. Katie grins at me.

"She's all yours, Hunt," she says, gleefully shoving me towards Hunter with enough force that I stumble.

Hunter's hands land on my waist, his fingers tightening to steady me. I feel each individual point of pressure and it makes my pulse rate skyrocket.

"That girl's a fucking menace," Hunter growls, pulling my body flush against his. A wave of lightheadedness washes over me at the contact.

"It's most of her charm," I manage to choke out.

Hunter laughs softly, a smile curving his mouth as he looks down at me. I reach up and trace the shape of his bottom lip.

"Does it bother you when she calls you Hunt? I can ask her to stop."

Hunter sighs, settling his arms around me more comfortably. "Don't you ever tell her I said this, but I kind of like it. Only from her, and only because I know she's trying to piss me off. It doesn't, not anymore, but I'm not going to let her know that. At first it was like a jump scare every time she said it, but I like the fact she doesn't pussyfoot around me. Mum and Dad would have adored her."

"They would have," I agree, leaning in to rest my head against Hunter's shoulder.

I float in a bubble of bliss inside his arms, his chin against my temple, until a slap to Hunter's shoulder jerks us out of it.

"Big Woods is here!"

I glance towards the booming voice to find Max Sheridan grinning at Hunter.

"I'm out," Hunter grumbles. "Want a drink?" he asks me and when I nod he spins on his heel and heads for the bar.

"And Willow," Max says, turning his grin on me. "I heard you were back."

"Wasn't like it was a secret," I grumble, my hackles rising. This guy was Olivia's best friend, along with Flynn, all through childhood, but when Katie moved to town when they were sixteen, Max took an instant dislike to her.

It was like he had a personality transplant and he cut ties with Olivia. I'm never going to forget the night she crawled into my bed crying and told me he wasn't her friend anymore. He then proceeded to make Katie out to be some kind of villain.

When she came back to Kauri Creek she never intended to stay, because of Max. For my sister's sake, I'm glad Dallas was a big enough drawcard to keep Katie around, because Olivia deserves all the love in the world.

"How long are you back for?" Max asks, as though he's not public enemy number one when it comes to my family. He's acting like he didn't just interrupt one of the greatest moments of my life.

"Is that any of your business, Max?" I ask and he recoils.

"I was only asking," he says, dropping the fake cheer. Once the facade is gone, he looks defeated and a little lost.

"After what you did you don't get to ask me things like you didn't hurt my sister," I hiss, leaning in to emphasise my point.

Max's face drops. "I know," he mumbles, staring at the floor. He lifts his gaze, fixing it on mine. "I know," he says again. "I know what I did. I know it was wrong. I'm going to make it right, somehow."

"Good, now go away." I turn on my heel. If Max makes it up to my sister, good on him. If she never forgives him, then good on her.

But right now, I've been away from Hunter too long.

I find him leaning against the bar, no drinks in sight.

"I thought you were getting me a drink," I say, stepping right into his space.

His arm settles around my waist like it's the most natural thing in the world. He tugs me close and drops his free hand to the hem of my skirt.

"I was going to," he says, slowly lifting the velvet fabric. "But then I realised another drink means we stay here longer." His hand slips under my skirt and traces a line up the centre of my thigh.

I glance around, but no one's bothering to look in our direction, even if they were, the chances of seeing what Hunter is doing are slim. He's somehow perfectly positioned me between him and the bar so no one can see his wandering hand.

"That is true," I breathe.

He leans in close, his mouth a hairsbreadth from mine. "And that would mean I have to wait even longer to see what's under this skirt." His fingertips reach the edge of my underwear and trace along the lace edge, creeping towards my pussy.

"I'm not thirsty anyway," I choke out.

Hunter ghosts his mouth over mine, flicks the edge of my panties again, then pulls back, dropping his hand at the same time, leaving me a quivering mess, barely able to stay on my heels.

"Sure you're not, kitten," he laughs. "Say your goodbyes. I'm done with waiting."

34

HUNTER

WE DON'T BOTHER with the goodbyes.

The dance floor is a mess of bodies, with all of Willow's friends out there. She spares them all a three-second glance and waves in their general direction.

"Bye," she calls out even though no one can hear her, then she grabs my hand and all but drags me out of the pub.

The door slams behind us and we're thrust into the cold night. Willow shivers.

She hasn't bothered to put her jacket on.

"In a rush?" I ask, tugging her to a stop and taking the jacket from her clenched fist. I hold it up and Willow turns, letting me slide it up her arms. Once it's settled on her shoulders she spins back to face me.

"Are you being a hypocrite Hunter Woods?" She arches a brow.

I shrug. "Well, considering I was at least going to say goodbye to everyone, I don't think I am." I take a step closer, then another, backing Willow into the wall of the hotel. "Do you want something from me, kitten?"

I crowd her body with mine and let my hands linger on her waist, the velvet of her dress smooth and soft under my hands. I know what'll be smoother and softer though.

"Yes," Willow breathes, clutching at my biceps to steady herself.

I press myself against her and she moves her feet apart so my thigh slots between hers.

"What do you want from me, Willow?" I ask as I drag my mouth down her neck. She whimpers and shifts again, dragging her pussy along my jeans.

"Everything," she gasps as I lick a stripe back up her throat.

I pull back and study her, back pressed against the wall, vivid blue eyes filled with want staring up at me, her tits heaving beneath the bodice of her dress. She grinds on my leg again, her eyes fluttering closed as she lets out a long, low moan.

Everything.

She said she wants everything, but in what context? Does she want everything as in a life together, or everything as in she wants me to fuck her every way I know how?

Either way, the second one is happening.

I drag my hand up her body, pausing to roughly jerk the front of her dress down to expose the lace edging of her bra. I give her breast a firm squeeze, then lift my hand higher, resting my fingers along the side of her neck.

I cup her throat with my palm and gently stroke my thumb down the other side of her neck.

"Everything, huh?" I say and she nods hurriedly. "You'd

better get that sexy little ass of yours inside then, before I fuck you right here against this wall."

Willow shudders, then lets out a throaty little laugh. "That'd give this town something to talk about."

"Are you stalling on purpose?" I ask, pressing my thumb to her chin. At the silent command, she drops her mouth open, allowing me to dip my thumb inside. "I want this mouth, kitten, and you're making me wait for it." I lower my hand, dragging it back down over her tits where it lingers. "I thought you were in a hurry."

"I. Am," she pants. "Just. Can't. Think or move."

I chuckle softly and press a gentle kiss to the side of her neck. I withdraw my leg from between hers, then tap my shoe against hers, kicking her feet apart. "Well, if you aren't going to move, I'll have to give you a little teaser right here."

I walk my fingers up her thigh while her pliant, quivering body rests against the wall. My hand disappears under her skirt and her glazed eyes drop, registering where it's going.

God, her skin is smooth, and soft. I bet it tastes delicious. I can't wait to have my mouth on her.

I brush a knuckle over the front of her satin and lace panties and let out a low hum when she gasps. I hook her underwear to the side and circle her entrance with the tip of my finger.

I want to tease her, take this slow and take her apart piece by piece, but also, god damn, I want to fuck her senseless and I'm tired of waiting.

I slide a finger inside her.

"Hunter," she cries, her voice muffled from where she's pressing her face into my shoulder. "We can't. Not here."

"I warned you, kitten," I whisper against her throat. I give my hand another thrust, then pull it back.

Willow whimpers that same desperate sound that's been leaving her lips each time we've been together lately.

I want to know what she sounds like when that desperation turns to satisfaction.

I hold up my hand, sucking on my finger to finally taste her sweetness. God, my self-control is crumbling by the second and if she doesn't move her ass I really am going to fuck her right here against the wall.

"This taste is only going to last me so long, so you'd better get that dripping pussy inside so I can get my fill."

I take a giant step back. I have got to stop touching her or we'll never make it back to my place and it's only down the block. But Willow is addictive. Everything about her draws me in and makes me want more, more, more.

She blinks up at me, surprised at my withdrawal. I gesture for her to go ahead of me.

"I'm hanging on by a thread here, kitten. Get your ass inside my front door."

Willow grabs my hand and tugs me down the street, moving impossibly fast in her heels. We reach my door a moment later and Willow punches in the code with shaky fingers.

We tumble inside and I expect Willow to race up the stairs. I'm looking forward to the view.

But she spins and backs me against the door.

"Kiss me, baby," she whispers against my mouth. Her voice still has that thread of need in it, but there's something else here too, something deeper.

I try to will my heart rate to slow and settle a hand on her waist, trying to ground myself. Willow needs something more right now than my horny dick trying to bang her in the street.

I cup her cheek, marvelling at the way it fits so perfectly into my palm and sweep my thumb over her mouth, before leaning in and pressing a soft, chaste kiss to it.

"Like this?" I whisper.

"You're such a fucking tease," she grumbles. "I meant like this."

Then she pushes onto her toes and fuses our mouths together. Her hand curls around the nape of my neck and I can feel that delicious scratch of her nails against my scalp.

I relax into Willow's touch and let her lead the kiss. When she drags her tongue along my lip I open for her, allowing her to lick into my mouth.

Our tongues tangle, mouths moulding together as we cradle each other.

Something about the softness of this moment, compared to the heated, horny fumbling outside, makes pressure build in my chest.

How can one person be so many things to me?

Obviously she's hot as fuck and I'm desperate to bury my cock in her. She lights my blood on fire and I've never spent so much time hard as I have in the past two weeks, and I was once a teenage boy.

But, there's more here, because it's Willow.

She's the goddamn love of my life and I never, ever thought I'd feel her mouth on mine again.

I never thought I'd get to hold her in any capacity, let alone up against my door while she kisses me like I'm the air she needs to survive.

I try not to get too caught up in what this means. I've been spiralling on and off about it for days and I'm no closer to a resolution. At this point, I'll take whatever Willow is offering.

I once thought I'd move on from my love for her but, as the years passed, I realised that was never going to happen. Willow is it for me and I'm going to enjoy this as much as possible, for as long as she wants it to last.

Willow breaks the kiss, panting softly. Her blue eyes meet mine and there's a thread of vulnerability there.

"Thank you," she murmurs. "Now, where were we?" She narrows her eyes. "Oh yes, I was getting my ass upstairs so you can finally make good on all this fucking teasing." She spins on her heel and starts up the stairs, glancing back over her shoulder to where I'm still leaning against the door, stunned by her abrupt change in pace.

"You coming, baby?" she asks with a smirk, the endearment slicing my heart open.

Shit, I need to keep it together. Now isn't the time to declare my lifelong, never wavering, complete and utter devotion to her.

If I'm lucky, I'll have that chance later. And if I don't, at least I get tonight.

"Just enjoying the view," I say, dropping a hand to my groin.

Willow continues up the stairs, shaking her ass a little more than strictly necessary with each step.

"Is it a good one?" Willow asks, her voice sugary sweet, full of phoney innocence.

"You know it is. That skirt is criminal."

She lets out a laugh. "You should see what's under it." She pops her ass out and I can see the creases at the tops of her thighs.

"I plan to." I grip my dick through my jeans, hoping the pressure will make the ache subside. It doesn't help. "What's that on the step in front of you?" I ask, finally pushing off the door and starting after her.

"Hmm? What?" Willow asks, confusion lacing her expression as she glances between me and the empty step in front of her.

"Your hands," I growl and realisation crosses her face.

Immediately her hands drop to the floor and for good measure she widens her stance. She tilts her hips and the skirt of her dress rides up, exposing the slightest glimpse of her panties.

"Fuck me." I pause in my climb up the stairs. "How is this even real?" I mumble.

"I keep asking myself the same thing," Willow says, her voice breathless.

Closing the gap between us, I pinch the hem of her skirt between thumb and finger and toss it forward, exposing the smooth, full curve of her ass, wrapped in satin and lace.

I kneel on the step below her, bringing myself inline with her pussy. I stroke my palms up her thighs, watching goosebumps spiral across her skin at my touch.

Leaning in close, I inhale, eliciting a moan from Willow as my nose brushes her skin. I sink my teeth into the spot, the bite gentle.

There's a scrabbling noise as Willow shifts, then a foil

packet is tossed back between her legs, hitting me in the stomach before falling to the ground.

I laugh. "You came prepared did you?"

"Wasn't letting something as stupid as a condom fuck this up. Can we use it now? Please?"

I sink my teeth into her other ass cheek. "Not yet, kitten. Turn around and sit this pretty ass on that step. I'm hungry."

35

WILLOW

I REALLY THINK I might die, sitting with my bare ass on Hunter's stairs as he shoves my skirt up past my hips.

"Spread these," he says softly, tapping on each of my knees and I let them fall apart.

Hunter rears back, his hand dropping to his crotch again. It's been straying there more and more often since we got inside. He squeezes the bulge in his jeans as he drinks in the sight of me, his eyes dark with lust and hunger.

"This doesn't feel real," he murmurs as he crawls closer, pressing a kiss to the place on my knee he nudged.

He leaves a trail of kisses up my thigh before he drops back to my knee on the other side.

"It's real, baby." I lean back on my elbows and moan as his mouth teases the satiny soft skin of my inner thighs.

But I can understand the feeling. I've dreamed about this moment for days. For years. I never actually thought it would happen and in moments it does feel like an illusion.

But even my dreams haven't been this good.

Hunter hooks his fingers into the waistband of my panties and tugs them down, peeling them down my legs and off over my shoes.

I feel exposed and vulnerable, but it's *Hunter* and he's staring at me with adoration in his eyes. A deep longing flares in me as I see the expression on his face. This is what I've wanted for so long.

His gaze drops and now he's staring at my pussy like it's one of the great wonders of the world.

He traces a finger along the crease of my thigh and groin and I shiver.

"Come on," I whine. "The time for teasing is over."

His finger strays closer to where I need it. I want him to thrust his finger back inside me, add more and fill me up. I want him to replace his hand with his cock.

Having that brief moment outside when he slipped inside me has coiled the need for him even tighter. Everything he's done, every time he's touched me, has been a tease, a taunt.

I need him for real this time. No more lingering touches or barely-there caresses.

He smirks. "No more teasing?"

"No. Get on with it," I whine again as his touch ghosts over my pussy and draws a line along my thigh.

"You should be careful what you ask for." Then, without further warning, he buries his face between my legs.

The time for teasing really is over as he commits fully, stroking the flat of his tongue over my clit while I convulse on the step, waves of pleasure shuddering through me.

He licks and sucks and flicks with his tongue, his fingers sinking into the flesh of my thighs as he pushes them wider, pinning them exactly where he wants them.

My moans and cries echo in the stairwell and Hunter hums against my pussy.

He lifts his head. "This better than the teasing?" he asks, evidence of how fucking horny I am glistening in his stubble.

"God yes," I moan, reaching out to cup his cheek.

"A god, huh?" He grins and pushes my knee up, towards my chest, exposing me even more. "I'll take it, I suppose."

My hand runs up the side of his face to rest on his hair. The short bristles rub against my palm and I press down.

"Shut up," I say, the last word a drawn out moan as Hunter takes the hint and buries his face in my soaking, aching pussy again.

He works me over like a master, his tongue coiling me tighter and tighter. He sucks my clit into his mouth, rolling his tongue across it and my world blinks out of focus.

I come so hard I nearly levitate off the stairs and it's only Hunter's firm grip on my thighs that keeps me in place.

"Hunter."

I cry out as shudders wrack my body and Hunter presses his cheek against my thigh, his body tense as he lets out a long groan when my body finally settles.

My breath comes in stilted gasps as I lie back on the stairs. It's not the most comfortable position now I'm not distracted by Hunter's mouth on me, but my limbs feel like jelly and I'm not sure I can actually move.

"I can't feel my toes," I mumble. I feel Hunter's laugh as his breath puffs across my heated skin.

He sits up, eyes still a little glazed and cheeks flushed. He carefully takes the hem of my dress and tugs it down, smoothing the fabric reverently.

"More time for that later," he says, voice rough and gravelly. Then he reaches down and unbuckles the tiny ankle straps on my shoes. He slips the heels free and places them on the step. Picking up a foot, he massages it gently, then gives my big toe a soft squeeze. "Toes are still intact," he says.

I roll my eyes. "Shut up and come here."

He crawls up beside me, lying awkwardly on the stairs and reaching over to gently brush the hair back from my face.

"You're fucking beautiful, Willow," he says, his voice soft with reverence.

"So are you," I whisper back. And he is, with shining hazel eyes and his mouth tipped up into an easy smile.

He smirks. "I'm going to have to grow my hair again, even if it's fucking annoying." He leans in and brushes his lips over mine.

"Why?" I manage to croak through the dizzying waves of desire and lust and love for this man.

Shit.

Love. But that's true too. I never stopped.

"Give you something to hold onto," he says, his lips brushing my ear with a featherlight touch.

I groan and reach for him, angling for the button on his jeans. I manage to get it undone and am fumbling for the zip when he scoots his hips back, out of reach.

"Where are you going?" I ask, clinging to him as he drags himself upright so he's sitting on the step beside me, elbows resting on knees.

I shimmy around until I'm kneeling between his thighs, then aim for his fly again. I thought he'd already have those pants off and be sliding his dick between my lips by now, but it's almost like he's reluctant.

My hands slow, then come to a stop and I rest them on his legs, feeling the solid muscle through the dark wash denim that makes his ass look edible.

"Do you not want me to?" I ask, voice suddenly shaky, completely in the dark about why his pants are still firmly attached to his body.

He cups my cheeks and leans in, pressing a gentle but firm kiss against my mouth.

"Oh, I want you to," he murmurs against my lips, then hesitates. I can feel reluctance radiating off him.

"I want to." I pull back and eye him. "Are you going to make me beg, Hunter?" I bat my lashes and pout, trying to make my eyes go big and round. "Pretty please can I suck your dick?" I ask in a sickly-sweet voice.

He barks a laugh. "Save that for later, kitten, when I really do have you begging." He leans in again, but this time instead of a sweet kiss, it's filthy, his tongue owning my mouth as he tips my chin back to an angle that suits him. "I don't need you to suck my dick right now," he grumbles, breaking the kiss, "because your hot little moans and the way you said my name as you fucked my face sent me over the edge, Willow. That sweet pussy I've been dreaming about made me come so hard I nearly fell down these stairs."

His mouth is back on mine before the words register fully in my mind, his tongue plundering and searching, owning me.

I pull back, chest heaving as I try to catch my breath. Hunter drags a hand down my throat, along my collarbone, then cups my breast, massaging and moulding the flesh. Heat is pooling between my legs again.

"You came?" I pant. "You already came? I didn't even get to touch you."

Hunter pinches, my nipple tight between his fingers and I let out a hiss of pleasure. "Don't worry, we've got all night, and with you around it won't be long until I'm hard as fuck again."

He pinches my other nipple, then pushes to his feet in one swift, fluid movement.

"Come here, let's get you inside."

He hauls me to my feet, then sweeps me off them, carrying me the last few steps and into his flat, leaving my discarded shoes and a pair of lace panties on his front steps.

I'm not thinking about them for long though as he tosses me onto his bed.

"Get naked. I'll be right back, and this time my cock's all yours, kitten."

I STEP BACK into my room and almost come again at the sight.

Willow is in my bed, sitting right in the centre with the sheet tucked around her looking all sweet and demure, wearing nothing but the fine gold necklace I gave her years ago. At the foot of the bed her dress is lying in a crumpled heap, a lace bra that matches the panties I left on my front steps strewn across it.

Fuuuck. My dick twitches. It's not quite ready for another round, but it isn't far off, and this time I'm not coming in my pants like a horny teenage boy.

This time I'm coming with my cock buried so deep inside Willow we'll both be feeling it for days, months, years, a lifetime.

"That's far too many clothes," Willow says, a cheeky smirk on her puffy lips. They're redder than usual, slightly swollen from my harsh kisses. God, I want to see them wrapped around my dick.

I yank my shirt over my head, tossing it on the floor with her dress, then shove my jeans down that I hadn't bothered to fasten after my quick clean up in the bathroom.

I can't believe I did that, but Willow crying my name as her sweet taste filled my mouth sent me over. I kick off my jeans and stalk towards her, reaching for the blanket to pull it back and climb in beside her.

"Nope," she says, yanking it out of my reach and tucking it tighter around her. "Still too many clothes." She eyes my navy boxer briefs with a raised eyebrow. "I'm in here completely and totally naked and you're standing there overdressed for the occasion." She pouts again and bats her eyelashes at me.

It makes me want to get on my knees for her, follow her every command, make her every wish come true.

It also makes my dick hard again. Thank fuck. I was a little nervous I'd come so hard that it was down for the count tonight. That would have been seriously uncool considering it's taken Willow and I two weeks and ten years to get back here.

I shove my underwear down my thighs and step out of them, resting my hands on my hips and glowering down at her. I have no idea what kind of dynamic we have between us, but it's hot as sin and fucking fun, which I never expected when it feels like there's a lifetime of pressure on my shoulders.

But the way Willow weaves together playful and sultry is a masterpiece and I cannot get enough. One minute she's like a sex goddess and the next she's making me laugh even though this whole situation is so wild I can barely think straight.

Because Willow is here.

In my bed.

Naked.

And I'm getting in there with her.

She lifts the blankets and I slide against the cool sheets.

Our skin connects and there's nothing cool about it. Heat and fire sizzle through me as Willow lets out a satisfied little hum.

"Oh, that's better," she murmurs. "I was lonely before." She says it in that silly little voice, but I ignore that as I wrap my arms around her and pull her into me, fitting her perfectly against my side as I stretch out.

"You'll never have to be lonely again," I murmur, then capture her mouth with mine.

This time the kisses are slow, our tongues tangling together as hands skim over miles of bare skin. I explore her body by feel alone, learning the places that make her breathy with desire or sensitive and ticklish.

I savour the moment, feeling her hands splayed across my chest, her nails gently biting into my skin.

I've lost all track of time, floating in this bubble with Willow in my arms, cocooned in my blankets, the rest of the world fading away until it's not even white noise.

Her kiss turns greedy and a moment later Willow pushes me back and rolls, sliding her leg over my hip so she's straddling me.

I can feel the wet heat of her pussy against the base of my shaft as she lets the blankets fall from her shoulders.

"This is gorgeous," she says, tracing the outline of my tattoo with a fingertip, causing shivers to ripple through me.

I glance down at the design, watching her finger move over

it. It's been a part of me for so long I barely think about it anymore.

"I guess you've never seen it up close," I say for lack of any better words in my head. It's hard to focus on talking with the tingles that shoot to my balls every time Willow shifts, her pussy rubbing against my cock. I'm not even sure she's aware of how much it's affecting me.

"I've never seen it at all," she says.

"You must have." Surely. I got the tattoo the year after my parents died.

"Nope." She trails a finger down my ribs and across my abs, skirting around my hard cock. "You've been hiding all this from me for years. I can't believe you've been holding out on me all this time." She reaches back and rakes her nails up my inner thigh.

A shudder wracks my body and I groan, reaching up to grasp the nape of her neck and tug her down to me, covering her mouth with mine.

She opens for me, supple and willing as I control the kiss. Her hips tilt and grind, bringing her pussy into contact with my cock over and over, coating it with her wetness.

"Fuck, you're so wet I can feel it dripping all over me," I breathe against her cheek as I hold her in place with a hand tangled in her hair. I wrap my other hand around her throat, stroking my thumb down the length of her neck, the skin pale and smooth against my calloused hands.

Willow bucks her hips, her movements growing more frenzied. She lets out a tiny whimper.

"I can't wait to taste you again. Your cunt is the sweetest thing I've ever had."

"Yeah?" she asks, a thread of uncertainty in her voice.

"Mmhmm. I'll bet you'll be able to taste yourself when you suck my cock with the way you're sliding all over it."

Nobody has ever moved as fast as Willow in that moment as she pulls free from my hold and wriggles down the bed, laying between my thighs. She looks up at me with those big blue eyes, then opens her mouth and drags her flat of her tongue up the underside of my cock, never breaking eye contact.

She hums, licks her lips with a smile and goes in for another swipe.

Holy shit. I can't believe this is happening. I know this isn't the first time I've actually had Willow in my bed, but it wasn't like this last time.

Back then we were two fumbling virgins and while I tried to make it good for her, there wasn't this level of foreplay. There was no pussy licking, no blow jobs, just awkward hands and the quickest fuck in the history of time.

But at the end, Willow had wrapped me in her arms, kissed me soundly and told me she loved me, so it can't have been totally shit.

Being with Willow was one of the best moments of my life and I've held onto that feeling for the past decade, never expecting for us to have another chance.

Never expecting that one day she'd be between my legs, swirling her tongue around the head of my dick like she's sucking a goddamn lollipop.

I prop myself up on an elbow so I can get a better view of her lips stretching wide over my length and Willow looks up at me again as she sucks my tip into her mouth.

"Holy Jesus fucking shit," I groan.

Her mouth is hot and wet and the suction is absolutely perfect as she inches my dick into her mouth.

My body strains as I lock it down, forcing myself to stay still and not thrust my hips up to fuck into her throat.

This moment is Willow's and she gets to set the pace, but it doesn't stop my thighs shaking with the intensity of it all.

My cock brushes her throat as she swallows me down, holding it for a moment before popping off with a lusty moan.

I'm about to grab her, lay her out on the bed and slide my cock into her pussy when she drops her mouth over my cock again, this time bobbing her head and working me over, alternating between quick, shallow sucks and slower, deeper ones.

She rolls my balls across her palm and tingles zap up and down my spine.

I fist a hand in her hair, happy to hold her and let her control the pace, but as heaviness pools in my balls and the tingles settle at the base of my spine, I tug her free.

She looks up at me from between my spread thighs with that ridiculously sexy little pout on her swollen lips.

"I'm sorry to ruin your fun, my kitten. But the next time I'm coming tonight, I want my cock buried in your pussy."

Willow's eyes flash with desire and she loses the pout real fast. "Yes. God, yes. Fuck me, baby, please." Her voice is husky and rough, like I've never heard from her before, as she crawls back up my body, grabbing my cock and angling it for her pussy.

I grip her hips, holding her back from sinking down on it. "Hold up. As much as I love this enthusiasm we've got to wrap it up first."

Willow's pout is back as she flings herself off my lap and into a pile of limbs on the bed beside me. "Fine, be all responsible and shit," she grumbles.

I laugh, grab a condom from my bedside table and roll it down my aching shaft. "Apparently someone's got to be. Never thought I'd see the day when it'd be me instead of you though."

She mock-glares at me from under her tangled hair and I reach out to brush it back from her face.

"Thank you," she says, voice soft.

"Of course. I'm always going to look after you," I whisper, voice husky. "Now come here." I drag her into the middle of the bed and push her thighs apart.

She's relaxed, letting me arrange her how I please, and her complete trust in me, in this moment, has my heart singing.

I kneel between her legs, sliding my cock through her wet pussy a few times, causing Willow to writhe and moan. The sight is incredible, from her flushed cheeks to her heaving tits, to the way her pussy was made to hug my shaft.

"Just fuck me already," she gasps.

"Patience, kitten," I murmur, giving her cunt a slap with my cock before lining myself up with her entrance. "I've waited a long time for this, you can bet I'm going to make the most of it."

She moans again and wraps her legs around my waist as I ever-so-slowly sink inside her, my eyes locked on hers.

Her pussy is as hot and tight and wet as I'd imagined and she fits like she's made for me.

Willow reaches up, wraps a hand around the back of my neck and, digging her nails into my skin, drags me down for a heat-filled, sloppy kiss.

It's utter fucking perfection.

It's magic and happiness and all of my dreams coming true.

37

WILLOW

MY EYES WANT to roll back in my head, but I refuse to look away from Hunter's intense stare as he inches his cock inside me.

God, he's big. It was a struggle to get my lips around it, but I always was an overachiever so there was no way I wasn't getting his length in my mouth.

He was right. I could taste myself on him, and it was the hottest thing I've ever experienced.

That and having him eat me out on the stairs while he came in his pants because he couldn't hold back.

Over me.

He bottoms out and a hoarse sound escapes the back of his throat. As disappointed as I was when he stopped me blowing him, I appreciate it now.

He rolls his hips and this time I can't hold his stare. I gasp and drop my head back. Hunter takes my arched neck as an invitation and lavishes my throat with his tongue, biting down on the sensitive spot below my ear.

"Hunter," I gasp. "Please."

"Please what?" he asks with another slow roll of his hips.

"Harder. Faster. More."

"You'll get that, kitten. I promise." He kisses me roughly. "But right now—" he cuts off with a curse when I clench around him. He stops the slow, sensual hip rolls and instead pulls almost all the way out, holding himself with only the tip of his cock inside me.

"Baby, *please*," I whine.

He smooths a hand over my hair and down my cheek.

"I'll give you anything you want, Willow. *Anything*. I just need this right now." He ever-so-slowly thrusts back inside me. My toes curl at the sensation. "If you're going to be a brat about it I'm going to take even longer," he mutters in my ear once his cock is fully seated in me again.

I dig my nails into his shoulders and he groans. "You can't blame me for scratching you up then," I whisper, dragging my nails forward, down his pec, leaving a trail of red lines.

"You can fucking shred me anytime you like." He gives another roll of his hips, then another, slowly increasing the speed.

Tension coils in my belly, my core tightening as I brace for him to finally unleash. I'm a quivering mess, my legs wrapped tightly around his hips, holding him to me.

Just when I think he's about to snap he slows down again.

I emit some kind of frustrated, growling shriek and drop my head back again.

"How are you so fucking *patient*?" I hiss.

"Ten. Years. Willow," he says, breaking between each word to cover my mouth with his. "I'm not letting it all be over in ten seconds."

"Argh. Fine," I grumble, then gasp as Hunter pulls almost all the way out again, and slides in achingly slow.

I give in and let him set the pace as he draws me closer to the edge and backs off time and time again.

His eyes are dark with heat and lust, the muscles in his arms quivering as each thrust of his hips gets a little faster, a little harder.

I'm hanging right over the cliff, stars dancing at the edge of my vision, when he finally snaps. His next thrust is so hard he shunts me up the bed and I let out an appreciative sound as I finally get what I need.

Hunter grabs my thigh, holding my leg tightly around him. "Better hold on tight, kitten. I'm done playing." Then, without warning, he snaps his hips forward again, and again.

My nails are tearing at the skin on his shoulders, his waist, his back and chest as I tighten my legs around him.

"Yes, baby, yes." Moans and whimpers and cries fill the room to the tempo of Hunter's headboard thunking against the wall.

"Come for me," he growls and, at his command, I do.

My world is rocked as Hunter thrusts into me once, twice, three times more. "Hunter, baby." The words are barely a breath.

"That's my girl," he manages through his grunt as he stiffens and comes.

My hands automatically caress his face, his head, smoothing over the scratch marks I've left on his shoulders and down his back.

Hunter rolls off me with a groan and we lie side by side, spreadeagled on his ruined sheets.

"Did you mean it?" I whisper into the silence.

He rolls his head to face me, a question on his face. "I said a lot of things," he says, reaching up to smooth my hair again. I savour the comforting gesture, because this conversation could tear it all away again.

"When you said I'm your girl?" I hold my breath, clenching my fist and hoping, hoping that I've read this right.

"You've always been my girl, even when neither of us could see it. And all these years, I've always been yours, no matter what I said when I was young and stupid. Of course I was waiting for you. There's never been anyone else."

I throw myself at him, somehow finding the energy even though my body is so completely wrung out that even my bones feel weary.

"You're right. I've always been yours." I wrap my arms around him and bury my face in his neck. "I'm sorry I was too blind to see it for so long."

Hunter trails his fingers down my spine, the touch sweet and gentle as his palm skates over my ass. "You weren't blind, Willow. I hurt you and for that, I'm sorry. There's not very many things I have regrets over, but hurting you, saying those things I did to you, I'll regret that forever."

I snuggle into him. "Maybe it was supposed to happen this way. Maybe if we'd tried to make it work back then it wouldn't have." I lift my head, wanting to look him in the eyes for my next words: "I understood, Hunter. You were hurting. Your world had been turned upside down. You had to stay, and I was way too optimistic back then. It wouldn't have worked and then we would have been even more heartbroken and devastated. Maybe we would never have been given this chance if we'd pushed our luck then. I've never held it against you, I want you to know that."

"God, I fucking love you Willow," Hunter says, pulling me in for a sensual kiss, his tongue stroking over mine. He breaks away, panting, before I even have a chance to process his words. "I know that might feel way, way too soon, but I do. I always have."

I kiss him again. "I love you too, Hunter." I snuggle back into him, his arms wrapped around me in the safest, cosiest embrace. "I need a nap," I say, yawning. "But then we're going to have another round, and another. I don't want to be able to walk tomorrow."

"Don't worry, kitten. I've got you."

Hunter presses a kiss to my forehead and we drift off to sleep, shrouded in blissful contentment.

38

———

HUNTER

I WAKE up with Willow tucked into my side, her hand splayed across the tattoo on my ribs.

I got the design not long after my parents died, a stand on native trees, tangled with a flowered vine of my mum's own design. She painted it on the ceiling of the shearer's quarters where her and dad lived right after they got married. It's still there.

The tattoo artwork is incredible, but it's all tied up in memories of grief, and the terrible ways I tried to cope with that. I was spending way too much money, trying to make it up to Flynn because our parents were gone. Somehow thinking that buying him the best of everything was going to help.

Then I got it in my head that I deserved something too, and spent way too much on a tattoo.

Thankfully, Henry and Violet stepped in, calling me out before I could ruin everything, but it still wasn't good for a long time.

And now, it's probably due to my reckless spending years ago that I can't afford to buy the mechanic business unless I sell my dad's Torana.

I reach for my phone, trying to grab it without disturbing Willow. It's already mid-morning and I've got several texts from Flynn, sent last night.

FLYNN:

We can't find you or Willow. Where'd you go?

Don't worry Liv said you and Willow left. At least she let her sibling know

It was good to see you. Have a good night

I lock the screen and drop the phone onto the bed beside me, then pick it up again a moment later.

It was good to see Flynn, for us to hang out like that. It's not something we've ever really done and most of the times I see him now are across Violet's kitchen table when she invites us both for dinner.

Even though I'm convinced the whole night was a set up, it was still nice to sit with my brother and listen to him talk about his life over a beer. I didn't even mind hanging out with everyone else, especially because Willow was there.

HUNTER:

It was good to see you too.

We could do it again sometime? Maybe.

If you want.

Just us, I mean.

I sigh and toss my phone aside again. Way to be cool about it.

Willow stretches and blinks up at me. "Morning," she says, reaching up to run her fingers down my cheek.

"Morning," I reply.

"What time is it?" Her voice is a little croaky, still filled with sleep and she stretches out again, pressing her incredible body against mine.

"After ten," I say. My hand finds its way into her hair, gently combing through the silky strands.

"Wow. I haven't slept this long in ages." She shuffles so she can look up at me. "Everything okay? That was a big sigh you made."

"Yeah, it's all good, kitten. Just replying to Flynn's messages from last night."

Her grin turns wicked. "I guess we weren't very subtle."

"Like a sledgehammer," I deadpan.

"You know what else isn't very subtle?" she asks, pushing up onto her elbows.

"What?" I ask, wary of what she's about to throw at me.

"Me."

She slides down the bed until her face is in line with my cock. She tentatively licks the tip, then sucks me into her mouth.

"Fuck," I groan. "You're insatiable."

Willow hums, her gaze flicking up to meet mine as she works me over.

We'd fucked again sometime during the wee hours of the morning and at this point I'm surprised my dick has anything left in it to stand upright.

But it is, and it isn't long before my balls are tightening.

I wrap my hand in her hair and tug her off. As expected, her lips form a pout and she looks at me like I've ruined Christmas.

"You're so good at that," I murmur. "Do you want to finish me like that, or have me fuck you again?"

The pout vanishes. "Fuck me again." Her voice is already desperate and pleading. She's tearing open a condom before I even have a chance to move.

She rolls it down my shaft, then sits back on her heels, demeanour suddenly shifting to sweet and a little shy. "How do you want me?"

I lie back against my pillows, resting my arms behind my head. "I want you to ride me, kitten. That way I can see all of you. I want to watch you make yourself feel good."

She bites her lip, eyelids fluttering as a low moan rumbles in her throat.

Straddling my lap, Willow notches my dick at her entrance, then slowly slides down my shaft. I regret teasing her so damn much last night now, because I'm pretty sure this is payback.

Once I'm fully inside her, she pauses, her palms pressing against my pecs, the now-familiar bite of her nails on my skin.

My hands itch to touch her and I bring one forward, aiming for her full tits. Her nipples are so sensitive and I want to make her squirm.

But Willow bats my hand away. "I thought this was my show."

"My bad." I tuck my hand back behind my head. "Go right ahead."

And she does, riding me until my thighs are shaking. She

cups her tits, tweaking her nipples as she grinds on my lap. She tips her head back, exposing the soft skin of her throat. She bounces and grinds and fucks me until I can't see straight.

I want to touch her so badly my palms burn, but I hold off until I finally blow and I can't stop myself anymore. I grip her hips and slam her down, holding her against me as I pulse inside her.

When my vision clears again, it's to see the most incredible sight I've ever witnessed: Willow still straddling me, her naked body a work of art, but it's the expression on her face as she gazes down at me, her eyes filled with love and a soft smile on her perfect lips.

"Get up here," I growl, grabbing her thighs and dragging her forward until she's sitting astride my chest. She reaches out to balance herself with a hand on my headboard.

"What? Why?" she gasps and giggles.

"Because you didn't come, so you're going to ride my face until I make sure you do."

The noise that leaves her is so feral I know I've made the right call. She's filled with hesitation, but lets me arrange her knees on either side of my head.

"Are you sure?" she whispers. "I feel like I'm going to smother you."

"Then I'll die a fucking happy man. Now, sit."

Willow lowers herself, but she's still too hesitant, and this time I'm allowed to touch, so I grab her hips and yank her down, spearing my tongue into her pussy as she comes within reach.

She lets out another rough sound and after another couple

of licks, she lets go, riding my face with the same enthusiasm she did my dick.

I savour every second, every taste, and when she comes with a cry, thighs shaking, I hold her in place until I'm well and truly done with her.

We collapse back onto the bed, Willow a tangle of blissed-out limbs beside me.

"I've been thinking," she says as her breathing settles, her voice languid and dreamy. "I don't want to stay here."

"Stay here? Like right now?" I roll up on my elbow to gaze down at her. "I wasn't planning on wearing pants today, but if it's what you really want."

"No, not right now." She waves a hand in the air, a smile on her lips. "Long-term."

"Oh. That makes sense." I smooth her hair back and lean down to kiss her. "We'll find another place." Ideas and images are already filling my mind. Maybe we could build a place at Wildflower Ridge, one full of windows so every time we look outside we know we're home.

Willow watches me for a moment, a crease between her brows. "No ... I mean Kauri Creek. I don't want to stay in Kauri Creek."

And, just like that, everything shatters.

39

WILLOW

HUNTER JERKS back at my words, his face stricken. I don't think anything could have shocked him more, which I don't fully understand.

"You want to go?" he asks, gravelly voice barely audible. He shakes his head. "But, I thought … I thought …" He gestures between us and realisation dawns.

"Hunter, baby. I want us to go together." I reach out and grasp his arms, wrapping my fingers tightly around his wrists to hold them in place. I can feel the tension radiating through the tendons and muscles.

His jaw clenches over and over, his wild eyes searching the room for answers, looking everywhere but at me.

"I can't," he says. His voice is wrecked in a way I've only heard once before, ten years ago, the day after his parents' funeral.

I blink at him and he takes my moment of stunned silence to break out of my hold. He shoves to his feet, searching the room for his underwear which he pulls on with rough, clumsy movements.

"Why?" I whisper, unsure if I really want the answer.

When I mentioned my idea I never expected this response. I thought he'd be excited. We could go off and live all the adventures we'd talked about doing before.

"Because ... Because ..." Hunter huffs. "I *can't*, Willow. Flynn is here, my job is here. I'm planning to buy the business. I can't leave." He drags a t-shirt over his head and tugs on sweatpants, then he spins on his heels and leaves the bedroom.

I don't know what happened and I'm left sitting here in his bed that smells like sex, an ache between my legs from our activities last night, and an overwhelming, desperate pain in my heart.

Fishing my dress off the floor, I pull it over my head, spending a moment searching for my panties before realising they're on the front stairs with my shoes.

Fuck it. I guess we're doing this bra-less and panty-less.

I grab my discarded bra and stalk into the main living area of the flat, shoving the bra into my handbag before turning eyes on Hunter.

He's leaning on the windowsill, staring down at the street below. Tension lines his frame, his shoulders bunched tight.

"Maybe you don't buy the business," I say, struggling to keep my voice calm. "Maybe you come with me. We could finally do what we planned to do all those years ago."

"And Flynn?"

"He's an adult now. He's got Abi, my whole family. He's happy, Hunter."

I step closer, hesitantly resting a hand on his shoulder, but he shrugs me off immediately.

"I can't. He's the only family I've got. I can't leave him." He turns and walks away from me again.

"What if I can't stay here?" I ask, heart in my throat. "I don't know that I'm ready to come back forever."

Hunter finally turns his eyes on me. He looks tortured. "Do you want me?"

God. I've never wanted anything more in my life, but I know there's so much of the world I want to see before I come back to Kauri Creek and settle down forever. I've been thinking about it more and more as things have developed with Hunter. We could have the adventures we always dreamed of.

I thought Hunter might feel the same way. Once upon a time it was him counting down the days until he got to leave this place.

I guess a person can change a lot in ten years.

"Yes," I whisper. "I want you Hunter. I want you to come with me."

He shakes his head. "I'll wait." His voice is so low and gruff I think I've misheard him for a moment.

He'll wait? Haven't we waited long enough? I think about leaving him here and there's a hollow echo in my soul.

"I can't leave, Willow, but I can wait for you. You do what you need to do and I'll be here when you come back. It doesn't matter how long you go for, I'll always wait for you."

My heart breaks. He means it to be a romantic declaration, I know he does, but it's not what I want. I want him. I want waking up with him every single damn day.

"I don't want you to wait," I cry, the exasperation and heartbreak overwhelming me as my voice splinters. Hunter's face falls, his expression shifting from hopeful to desolate. "I want you to come with me."

"I told you I can't do that." He rubs a hand over his face. "You don't get it." The defeat in his voice is ... I don't even have a word to describe it. A yawning ache starts in my chest. "I understand if you want to go," he whispers. "But I can't go with you."

I stare at him as he crosses his arms, completely resolved in his decision.

If I go, Hunter isn't coming with me.

I could stay. It would be easy. I've made the decision to leave my job anyway, to bring all my possessions back to Kauri Creek and store them at Wildflower Ridge. Maybe instead of going into storage Hunter and I find a place to fill with all my random stuff?

But there's something in my bones screaming at me that isn't the right choice.

"That's it then?" I rest my hands on my hips, my devastation turning to anger. "You're not even going to consider it? Not even give it a chance? If I want you, I have to stay here?"

"It's home, Willow," he says, his voice growing gruffer the longer this conversation continues. "I don't want to leave. I can't leave."

"Fine." I snatch up my handbag. "I guess I have some things to think about then."

Tears are welling fast and I need to get out of here before

they spill over. If Hunter's going to let me go this easily I'm not going to give him the satisfaction of me crying over it.

"Willow," he says, voice wavering as he reaches out as I push past him. "Don't go." I spin to face him. "Please."

"I have to," I say, fingers clenched around my handbag strap. My knuckles ache with the tension. "I have to figure out how this all fits together. I thought you'd want to come with me."

"We can figure it out," he says, holding out his hand. "Please stay."

"There isn't much for you to figure out," I snap, eyes burning and heat rising in my throat. "You intend to stay here regardless of how I feel about it. Meanwhile I have to decide what I want to give up—you or a life outside this town."

"You can have both. I said I'd wait."

"You don't get it!" My voice is rising, growing shriller with each word out of my mouth but I can't stop it. "We once talked about Paris, Italy, the fucking Scottish Highlands, and I thought maybe you'd want to see those places with me. But maybe I'm still some naive, stupid girl for believing that was a possibility. We've wasted all these years, and you're happy to sit in this shit-hole town we both used to hate and waste even more time."

"Fine," he shouts. "I won't wait. Is that what you want to hear?" He rubs both hands over his face then turns to face me, hands on hips as he glowers down at me. "I don't want to leave my brother, is that so criminal? Your family's here too. Don't you think they'd be happy for you to come home?"

"They want me to live my own life, the one I choose for myself," I say between gritted teeth. "At least this time you're giving me some kind of a choice." Last time he made the call, he ended it and didn't let me have an opinion on the matter. This time at least I get to choose whether I have part of him, or none at all.

The problem is that I want all of him.

Every day. Every morning. Every night.

I want to wake up with him and fall asleep on his chest. I want to explore the world with him. There's nothing left in Kauri Creek for us to discover.

"I need to go," I say, voice wavering.

I head for the stairs, only stopping long enough to collect my discarded underwear, shimmy them up my legs and pick up my shoes.

I hold my breath the whole way down the stairs until the door slams shut behind me, hoping that Hunter will ask me to stay, hoping that he'll follow me.

But he doesn't.

He'd never ask me to give up my dreams for him, and while I might have done it for him when I was eighteen, I'm not sure I can now.

Not when he's not willing to fight for it, for us.

40

HUNTER

THE DOOR SLAMS shut behind Willow and all I can hear is the sound echoing in my mind.

My flat is eerily silent, even though I'm more than used to being here on my own.

But after having Willow here for hours, whispering to me in the darkest part of the night, or letting loose the many, many sounds she makes on her way to orgasm, now it feels incredibly, desolately empty.

I want her to stay. I desperately want—no, need—her to stay. But how can I ask that, when I remember clear as day the hours she used to dream about the places in the world she wanted to visit.

I want to be able to go with her, but I can't. My entire life is here, as small and insignificant as it might look to someone else. Flynn and this job are all I've ever had.

I can buy this business and finally make something of myself. Maybe I can somehow make all my failings up to Flynn.

After last night there's a little hope shining there, that maybe that's a thing we can do.

God, a few minutes ago I had it all. My perfect dream life.

I should have known better.

And yet, I still can't ask Willow to stay.

And I can't go. What happens if Flynn needs me and I'm on the other side of the world?

I know things are still relatively new between him and Abi, but I know they're it for each other and it won't be long before Sadie gets a sibling or six.

I've never really considered it, but I don't think I want to miss out on being an uncle, not after spending time with Sadie.

Surely Willow can do her travels and when she's done she can come home and I'll love her so damn hard it'll make up for all the years we've missed.

I told her I'd wait, and I will.

I don't have a choice. I tried moving on. I've been trying, but having Willow home again has cemented the fact that there is no one else for me.

It's Willow or no-one.

So I'll let her go, and when she's ready, I'll be here, waiting for her.

41

WILLOW

I REALLY EXPECTED to walk into the kitchen in last night's dress and either burst into tears, or blush the colour of the dress from the catcalls my sister and her friends would subject me to.

Neither of those things happen though.

Instead, I walk into panic and chaos.

Mum, Abi and Tilly Sheridan are sitting at the table, sheets of paper spread out before them. Abi is frantically taking notes as Mum and Tilly point out various things on the paper.

Olivia is in the corner, elbows on the bench, face buried in her hands while Katie leans in close, an arm wrapped around my sister's waist, whispering in her ear.

"What's going on?" I ask, not sure I want to hear the answer.

Olivia glances at me, eyes filled with tears she's valiantly holding back. She opens her mouth, but no words come out. She shakes her head and buries her face in her hands again.

"The caterer flaked again," Abi says, voice steely with barely contained anger. I've never seen her like it. "I knew I should have found someone else." She glances over her shoulder at Olivia. "I'm so sorry, Liv."

Liv waves her apology away, never lifting her face out of Katie's neck.

"Big wedding," Mum mouths. "Very important."

Fuck.

This wedding venue is Olivia's dream and it's bad enough she doesn't get to handle the day-to-day running of it and had to employ Abi instead, but for an important event to be fucked up at the last minute because this town doesn't have a good catering option pisses me right off.

The front door slams and my breath catches.

Did Hunter follow me after all?

But it's two sets of footsteps in the hall and two male voices. Unless he found Flynn or Dallas on his way in?

Dallas does step through the door, but it isn't Hunter with him. It's a man with shaggy black hair and facial hair that's probably too long to be stubble but not quite an intentional beard. He's wearing a black leather jacket with ripped jeans and looks more like he should be on some city street rather than my mum's quaint country kitchen. He's vaguely familiar, but I can't place him. He was probably at school around the same time as either Olivia or I and with the size of this town, we would have crossed paths.

The man scans the room, his gaze quickly cataloguing the chaos, and Dallas is doing the same thing beside him.

"What are you doing here?" Olivia asks with enough snark for me to know this isn't their first meeting.

"Olivia," the man says. He holds out a hand to her, which

I've got to give him credit for. "I was sorry to hear about Henry." He glances in Mum's direction and gives her a nod.

Olivia stares out his outstretched hand. "You didn't answer my question."

"He's here about the job," Dallas says, clearly confused about the situation, and Olivia wilts.

"Crap, I forgot about that. Does it really have to be Zane Harrison though?" She completely ignores Zane—who I can place now I have a name, but I'd never have linked this man to the surly teenager with a bad reputation and an attitude to match—and speaks like he isn't even there. He doesn't seem to mind though, eyes bouncing between Olivia and Dallas as they discuss his job prospects.

Abi, Mum, Katie, Tilly and I all watch with rapt fascination as the conversation unfolds.

"He knows what he's doing, doesn't need housing and has great references," Dallas says.

Olivia makes a frustrated sound. "Ticks all the boxes, huh?"

"He's also best buddies with Max," Katie interjects, and now everything falls into place.

Dallas visibly flinches, so he must know of the bad blood between Max and Katie.

Olivia sighs. "Leave your CV. I need to think about this after we've finished averting this crisis." She waves at the table.

"What's this crisis?" Dallas asks.

"Caterer flaked on the wedding, so now we have to try and come up with a menu as close to the client's original one as possible, while also making it something we can actually cook."

"I can help," Zane says, sliding into a seat across from Tilly and snagging the paper out of her hand with a wink. Her cheeks turn the most violent shade of red in a second. "Matilda," he says, dragging out her full name. "Long time no see."

"Hi, Zane," Tilly squeaks, ducking her head as she tucks her long blonde hair behind her ear.

Zane reads down the list while my sister stands over him, arms folded, looking like she's ready to throw him out at any second.

"Do you have the ingredients?" Zane asks.

"Most of them, yes," Abi answers. "I've managed to get my hands on pretty much everything, but we don't have the expertise to cook half of these things."

"Well, I can't do much with desserts, but I can handle the mains, with some extra hands," Zane says, his confidence enviable.

Olivia opens her mouth, hands dropping to her hips and I know she's about to let him have it, then kick him out for his audacity, but Dallas thrusts a piece of paper in her face.

"He's actually qualified," Dallas says quietly. "He worked as a chef in Australia, has a qualification and everything."

"He's a good cook," Tilly says, her voice not quite its usual soft melody. "Miles better than me. He worked at the Hotel all through school."

"Fuck my fucking life," Olivia groans, then, before she can say anything else, I grab her hand and tug her from the room.

"Management meeting," I holler back down the hall as I drag my sister up the stairs.

I obviously need to be helping out today, and last night's dress with no bra is not the best attire for the occasion.

"Sit," I push her down on the edge of my bed. "Is your only issue with Zane his connection to Max?" I ask as I yank a pair of faded jeans from my dresser drawer.

"I don't know. Probably, yes," Olivia says, chewing on the edge of her thumbnail. "He's got a shitty reputation, but I don't actually give it much weight. I think it's more he was in a shitty situation."

I slap her hand away from her mouth, then turn away to tug my dress over my head and pull on a comfortable sports bra. Once my boobs are encased I turn back to her.

"If he has the relevant experience, is it going to hurt having him help get us through tonight?"

Olivia makes one of her frustrated grunts. "No," she says. She's already sulking and I haven't even hit her with the real kicker yet.

"And then," I say, popping my head through the neck of a t-shirt. "You're going to consider hiring him for the farm based on his work merits and not the douchebag he hung out with in high school. You need more hands around here, Liv." I sit down beside her and take her hands in mine, giving them a squeeze. "I've done the numbers and it's all fine from the budget side. You need more help, you need a break and so do Dallas, Katie and Flynn."

Olivia sighs, defeated—I knew mentioning her friends would get to her—and drops her head to my shoulder. "I'm so tired," she mumbles. "All the damn time."

"I know, Liv." I smooth her hair. "You're doing amazing though. Mum's so proud."

She snorts. "I always feel like I'm letting her down."

"You're not. Next time she's rambling on about how fucking incredible you are I'll try and record it for you." I hesitate, then wrap my arms around her. "Dad would be so proud too, Liv. I hope you know that."

She nods against my neck and lets out a little sniffle, then sucks down a deep breath and pushes back.

"Right, let's go hire Zane Harrison of all fucking people to save my ass."

I laugh and haul her up from the bed. "That's the spirit."

I'm about to head down the stairs when Olivia snags me by the wrist and pulls me to a stop.

"You stayed with Hunter last night?" she asks.

I nod, avoiding her eyes.

"And yet I get the sense you're not going to be staying here for much longer?"

I meet her eyes. "I don't know," I say, voice wavering.

Olivia hugs me so tight I can't breathe. "You do whatever you have to do to be fucking happy, okay? Promise me."

"I promise," I whisper into her hair. "But you have to promise me the same thing."

Olivia sighs and holds me tighter. "I don't know how, but I'll try, Will. I promise I'll try."

IT'S BEEN forty-eight hours and I'm done with waiting.

I grab the jacket Willow left tossed over one of the stools at my kitchen bench and storm down the stairs, crashing through my front door and into the gloomy Monday evening.

It's been drizzling all day and it matches my mood perfectly.

After Willow left on Saturday, I changed my sheets, then immediately regretted it when I couldn't smell her on them anymore. I went to the gym and did a gruelling workout, then sat at home and ate leftover chicken pasta because I didn't have the heart to cook the dinner I'd planned. The dinner I'd expected to share with Willow.

Sunday looked pretty much the same, except I also spent a good deal of it staring at my ceiling, missing the feel of Willow's body tucked in beside mine.

I haven't heard from her. Not a phone call or text or border-line indecent photo. Not that I need photos anymore after exploring her body in real time, watching her tits bounce as she rides my dick or the goosebumps spread across her skin at my touch. I don't need photos because I know exactly what she looks, smells, sounds, feels and tastes like.

But still, it would have been nice to know she was thinking of me.

I messaged her twice, once right after she left to apologise for letting her down, and the other a couple of hours later when I found her jacket. She didn't respond to either and I don't know what to think.

Is that it? Are we done? All over again, this time for good?

Or will Willow come back to me someday?

I trudge to my ute, ignoring the drizzling rain that sneaks inside the collar of my jacket. It's a quiet drive out to Wildflower Ridge and when I pull up in the driveway outside the main house I scan the vehicles. Willow's isn't here.

But then, it looks like it's only Violet's that is. Maybe the women are all together somewhere, maybe Willow is helping at the function venue. I think they had a wedding on Saturday night.

I climb out of the ute and head for the porch. I'll drop off the jacket and ask Violet where Willow is, then go and find her to clear the air.

We'll be able to talk it out, and she'll understand why I can't go anywhere. But it won't be like before. We'll still have each other, even if we aren't sharing the same space.

God, my body aches for her and the thought of her not being right beside me forever burns in my chest.

I don't want us to be apart, but I don't ever want to stop her from seeing out her dreams. I won't stand in her way. Ever.

I reach the top of the porch steps as Flynn opens the front door.

I blink at him, stopping in my tracks at his sudden appearance.

"Hey," he says, easy grin spreading over his face. "What brings you here?"

I hold up Willow's jacket. "Willow left this," I say.

"Oh right," Flynn says. "Are you going in to see Vi, or just leaving the jacket?" He's asking if I want him to leave the door open and instead of answering I shrug.

"Willow's not here?" I ask, even though I know the answer.

"No," Flynn says slowly, dragging out the word. His brow furrows.

My breath suddenly feels tight. "Where is she?" I ask through the thickness in my throat.

"She's in Auckland," Flynn says, reaching out a hand as I stumble sideways, then collapse to sit heavily on the porch step, Willow's jacket clutched in my white-knuckled hands.

Flynn slowly sits beside me. "I figured you knew," he says. "You've been in each other's pockets since she came home."

"Do you know why she's gone?" I turn and clutch at Flynn's shoulders. "Do you know when she'll be back? Is she coming back?"

God. The thought hits me at the same time as the searing heat behind my eyes. What if she isn't coming back?

What if she's decided her life in Auckland is what she

wants? Or if she's decided to go travelling but didn't tell me because she doesn't want me?

Flynn shrugs. "Sorry. I don't know. No one's really said anything. Like at all. It's been pretty hectic around here. Saturday night was all hands on deck, then Willow left lunchtime yesterday."

"Fuck," I moan, dropping my head into my hands. "Fuck, fuck fuck." I turn blurry eyes on my brother again. "I fucked everything up." My voice cracks, but I manage to restrain the tears.

Flynn's hand lands on my shoulder, squeezing tight. "Dude, why are you still here?"

I stare at him. "I— what?"

"Why haven't you gone after her?" Flynn shakes my shoulder gently.

"I only just found out she isn't here. I don't even know where she is. How am I supposed to go after her?" Also, if she wanted me to know where she was, wouldn't she have told me?

"I don't mean today," Flynn says, then lets out a long, aggrieved sigh. "I thought you'd be out of here the second I turned eighteen. Like, I was totally prepared for it. But you didn't go. You've never left."

"I wasn't going to up and leave you," I say. "I wasn't going to abandon you."

Flynn makes a frustrated sound. "You wouldn't have been abandoning me. Shit. You gave up *everything* for me."

I attempt to cut him off, to contradict him, but Flynn holds up his hand. "I know I was a dumb kid, but I knew how you felt about Willow. I saw you two holding hands when you walked into this house that night. It was the last time I ever saw it." He shifts so he can look at me fully. "You gave up everything for me, even when you didn't have to. We both know Violet and Henry would have taken me in if you'd gone to uni with Willow like you were supposed to."

"I wasn't going to leave you," I whisper.

"I know that," Flynn says, his voice soft. "I'm grateful for it. I love you for it." His cheeks turn pink. "I know we don't talk like this, but I do love you, Hunter."

I scrub a hand over my face. "I love you too. Of course I do."

"I know you do." He smiles. "You stayed for me. But what I don't understand is why you're *still* here? I've been an adult for years now. You could have left town the day after I turned eighteen and never looked back."

"I didn't want to leave you," I say. Isn't it obvious? Why is no one else getting this? He's my brother and we're all each other has.

"You know we'll always be family, even if we aren't living in the same place? You think Livvie doesn't think of Willow as family because she lives in Auckland?"

"Of course they're family," I mutter, the urge to roll my eyes winning out.

"And the same goes for us." Flynn lands a soft punch on my shoulder. "It doesn't matter where in the world you are, you're stuck with me, bro."

I snort. "You make it sound like a bad thing."

Flynn shrugs and turns so we're sitting side-by-side on the step, both staring out across the driveway. "Sometimes it feels like it. If you weren't stuck with me you'd be with Willow already. You would have gone to university and travelled and done all the things you wanted to do. Maybe you'd even be happy. Instead you got me, and stayed stuck in Kauri Creek."

"I'm happy."

He gives me the most aggressive side-eye I've ever seen. "Are you, though? You're sitting on Violet's front porch nearly crying because you're letting the love of your goddamn life get away again."

"That's— I— I mean—"

Flynn cuts me off. "Are you going to tell me Willow isn't the love of your life?" He's watching me closely, eyebrows raised.

I shake my head. "No. I'm not going to tell you that, because she is." I heave a sigh and bury my face in my hands. "She doesn't want to stay here."

"Fair enough," Flynn says. "You know Kauri Creek is a bit of a shit-hole in the middle of fucking nowhere right?"

"You live here," I point out.

"Yep. And I fucking love it. I want to be in the middle of nowhere. I have never once wanted to eat cheese in Italy, or see the Eiffel Tower. I have everyone I need here, my friends and Vi, and Abi and Sadie. And for the ones that don't happen to be close by there's email and this amazing invention called a phone."

I roll my eyes. "Yes. I do understand methods of communication," I mutter.

"So, why are you still here? Why aren't you wherever Willow is? Whether it's Auckland or France?" He pauses, then snorts. "Good luck to you in Auckland though."

I laugh. "Not my first choice."

"But if that's where Willow is, wouldn't it be worth it?"

I think about living in Auckland with Willow for a moment. It's likely I could find work easily. Everyone needs a mechanic at some point. A job in Auckland would pay more too. I wouldn't have the same flexibility as I do here, or a management role, but when I'm done with work for the day I'll get to go home to Willow. I'll cook her dinner, then sit on the couch while she tucks her body into mine, and each night I'll take her into our bedroom and explore the rest of her body by moonlight.

I could have a lifetime of nights like Friday night, if I choose it.

I could have a lifetime of loving Willow, and all I have to do is choose it.

"Can you find out where she's staying and text me the address?" I ask my brother, my voice hoarse with anxiety over what I'm about to do.

What if I put myself out there and she's already decided? She didn't even let me know she was leaving yesterday. Is that a hint I should take?

"Sure. Consider it done." Flynn's face breaks into a delighted smile and he claps me on the back with one big hand.

A big hand. A man's hand.

I turn and study Flynn. I've seen him countless times over the years, though admittedly a lot less since he finished school.

Sitting across from me is a man. A man with a partner and a stepdaughter and a job he loves.

All this time I've only been seeing the grieving kid I sat across the dinner table from every night until he turned eighteen.

"You're happy?" I whisper and Flynn's fingers tighten on my shoulder.

"The happiest," he says back. "I love this place. I love Liv and Katie and Violet. I love my job. I've got Abi, and I know that from the outside that looks complicated, but for me it isn't. We fit together and I love her, and Sadie. God." A wistful look crosses his face. "I love her so much."

"I know you do, and not that you need my permission or whatever, but I like Abi."

This wistful look vanishes and Flynn looks at me with suspicion. "You do?"

"Yeah, I do. I think with her around, maybe I'll worry about you less." I sigh. "Maybe."

Flynn laughs. "Thanks for saying that. Now, don't you have somewhere to be?"

He slaps me across the shoulders and stands. I push to my feet, picking up Willow's jacket. It's a long drive to Auckland to deliver it, but it's worth it.

Willow is worth everything.

Before Flynn has a chance to bound off to do whatever it is he's supposed to be doing, I reach out and grab him around the shoulders, tugging him to me for a hug.

He freezes at the contact, but after a second, melts into it. His arms band around my back like steel rods and we stand there for a long, long time.

When we finally break apart, we don't say anything about it. I turn for my ute.

"Go get your girl," Flynn says, stopping me in my tracks.

"Just don't forget me while you're off travelling the world and living your dreams alright?"

"As if I could ever forget you," I mutter. "Even if I wanted to."

Flynn grins and heads back inside, I assume to get Willow's whereabouts from Violet.

I climb into my ute and head for the road. When I reach the main road, I head north.

43

WILLOW

I'M STILL NOT QUITE sure how we did it, but we pulled that wedding off without a hitch. Well, another hitch. I guess the caterer cancelling the morning of is quite a major one.

But with Zane on board, we nailed it. Got to hand it to the guy, he knows how to operate a kitchen. The rest of us all pitched in, following his directions as best we could, and while we're definitely not caterers, it was actually a lot of fun.

Tilly pulled together the desserts like she'd been prepared to do it all along, and luckily she was already sorted with the wedding cake.

I need to talk to Olivia again about keeping Zane on, especially if he's a reliable chef. The function centre isn't big enough to employ a chef full-time, but if he was working on the farm during the week as well, that should be enough to keep him occupied. My sister just needs to deal with his connections to Max Sheridan first.

Saturday night was utterly exhausting, but at least it didn't allow much time for dwelling on things with Hunter.

He sent me two messages on Saturday. One to tell me I'd left my jacket behind, the other to tell me he'd wait for me. He hasn't called, or come to the farm, or sent me a smoking hot photo of his abs.

He probably thinks he's doing the right thing and giving me space, but I miss him. I missed him the second my feet hit the footpath outside his front door.

It's been two days, but feels like weeks, months, years. And I'm still no closer to deciding what I'm going to do.

What I do know is that my time in Auckland is done.

I drove up Sunday afternoon to stay with Margot. I went to work yesterday and handed in my notice. I'm meeting with Mark this morning to tie up any loose ends from our relationship.

When I messaged him yesterday to set up a time, he even apologised for the way he spoke to me when he came to Kauri Creek, for the way he booked the wedding venue without even considering me in it.

It changes nothing, but it was nice that he said it.

I check the time, then haul my ass out of bed. Mark will be here any minute.

Two weeks ago I would have been up for an hour already, trying to make myself look perfect, so I'd feel confident, or he'd feel regret, I'm not actually sure. Probably both.

But this morning, I don't care.

We lived together. He's seen me in my sausage dog pyjamas.

He's seen me without makeup, so when there's a knock on the door that's exactly how I answer it.

"Hey," I say as I swing the door open to reveal Mark standing outside, a cardboard box in his arms.

"Here I was thinking I was the dog you won't let in the house, but you actually make him sleep on the front porch," he says instead of hello.

"What?"

Mark steps aside to reveal a hunched figure leaning against the verandah post.

"Hunter?" What the hell? Why is he here? Why is he sitting on my porch at six-thirty on a Tuesday morning? It's freezing out here.

I crouch in front of him and place a hand on his cheek. Shit he's cold.

He blinks slowly then the softest smile I've ever seen curls his lips. "Will," he says, still sleepy.

"What are you doing here?"

He holds up my jacket. The one I left at his place on Saturday morning when I ran out of there feeling like my heart was going to break.

"I didn't want to miss you if I waited in my car," he mumbles. He shivers violently. "Thought it was supposed to be warmer up here."

I laugh softly, my heart singing because he's *here*. "Let's get you inside."

I help pull him to his feet, then turn to lead him inside. He freezes when he spots Mark, who's set the box down and is leaning against the wall with his arms crossed. Hunter's eyes narrow, then flick between me in my dachshund pjs and Mark.

"I didn't mean to interrupt," Hunter says, taking a step back, pulling his arm out of my grip.

"You're not," I say, grabbing his arm again and purposefully digging my nails in a touch. I'm not letting him get away, not again. Never again.

Hunter's gaze darkens as he turns it on me.

"Inside," I say, ushering him ahead of me.

"You're playing dirty, kitten," he mutters low enough that only I can hear as he stalks past me.

"Come on," I say to Mark, waving him inside too. This should be fun.

I usher Mark into the kitchen and tell him to make a coffee, while I drag Hunter down the hallway into the bathroom. I turn the shower on and toss a towel at him.

"Get warm you giant, stupid idiot," I say, trying and failing to keep my expression flat.

I want to squeal and sing and dance.

Because he's here.

He's here.

He's *here*.

He followed me.

He did the thing I never thought he'd do, and while I'm not naive enough to think this means everything is going to be perfect, he *followed* me. He came after me and that has to mean something.

I'm going to find out what as soon as I get my ex out of the kitchen.

At least Margot has an early shift this morning and isn't home to witness this chaos. She'll never let me hear the end of it.

"Willow," Hunter starts, eyes filled with emotion; love, pain, regret, lust.

"Soon, baby," I whisper. "You get warmed up and I'll go deal with ... that." I wave in the direction of the kitchen.

"Why's he here?"

"We're sorting everything out. He just got here. This is the first time I'm seeing him. Now, please." I push him towards the shower where steam is beginning to billow out. "Get warm."

"I know a more fun way to get warm," he says, a smirk on his mouth. God, I've missed that mouth. I've missed this horny, complicated man.

I give him a stern look and he drops the smirk. "Willow, I'm—"

"Soon." I hold up my hand and Hunter cuts off. "Shower. I've got to go talk to Mark."

"Okay, okay," he says. "We'll talk soon."

"We will." I head for the door, pausing when I reach it and turning back to him. "Hunter," I wait until his gaze locks with mine. "Thank you."

44

HUNTER

I WANT to have the fastest shower in the world and get back to Willow.

But I really don't want to see whatshisname again.

So I take my time and marvel at how clever Willow is to separate us like this.

I stand under the hot water, letting the warmth seep into my bones. I should have stayed in my car, but I didn't want to fall asleep and miss Willow if she was heading out early this morning, and I didn't want to knock on her door in the middle of the night either.

Though maybe that would have been preferable to being found asleep on the front porch by her ex-boyfriend of all people.

When the hot water runs out, I shut off the shower and dry myself off, putting my clothes back on slowly, wondering how long Willow needs before I head back out there.

I lean against the vanity and check my phone. There's a

message from my boss in response to my voicemail saying I wouldn't be at work today. I'm really fucking lucky he's such a good guy, because I'm really leaving them in the lurch and he's not even giving me a hard time about it.

There's also a string of messages from Flynn asking for updates.

HUNTER:

Was waiting on her front step this morning when her ex turned up.

No need to tell him that I was actually asleep at the time. That little secret can die with me.

FLYNN:

Her ex? Ew. Why? What does he want? Why is he there?

Did she send him packing?

Abi informs me that not all exes are bad. I told her she has extenuating circumstances

And also I can't slag off her ex because he's sort of my boss

and I actually like him

Willow's we don't like.

HUNTER:

They're talking now.

FLYNN:

Why?

HUNTER:

I don't know.

FLYNN:

Did you confess your undying love yet?

HUNTER:

Haven't had the chance.

FLYNN:

You have to make the chance. It's your undying love. You can't just let it die

HUNTER:

Can I take back the us staying in touch more thing?

FLYNN:

Nope. I told you. You're stuck with me for everrr

I laugh, but the warmth in my chest is anything but funny.

HUNTER:

Wouldn't have it any other way.

I hear a noise out in the hallway that might be the front door closing, but the bathroom is facing the back of the house so I can't check out the window if Mark is on his way out.

There's a soft knock on the door and Willow's voice filters through.

"He's gone. You can come out when you're ready." Then I hear footsteps retreating down the hall.

I pocket my phone and take a deep breath, staring myself down in the mirror.

I can do this. Whatever Willow asks of me I can handle. I'll do it. I'll move here, I'll travel, I'll go home and wait for her.

I'll do anything.

The only thing I can't handle is if she decides to end things for good. But if that's her choice, I'm going to have to suck it up.

I find Willow in the kitchen. It's a small space, but cheery, even with only weak morning sunshine filtering in the windows. The cabinets are white, the walls a bright yellow, which should be garish, but it's not. There's a photo of Willow and another girl stuck to the fridge.

There's a small table to one side, where Willow is sitting, a mug in front of her, hands tucked in her lap.

"Are you okay?" I ask as I approach, then hesitate when I reach the table. Am I supposed to be invited to sit down?

I charged up here and intruded on her life with zero warning. She didn't have to let me in the front door.

Willow smiles at me, but it's as weak as the sunlight.

"Sit down, Hunter," she murmurs, then returns her gaze to the tabletop.

"I'm serious," I say, taking the seat across from her. "Are you okay? After seeing him?"

"Yeah, I'm fine," Willow says, fiddling with her mug, turning it a quarter turn, then another, and another. "I'm sorry," she blurts out, wild eyes shooting up to lock with mine. "I'm sorry I ran out and didn't even bother to text you to say I was coming here. I was caught off guard I guess."

I shake my head. "I'm sorry. It caught me off guard too." I rub a hand over my face. "Having a bit of time to think about things was probably good for both of us."

Willow nods slowly, then returns to making the precise movements with her mug.

"Can I ask why you're here?" I ask.

"I quit my job. And I needed to finalise things with Mark. I needed to pick up my stuff from here."

All of that makes sense. But none of it tells me what she's actually decided to do. All it tells me is that she's not intending to stay in Auckland anymore.

"Have you made any decisions?" I ask, my breath thick in my throat.

Willow glances at me and gives the most defeated shrug I've ever seen. "I don't know what to do."

Her voice wavers and a tear races down her cheek.

I want to rip my heart right out of my chest and hand it over. I fucking made her cry. Again.

Pushing out of my seat, I fall to my knees at her side and spin her chair so she's facing me.

I reach up and drag my thumb down the tear track, wiping away the moisture.

"Willow," I murmur and Willow hiccups a sob as more tears fall. "Kitten."

"I don't know what to do," she repeats. "I want you, so much, but—"

"You have me," I interrupt, attempting to wipe away more tears as they fall, but giving up and cupping her cheeks between my palms. It's always been a perfect fit. "Wherever you want to be, Willow. Here, Kauri Creek, the other side of the world, I am always yours."

She tries to shake her head. "It can't be that simple."

"It is."

"But you don't want to travel."

I sigh and drop back onto my heels, my hands grasping the

edge of the chair on either side of her thighs. She's wearing ridiculous pink and purple flannel pyjama pants with little sausage dogs all over them. I love them. "Yeah, I do. I've just been a fucking coward about it all." I lean forward and rest my head on her lap. Willow's fingers immediately find their way to my scalp, then trace the edges of my face. "I was scared to go," I say, "because I was worried about Flynn. Not even really that he might need me, because he doesn't need me. He has a whole family now, and he's an adult. Which, by the way, is still a terrifying thought."

Willow lets out a soft laugh. "It is, right? That means we must be adults too."

"Yeah. Apparently." I sigh and try to pick up the threads of what I was saying. "I think I was scared that Flynn *wouldn't* need me, and being anywhere else but in Kauri Creek would mean he'd forget about me too easily."

Willow's fingers tighten on my head. "He would never—could never—forget you, Hunter."

"I don't mean actually forgetting. But when our parents died, I was a mess and I didn't really take to the whole guardianship thing very well. I was caught up in trying to learn a brand new job and grieve for my parents. I was terrified of being responsible for someone else when I could barely sort my own shit out. Flynn and I, well, you know what our relationship has been like. We barely have one. If I moved away, we wouldn't have anything. There'd be nothing left. We wouldn't see each other in passing in town, or at a random dinner at Wildflower Ridge."

"Oh, Hunter, I'm sorry." Willow lifts my chin with the tips

of her fingers and when our eyes meet, I know the tears shining in hers are for me. "We don't have to go anywhere."

I shake my head. "I went to Wildflower Ridge looking for you, ready to convince you of all the reasons you should stay in Kauri Creek. And instead I saw my brother." I take a deep breath. "I don't have to worry about losing him." A smile tugs at my lips. "Apparently I'm stuck with him forever, whether I like it or not." I roll my eyes, but the smile is taking over.

"You like it," Willow says, shoving me in the shoulder. Then her smile dims. "What does this mean?"

"It means we better book some plane tickets. We've got a lot of the world to see."

"But, but ... there's so many things to consider. Are you sure?"

"I've never been surer of anything in my life. You're everything to me. You're right, we've wasted enough time. If I have to follow you to a city, or halfway across the world, I'm going to do it. I'll follow you anywhere."

"I don't want you to follow me," she whispers and for a moment my heart twists. "I want you right there beside me, always."

Then she leans down and presses her mouth against mine.

45

WILLOW

I HAVE TO ADMIT, Hunter on his knees, expression wild with torment, tears in his eyes and pouring his heart out is a sight to behold.

But the look he's giving me now, one filled with passion and hope and love, this one is *everything*.

I still can't believe he drove through the night to be here, or that he's agreed to come travelling with me.

I feel like I need to pinch myself in case I'm dreaming.

Hunter drops his head into my lap again and I feel another twinge of embarrassment over my choice of attire. In my defence I didn't expect to see him.

The conversation while Hunter was in the shower was civil and direct. Mark and I sorted out the last of our financials and went our separate ways. I'm sure he still has some feelings about it all, especially with the way he found Hunter. But things between us are amicable and he admitted we were never going to work in the end. He didn't need to add it was because I've been in love with Hunter my whole life. We both know it.

And while I feel bad about it, it's not bad enough not to savour the warm weight of Hunter's head resting in my lap. His eyes drift closed and I realise he must be exhausted. I'm exhausted and I didn't drive half the night and spend the rest asleep in the cold on a porch.

"Come on," I say, gently pushing his head off.

"No," he mumbles, burying his face in my thigh.

"We need to get you to bed."

He lifts his head immediately. "Bed sounds like a fantastic idea," he says, a wicked gleam in his eye.

Fuck. That single expression is enough to turn me on and take me from exhausted and emotional to so desperately horny I don't know if I'm going to make it down the hall to my room.

"You need to sleep," I say, but my voice is thick and raspy, a dead giveaway.

"I'll sleep later. You have no idea what you do to me."

Oh, I have a pretty good idea.

"It's the sausage dogs," I deadpan.

Hunter traces the outline of one of the dogs. "I fucking love the sausage dogs. I'm going to love getting you out of them even more though."

I laugh and Hunter grins. His smiles come so easily and there's a different quality to them than just a few weeks ago. Now, he actually seems happy.

His hand creeps up my thigh and disappears under the sweatshirt I'm wearing. I gasp when Hunter's fingers brush bare skin at my waist, then tug free the drawstring of my pants.

"You need food," I say, my voice barely able to make the sounds as need pulses through me.

"Hmmm. I haven't had breakfast yet," Hunter says. "And I am starving." He tugs on the waistband on my pyjamas, then drags my ass forward so I'm perched on the edge of the seat, my knees forced to spread around his shoulders.

I don't mean to, but a low, needy groan slips out of my throat. "You need actual food," I gasp as his hand dips inside my pants, finding the edge of my underwear. "And sleep."

"I can have both of those later," he murmurs. "There's only one thing I really need right now, and it's you, kitten."

"After breakfast." I gently push his shoulder back, then try to stand, but he's in my way and I can't catch my balance. I teeter, then sit back down, but not before Hunter yanks my pants down.

"I love your ridiculous pyjamas," he says, "but they have got to go." He drags them off my legs, never taking his gaze from the spot between my thighs that's beginning to ache in desperation.

"Yeah, okay, they do."

Hunter reaches back and yanks off his hoodie, his t-shirt coming off with it so I get the truly glorious sight of his entire naked torso crowded between my legs. "Sit back, kitten. Let me look at you."

He pushes my knees wider and I lean back, bracing myself against the table as I drag the hem of my sweatshirt up to expose my stomach.

A heavy groan escapes Hunter on his next inhale. "You're already wet for me," he moans. "I can see you soaking your panties. God, I can't wait to taste you."

"I don't know what you're waiting for," I rasp. "I thought you were starving."

He smirks at me, then takes me by surprise as he buries his face in my pussy.

"Holy shit," I gasp, a wave of desire hitting me so hard I almost topple off my seat. "Oh my god."

"You praying for me, huh?" Hunter nips at my thigh, then hooks his finger around the edge of my panties and tugs them to the side.

"That thing you do where you roll your tongue over my clit is a fucking religious experience."

Hunter growls and does that exact move, sucking my clit into his mouth, then strumming his tongue across it.

"Yes. That." Words are failing me. Common sense is failing me. I have no idea when Margot is going to be home from her early shift at work. Is she going to walk in here to find me grinding my hips against Hunter's face?

I'm too far gone to care, especially when Hunter pushes a finger inside of me, and another one a moment later.

I hook my leg over Hunter's shoulder and clutch at his head, guiding him with pressure from my fingertips. Not that he needs much guidance. The man knows his way around a pussy.

I clutch at the table, knuckles white as I try to keep myself upright and when my orgasm hits I arch backwards, only avoiding hitting the floor because of Hunter's strong arms banding around me to keep me in place as he continues to lick and suck, working me over until the waves of ecstasy subside.

I groan and slump against the table, reality blinking in and out. When I can finally focus again, I look down to see Hunter grinning up at me, his smile smug and satisfied.

My attention is caught by the red scratch marks across his shoulder though.

"I'm sorry," I breathe, tracing the marks with a finger tip.

"I'm not," Hunter assures me. His grin turns wicked again. "But if you like I can even the score."

God, that shouldn't turn me on as much as it does. I'm surprised my body can even respond after what he's put me through. I raise an eyebrow, asking the silent question.

Hunter stands, planting his hands on the chair either side of my hips and leaning in close so his words ghost over my skin.

"I can spank your ass until it turns just as red."

My eyes roll back and I gulp, pressing my thighs together to stave off the wave of want that hits. Hunter takes my head dropping back as an invitation and licks a long stripe up my neck.

"Your neck is so pretty and delicate," he murmurs a moment before settling his hand around it. He lets out a satisfied hum. "You like the idea of me spanking you, don't you?"

I bite my lip and nod.

He doesn't release his hand from my throat, but uses it to gently guide me up out of the chair, then leans in for a deep, filthy kiss.

"Turn around," he murmurs, gently biting my bottom lip. "Put your hands on the chair."

I do as he says and moisture floods my pussy when he makes an appreciative noise.

"Something's not quite right," he mutters a moment before the yanks my underwear down my thighs. "Better." He kicks my feet apart, then presses a hand in the centre of my back, forcing me to bend over more.

Hunter's hands land on my hips, then glide up my sides, pushing up my sweatshirt and the tank top I'm wearing underneath that I use as pyjamas. He pauses where the band of my bra would sit if I was wearing one.

"You've been braless this whole fucking time," he groans. "And I had no fucking idea under that huge sweatshirt."

I grin, hiding my face in my shoulder.

"Get them off," he growls and I scramble to discard the garments without moving from my position.

A heavy breath behind me, then one uttered word.

"Perfection."

God, every part of me is on display. I feel vulnerable and exposed, and also as safe and cherished as I've ever felt in my life.

"You want me to do this, Willow?" His hand settles on the curve of my ass. I nod and he pats me lightly. "I need you to say it."

"Yes," I breathe. "But hurry up."

He laughs. "Oh, kitten, the tension is the best part." He drags his palm across my skin, his callouses giving the slightest bite of roughness.

A moment later his palm cracks against my ass and I let out a squeak of surprise. It wasn't a hard hit and it barely stings, but the suddenness caught me off guard.

Hunter continues to tease, stroking gently, working closer and closer to my aching core, then slapping his hand down when I least expect it. Sometimes he does one, sometimes two or three. They're never too hard and with each smack that echoes around the kitchen I get more and more desperate for him.

His next smack nearly brings me to my knees as I let out a groan so deep I feel it in my belly.

I glance back over my shoulder and the sight is incredible. Shirtless Hunter with his jeans undone, his thick cock sliding through his fist as he smooths my stinging skin with his other hand.

"Fuck me, baby. Please, please fuck me," I whimper.

"You want this?" he asks, dropping his gaze to where he's giving himself several short, sharp tugs. I nod and he reaches for his back pocket. "Fuck," he mutters. "I don't have a condom." He holds up a hand. "Stay like that and I'll get one from the ute."

I shake my head. "No. Just fuck me. I have an IUD. I've been tested. I trust you."

"Are you sure?" Hunter asks, eyes locked on mine, assessing if I'm serious. "I got tested a few months back. I haven't been with anyone but you."

"Fuck me bare. I want to feel every inch of you with nothing between us."

"You keep saying shit like that and I'm not going to be able to make this last." He grunts as he steps forward and drags the head of his cock through my soaked pussy. He leans down, his chest blanketing my back. "You can say no," he murmurs. "We don't have to."

"I don't want to say no. I want to feel you inside me."

He doesn't make me wait, his blunt head stretching me open a moment later.

I groan as he bottoms out, my ass meeting his thighs.

"You have no idea what this looks like," he groans. "How incredible you look taking me, bent over and all stretched open. God, you feel so fucking *good*, Willow. It's like you were made for me."

"That's because I was," I pant. "Just like you were made for me."

Hunter makes a guttural noise, then pistons his hips, his thrusts long and hard and my body reacts immediately, tension coiling tight in my belly until my limbs are shaking and I'm barely upright.

"Come for me, kitten," Hunter commands.

"Come with me," I manage on a strangled breath.

And he does, exactly like he promised.

46

HUNTER

I COULD BE DEAD, but I'm not actually entirely sure.

Is it even possible to die from coming too hard because the woman you've been in love with your entire life is right here making all your dreams come true, and being the fucking sexiest thing you've ever seen, heard, felt before?

After I fucked Willow until I nearly blacked out, we stumbled down the hall to her bedroom, collapsing into her bed in a tangled pile of limbs.

She snuggled into me and I fell asleep almost immediately.

I stretch and reach for her, but the rest of the bed is empty. It smells like her though and I take a moment to savour it before opening my eyes.

Was this all a dream? Am I going to open my eyes and Willow's changed her mind in the time I've been asleep?

Only one way to find out.

I sit up and glance around the room.

"I'm here, baby," she says, and immediately my anxiety settles.

She's standing by the dresser, folding clothes and packing them into a duffel bag. She's wearing the sausage dog pants again. She drops a t-shirt into the bag, then crosses the room to perch on the edge of the mattress.

"How'd you sleep?" she murmurs, leaning in for a kiss. She tries to keep it chaste, but I haul her to me and deepen it, because I will never be over being able to do that. With Willow Austin.

"I slept like the dead actually," I say, finally breaking the kiss that leaves us both panting. "What're you doing? Why aren't you in here with me?"

She laughs. "Because unlike you I actually got a full night's sleep and zero percent of it was sitting on a freezing cold front step."

"Okay, that's fair. By the way this bed is a million times better than the front porch."

"What a shocker."

"What're you doing?" I ask, pointing to the boxes.

"Packing," she says simply. I suppose I could have figured that out. I was hoping for a little more info though, like for her to tell me she's moving to Kauri Creek immediately for us to plan our trip, because if she's staying in Auckland until we leave I'm not sure what I'm going to do with myself.

She notices my frown and continues. "I've got a few more things to pack up, then my plan was to head back to KC today. I can work out the notice on my job from there. And what comes after that ... I guess that's up to us."

Us.

She says it so simply, like that tiny two-letter word isn't everything I've ever wanted.

"If that's still what you want?" she whispers, peeking up at me from beneath her lashes.

"It's what I want." My voice is so rough from sleep and emotion. "Was it always your plan to go back today? If you were planning to stay longer, then don't change your plans on my account."

Willow shakes her head. "It was always the plan. Sort out things with whatsisname, see Margot, get the rest of my things, head home as soon as possible and fix whatever was going on between us."

I pull her into my lap. "Looks like you've ticked everything off your list." I nuzzle her neck, pressing tiny kisses from her jaw to her collarbone. "You deserve a reward."

I slip my hand under her sweatshirt and cup her breast, my cock twitching when I find she still hasn't put on a bra. I brush my thumb over her nipple, feeling it harden under my touch.

Willow leans into my shoulder and lets out a breathy groan. The sound is like pure joy to me.

"Are you ever not horny?" she gasps as I gently pinch her nipple and roll it between my thumb and finger.

"Blame the sausage dogs." I suck on the delicious point where her neck meets her shoulder.

Willow tips back her head and laughs. The sound is so pure and unfiltered that my heart feels like it might burst. For years I missed out on this laugh. On her smiles, her gentle touches, and the not so gentle ones.

I never want to miss another day, another moment, that I could be with Willow.

The thought of travelling is kind of terrifying, considering I've rarely left Kauri Creek my entire life, but at the same time, I can't help feeling excited about the places we'll go, the things we'll do. And the itty bitty, teeny tiny fact that we'll get to do it together. Sure it's ten years later than we originally planned, but I'm not wasting another moment.

Willow splays her hand across the back of my head as I continue to drop kisses along her neck, interspersed with light sucking, gentle bites and a few stray licks. She squirms at the attention, her perfect round ass rubbing against my thickening cock.

I truly don't know how it's rallying again, but it's trying.

There's a light knock at the door and it swings open.

"How'd it go?" a voice asks softly, like she's worried Willow's going to be upset. "Oh my god! I'm sorry!" The woman in the doorway claps her hand over her eyes and gropes blindly for the door handle.

Willow giggles and climbs out of my lap, grabbing the girl's hands. "It's okay, we're decent."

"Phew." She finally drops her hand from her eyes and lets Willow lead her into the room. She assesses me as I arrange a pillow across my lap. "You think you're being subtle there?" she asks me.

"Not at all," I say, a smile on my lips. "It's not my fault I was interrupted."

She studies me for a moment. "You must be Hunter."

"And you must be Margot." I hold out my hand and she

studies it cynically for a moment before she shakes it. "Sorry, I'd get up but…" I gesture towards my lap.

"Yeah, yeah. I don't need to see it."

Willow climbs back onto the bed, nestling into my side, while Margot perches on the edge and I suddenly feel like I'm preparing for an inquisition.

"What are your intentions with my best friend?" Margot launches right into it.

"Love her forever," I say without hesitation, and I will, whether she loves me back or not. It's not my choice anymore. I don't think it ever was. "Anything she wants. Travel. Marriage. Kids. Anything. I'll do whatever I can to give it to her."

"You want kids?" Willow turns to me, eyes wide with shock. "I didn't think you would."

"I never really considered it until recently. But if that's what you want. Sadie's going to need cousins, right?" My cheeks feel hot as the two women stare at me.

Willow nods silently, then turns to make eye contact with Margot. I don't know what passes silently between them, but a moment later Willow's head is back on my shoulder so I take it that was the right thing to say.

Margot studies me, lips pursed and I know she's not done. "Last I heard you never wanted to leave Kauri Creek and were intending to buy a business there."

I nod. "That was the plan last week."

"What changed?"

"Everything. The only way I could afford the business was to sell my dad's old car—"

Willow lets out a gasp. "You can't. That car means too much to you."

"I know." I smile down at her. "I kissed you for the first time in it."

"So I can't afford the business anyway, even though I think I only wanted to buy it for that permanent link to Kauri Creek. I decided I can't part with the car, and I can't part with Willow. My brother was the main reason I was staying, but we'll be fine, even if I am on the other side of the world."

The number of text messages that he's been blowing up my phone with is evidence of that.

Margot crosses her arms, gaze still assessing, then she focusses on Willow. "You're happy?"

"Yes."

"And you believe him when he says he's actually going to leave that town?"

"Yes."

"Are you just super love drunk because he has a magical dick?"

I almost choke on my breath and Willow laughs.

"Yes," she says through her giggles. "But it's more than that." She laces our fingers together. "This is everything." She holds up our joined hands.

Margot smiles. "Then I'm happy for you. Wonderfully over the fucking moon for you, my friend." She leans over and wraps Willow in a hug. Her eyes meet mine over Willow's shoulder.

She doesn't need to say anything, but I get the meaning in her stare. I hurt Willow, and she'll gut me.

It's not something either of us will have to worry about.

"So what's the plan now?" Margot asks, finally releasing Willow and sitting back.

"Pack up and head back to KC," Willow says without hesitation.

She hides it well, but I catch the flash of disappointment in Margot's expression.

"Why don't you two hang out together a bit first?" I say. "We're in no rush to get back."

"Are you sure?" Willow asks.

I press a kiss to her temple. "Absolutely. I'll get out of your hair. I need to get Flynn something for his birthday anyway, may as well do that here."

For the first time, Margot looks at me with something closer to appreciation than disdain. "Brunch?" she asks Willow, who nods enthusiastically. "I'll go get changed then." She pushes off the bed and disappears down the hall, a moment later the shower turns on.

"You sure?" Willow turns to me.

"Of course." I kiss her forehead. "Spend time with your friend."

"And you'll be okay?"

I roll my eyes. "Yes. I'll be okay, kitten. I'm a big boy, and I'm going to have to get used to cities aren't I? Paris is a lot bigger than Auckland."

She squeals and tackles me back onto the bed, ending up straddling me while dropping kisses across both my cheeks. "I can't believe we're doing this," she says.

"I can't believe you woke my dick up again," I growl. I hold her hips and thrust mine up so she can feel how hard I am already.

She groans, grinding her hips into me.

"Nope. No way. Don't make it worse," I groan, lifting her off me. She collapses beside me. "You need to get changed anyway, unless you plan on wearing your saucy sausage dogs out."

Willow shakes her head. "I couldn't," she says. "I'd get too much attention. Everyone would be trying to get into my sausage dog pants. They're too sexy for their own good."

I roll on top of her. "No one else gets in the sausage dog pants. They're all mine, and so is what's inside them."

"All yours, baby. Only yours."

47

WILLOW

WE ARRIVE at Wildflower Ridge right on dinnertime.

It wasn't planned that way and I hesitate at the sight of the vehicles lined up in the driveway. *Everyone* is here.

Hunter parks his ute, then come to stand beside me, his arm automatically fitting itself around my waist. I lean into the touch.

"We don't have to make a big announcement," he murmurs, brushing his lips against my temple. "We can wait, talk to your mum first if you want."

I turn in his embrace and wrap my arms around his neck. "No more waiting," I say, accepting his soft kiss.

"Agreed," he says, lips against mine.

"You ready for this?"

"I've been ready forever."

I grin and slip my hand into his, leading him onto the front porch.

The moment is so reminiscent of the night ten years ago

when we first admitted our feelings for each other, but tonight, there isn't going to be a tragedy to tear everything apart again. I can tell the moment I open the front door because the sound of conversation and laughter is floating down the hallway.

I lead Hunter into the kitchen where, as expected, the entire family is gathered around the table.

Katie spots us first and lets out a whoop, then starts clapping. Hunter groans, but when I look over at him, there's a smile threatening to expose his true feelings about the moment.

Flynn takes one look at us, his gaze dropping to our joined hands, then leaps out of his seat and swings me into a hug. His arms are tight around me as I laugh at his enthusiasm. After setting me back on the floor and releasing me, Flynn turns to his brother. He hesitates, but the second Hunter opens his arms, Flynn falls into the embrace. I haven't seen them hug since before their parents died, and even then it was rare. When they break apart, Hunter's eyes are glassy, but he pretends he's unaffected by the moment. I know better.

"Well, I guess we don't need to make an announcement," I say, taking a seat at the table while my family congratulates us.

"Not really, no," Olivia says. "We've all been waiting for this for years."

"You have not." I roll my eyes.

"Oh, but we have," Katie argues. "Hard not to when he looks at you like that." She points at Hunter and I glance over to find him already watching me.

Katie might be right, he's not hiding his feelings at all. I can't believe I was so oblivious to it for so many years.

The only person at the table who seems slightly put out by

our new relationship is Sadie. She watches Hunter with disappointment in her eyes.

"Does this mean you're going to be kissing all the time too?" she grumbles, stabbing peas with her fork.

Hunter laughs softly, then reaches over to ruffle her hair. "Yeah, probably. I'm sorry, kiddo." She shakes her head then goes back to attacking her peas. Hunter leans towards me. "I feel like I've let her down," he whispers, brushing a kiss against my temple.

I laugh and dump a pile of mashed potatoes onto his plate. The announcement is done. It doesn't take long for usual conversation to resume, discussions of local town gossip, and work that needs doing over the coming few days, and what Sadie's learning at school.

"So, what's next? Are you leaving?" Olivia asks at one point during dinner, dropping the room into immediate silence.

I look to Mum, who gives me a nod and one of her infuriatingly knowing smiles, then back to my sister.

"Yeah. We're going to go travelling like we were supposed to after uni."

Olivia nods, smiles, does all the right things, but I can read her expression. She's happy for me, but there's some other emotion caught up in there too.

"When do you go?" Flynn asks.

Hunter shrugs. "We don't know yet. It's barely been a day." He smiles. "Give us some time to work out the details. But it won't be before your birthday. I haven't even given notice at work yet."

"He would have," I add, "except I said a text message wasn't appropriate for the occasion."

"It would have been a nice text message," Hunter argues.

The rest of dinner passes in a blur of discussions about the places Hunter and I should go. Everyone has an opinion or a tidbit of advice, even though none of them have travelled aside from a few days on holiday across the ditch or to the Pacific Islands.

Eventually, the family starts heading off to their various homes. Katie and Dallas go first, taking Sadie across the paddock to the farm cottage.

Flynn and Abi are next, leaving with more hugs for us both. Abi even hugs Hunter and he doesn't avoid the moment, hugging his brother's girlfriend back and whispering something in her ear.

Olivia leaves right after they do. I expect her to head upstairs to her room, but the front door closes behind her and a moment later I hear the farm motorbike start up. I glance at mum, who shrugs, a tiny frown on her brow.

"She spends a lot of time out on the farm by herself these days," Mum says quietly. "She doesn't sleep very well, but she hasn't talked to me about it yet."

"Do you think she'll be okay?" I whisper, throat tight as concern for my sister takes over. Am I leaving at the worst possible time? Should I be staying here and taking some of the load off her.

"She'll be okay," Mum assures me. "I'll make sure of it." She glances between me and Hunter. "She's happy for you, I know she is, but I think she's feeling a little left behind. First Katie, then Flynn, now you, all settling down."

I nod. "She's lonely."

"Yeah, but she doesn't want you to put your life on hold anymore than it has been. She'll be okay."

"I want her to be happy," I whisper, tears filling my eyes. "I don't want her to just be okay."

Mum's arms come around me and I lean into her hug, letting it strengthen me like it has my entire life. "She will be, given time."

"Did she offer Zane a job?"

Mum nods. "Yes, though she didn't really want to. But he proved himself. Him and Tilly were quite the team the other night." She has one of her knowing, satisfied expressions on her face, but rather than ask questions about it, I change the subject.

"Can Hunter stay tonight?"

"Of course," Mum replies immediately.

"Are you going to be ridiculous about it and make us sleep in separate rooms or anything?"

Mum snorts. "No. I didn't know I was supposed to be doing that when you're twenty-eight. Unless you want me to?"

"No, I don't want you to." I grab Hunter's hand and drag him after me as I head out of the kitchen. "Goodnight Mum, love you," I call back.

"Night kids. Don't keep me awake okay?"

Hunter groans and my cheeks heat. I stop at the front door, turning to bury my face in Hunter's chest.

"Please tell me she didn't just say that," I mutter.

"Can't. Sorry." He lets out an awkward laugh. "And, just so you know, we're never having sex in this house."

I laugh. "That's okay. There's plenty of other places we can do it."

Hunter shakes his head. "Do you want to go for a walk before bed?"

I pull back and study him. "Why?" Suspicion crawls into my tone.

He shrugs. "It's a nice night. We'll be leaving this place soon, seems like we should make the most of it while we can." He leans in close. "And if I can't make you come in this house, I'm going to need to use those other places you speak of."

A shiver runs down my spine and desire pools in my belly. I can't believe I still want it this desperately, but the idea of fucking Hunter in the moonlight makes my pussy clench.

"A walk sounds lovely," I say, keeping my voice prim and hoping he doesn't notice the lust coursing through me.

Hunter grabs a thick jacket from his ute while I pull mine from the hook in the hallway cupboard, then we walk hand-in-hand down the driveway, past the barn and up the hill in the paddock behind it.

It's a stunning night, with a huge glowing moon and a billion stars scattered through the sky. It's cold, but the sharpness of the temperature just makes the heat of my blood even more evident.

I watch Hunter as he walks—those solid thighs, broad chest and the way his fingers fit perfectly with mine.

By the time we reach the crest of the hill I'm nearly panting with need, the ache between my legs making it difficult to walk.

Hunter pulls me against him, his chest to my back, and wraps his arms around my waist, turning me so we look out over the farm.

"This place has always felt like home to me," he says into my hair.

"It is your home."

"You're my home, Willow. I never want to be without you, apart from you."

I sigh and lean back against my man. My man. I want him forever.

"This might be a little presumptuous but ..." he trails off as his arms leave my waist and he steps back.

It takes me a moment to catch up and turn. I don't know what I'm expecting to see, but it isn't Hunter kneeling in the grass, a tiny box held in one shaking hand.

"Willow Austin," he starts, then clears his throat before continuing. "I love you. I know this might feel soon, but for me it hasn't only been the past few weeks. I've loved you my whole life and I wanted you to know that, whenever you're ready, I am too." He cracks open the ring box, exposing a glittering solitaire diamond ring to the moonlight.

"Ask me," I whisper, voice shaking as much as Hunter's hands are.

"Willow, will you marry me?" Hunter's voice is hoarse, so overflowing with emotion he can barely get the words out.

"Yes."

EPILOGUE
HUNTER

WHEN I BOUGHT Willow's engagement ring while she had brunch with Margot, I only wanted her to know where I stood on our future.

I never expected her to say yes immediately.

I definitely didn't expect her to want to get married right away either, but she insisted it be done before we leave the country.

So, on a random Tuesday afternoon, Willow and I got married at Wildflower Ridge, like she's always dreamed.

The entire thing was perfect, from the bride to the location.

The only guests were the family, including Katie and Dallas of course, and Zane and Tilly, who were technically working that night, but that didn't stop Tilly from crying when Willow walked down the aisle, arm-in-arm with Violet.

I can't really judge though, because I did the same thing.

We wanted Margot to attend, but she couldn't get out of work at such short notice. Katie video called her and held the phone up for the majority of the evening so she didn't miss anything though and I think it was in the moment that the last of my defences against Katie crumbled and fell. I had to admit to myself that I actually like the woman. I won't be telling anyone else though.

After the ceremony and the dinner Zane and Tilly created for us, Willow and I headed back to my flat, where I loved her into the early hours of the morning, before dragging my ass out of bed to go to work and finish out my notice.

Today was my last day at the mechanics. I'll miss the guys, and the work, but I'm so ready to move onto the next chapter of this life, with my wife by my side.

I slam through my front door and jog up the stairs to the flat. I have time for a quick shower before I'm meeting the guys down at the pub for my farewell drinks.

I reach the top of the stairs and freeze though, because Willow is sitting primly on my couch.

"Hey, kitten. Didn't expect to see you," I say, stepping into the room.

Willow holds up her hand, gesturing for me to stop. I do as I'm told and lean against the doorframe, folding my arms across my chest and wondering what the hell she's up to.

She's wearing a white top with a low scooped neckline that shows off the swell of her tits and I'm desperate to go over and bury my face in them, but I wait as Willow lifts one leg, then the other, resting her feet on the edge of the couch.

The skirt she's wearing slips back, revealing her bare pussy.

I groan. I guess I'm going to be late for my own goodbye party.

I want to go to her, but I can't touch her anyway, not until I've scrubbed my hands again, and there's no way I'm leaving this room while she's sitting there all exposed like that.

Just when I thought the view couldn't get better, Willow picks up something from beside her on the couch and a moment later drags a hot pink toy through her pussy, letting out a little hum as it slides over her clit.

Oh, holy fucking shit. She's evening the score. I flash back to the night that started this whole thing, when she walked in on me jerking myself off on this very couch.

My cock is so hard it hurts and she's barely begun.

Willow's eyes don't leave mine as she works herself over, dragging the toy through her pussy over and over, her bottom lip caught between her teeth.

She lifts the toy to her mouth, dragging her tongue over it in a way I know feels amazing. She wraps her pretty lips around the pink silicone, sucking and licking before dropping it back to her pussy and slowly pushing it inside her tight hole.

She lets out a tiny whimper and I groan, striding forward until I'm standing over her, watching her stretch herself around her toy.

"You look so fucking good, kitten. Does it feel good?"

She whimpers again and nods, then does something to the toy. A low buzz fills the room as she thrusts the vibrator in and out of her glistening cunt.

It takes everything I have not to drop to my knees, push her hands out of the way and devour her. But this is Willow's show.

She alternates between thrusting the toy inside her and

dragging it across her clit, her breath becoming harder and faster with every stroke.

When she's a wild, panting mess, she reaches out for me. I take a step forward and she snags the waistband of my jeans, popping the button in one deft move.

"I need a shower," I murmur.

"I don't care," she whines, unzipping my fly with one hand while she continues fucking herself with the other.

She yanks my jeans down so they sit under my ass and shoves my underwear out of the way, revealing my rock hard, leaking cock.

Willow wastes no time, pushing herself off the couch until she's on her knees on the floor, spreading them wide to allow herself room to work.

She leans forward and sucks me into her mouth with a blissed-out groan in her throat.

Her mouth is hot and wet, the suction perfect as she works me over while doing the same to herself.

I want to touch her, tangle my hands in her hair and hold her still while I slide my cock over her tongue, between her stretched lips.

But I hold myself back, forcing myself to keep my hands behind my back.

It doesn't take me long to reach the edge. My balls tighten and I let out a muffled grunt as I fight against the urge to thrust into her mouth.

Willow must sense I'm close because she redoubles her efforts, riding that vibe with the same enthusiasm she's sucking my cock.

The nails on her free hand dig into my thigh and my orgasm crashes into me and Willow greedily takes every drop before pulling back, arching against the couch and grinding down on the toy.

"Come for me, kitten," I whisper hoarsely. "I want to watch my wife come fucking herself with that toy."

Willow cries out, body wracked with shudders and shivers as the waves of her pleasure roll through her.

She collapses back against the couch, completely sated, the toy beside her.

I'm too grimy to touch her, but I don't care at this point. I scoop her up and gently place her on the couch, pulling the blanket off the back and tucking it around her. The blanket is a new addition since Willow arrived and I'm more than grateful for it now.

"I'll be back as soon as I can," I whisper, dropping a kiss on her forehead as she snuggles into the blanket, humming a soft sound of contentment.

I collect the toy on my way to the bathroom, washing it, before having the fastest shower on record.

When I'm clean, I crawl onto the couch beside Willow, wrapping her up in my arms and dropping kisses on any part of her I can reach.

"Shouldn't you be going out," she murmurs, eyes closed and a smile on her face. I could watch her like this forever. I get to watch her like this forever.

"I don't want to," I whisper.

She gives me a little shove. "You should. We have forever."

And it's true. We do.

I have all the time in the world with Willow and she's right, I should go tonight.

Tonight, I say goodbye to my job and tomorrow is Flynn's birthday. He thinks it's a small family dinner at the hotel, not a full-on party.

We've been spending as much time together as possible, when we're not working and I'm not caught up in marrying the absolute love of my life. In a twist I wasn't expecting, most of the time we spend talking, it's about our parents and the past. The things we remember from childhood, the good memories, and sometimes, we even talk about the not-so-good ones. It's still hard for me to do, but I've been trying to be as open with Flynn as he's been with me and now, I don't know why I was ever worried I'd lose him if I wasn't in Kauri Creek anymore. He's my brother and we've got each other's backs. Always.

I can't wait to see his face tomorrow when we surprise him with his party.

Then, the following morning, Violet is driving Willow and me to the airport.

The thought of leaving is both exciting and terrifying, but I'm ready for the challenge, for the adventure.

I'm ready for anything, so long as I have my wife by my side.

Want to see where Hunter and Willow are at five years down the line?

Read a bonus scene here:

Already missing the Wildflower Ridge family?

Find out how Katie and Dallas went from one-night-stand to true love in In Full Bloom.

You can also catch up on Abi and Flynn's friends-with-benefits romance in Coming Up Roses.

Next up: Tilly Sheridan and Zane Harrison find their place at Wildflower Ridge in Buckle Up, Buttercup!

If you haven't read Violet and Henry's story, you can read No Shrinking Violet for FREE by signing up to my email newsletter here:

One of the best ways to support your favourite indie authors is to leave a review. I'd truly appreciate if you could leave one for Forget Me Not on your preferred platform.

Don't forget to follow me on social media to keep up to date with my work: @elle.ashwell.author

See you soon at Wildflower Ridge

ACKNOWLEDGEMENTS

I'm always bamboozled when it comes time to write the acknowledgements for a book, because it's really hard to thank everyone who has contributed in some way.

This time I'm going to start by sending a *huge* thank you to all of you, my readers! I would not be doing this without your support and encouragement, so THANK YOU.

I cannot write this page without thanking Amanda from A Dove Editing and Jennifer Rackham, my cover designer. Without these two this book would be a mess of bad grammar, overly complicated sentences and would likely have a badly drawn stick figure on the cover.

A big thanks to Sarah for doing a thorough content pull of my books for me! It saved me having to do *another* read through and I'm so appreciative.

As usual, Mon, Kelsey and Natalie got my first, messy draft of this story, complete with chaotic plot holes and undecipherable sentences. Big thank you to them for their feedback!

To my author friends: You absolutely rock and I love being a part of this community! It's the best.

And finally, the biggest thanks of all to my husband and kiddos who make this whole thing doable. One day I'll be less tired, I promise. X

ABOUT THE AUTHOR

Elle Ashwell has always been a hopeless romantic.

Dedicated to the swoon and happily ever afters, it makes perfect sense to combine her love of all things romance with the charm of small town life in New Zealand.

Her romances are sweet and a little spicy, with green flag guys and ride-or-die friendships.

When not lost in fictional small towns, Elle works in administration, is a farmer's wife and mum of three girls in rural New Zealand.